Hi Tom

Please read this!

Thanks,

Blair
4/24/06

★★★

D0422865

DANCING

WITH THE

ANALYSTS

A Wall Street Novel About The
Ultimate Financial Challenge

David A. Mallach

Penhurst Books

Copyright © 2003 by David A. Mallach.

All rights reserved. No part of this book may be used or reproduced in any manner whatsoever without written permission except in the case of brief quotations embodied in critical articles and reviews.

For information contact: David A. Mallach.
dmallach@aol.com

ISBN 0-9705684-2-8

Library of Congress LCCN 2002106512

Designed by Bob Wagner Design

Penhurst Books: Fax 305-675-0940
email: penhurstbooks@usa.com

Penhurst Books

Printed in the United States of America

Acknowledgements

Rarely is any work done alone, and this book is no exception. First, I want to thank my family, who have always given me the support and sense of purpose one needs when undertaking a large project such as this book. I would especially like to thank Jeanette Freudiger, my loyal and understanding assistant, for her constant support. Special thanks must be given to Todd Napolitano for his editing skills. Before Todd, this book had only a soul. With Todd, the book gained a heartbeat. Todd has always sought to bring a creative touch to his corporate life, and this book marks a milestone in his search for creative and economic balance. Perhaps his son Quinn will find in these words a legacy for personal growth and fulfillment. I would also like to thank my clients for their trust and respect. In return, I give them an investment discipline I believe to be the best.

Above all, though, this book is dedicated to Winthrop Smith, the former Chairman of Merrill Lynch International. Never have I met a man so dedicated to both corporate and personal growth. Winthrop Smith is a model of excellence to which we should all aspire, for "wealth" is nothing if we cannot acquire it in order to become better human beings. This, Winthrop Smith taught me.

From The Author

This book is a work of fiction. Therefore, it should not be assumed by any reader that any specific investment or investment strategy made reference to in this book will be either profitable or equal historical or anticipated performance levels. It should also likewise not be assumed that the performance of any specific investment style or sector will be either profitable or equal its corresponding historical index benchmark. Finally, different types of investments involve varying degrees of risk, and there can be no assurance that any specific investment or investment strategy made reference to in this book will be suitable or otherwise appropriate for an individual's investment portfolio. To the extent that a reader has any questions regarding the suitability of any specific investment or investment strategy made reference to in this book for his or her individual investment(s) or financial situation, he or she is encouraged to consult with the investment professional of his or her choosing.

David A. Mallach

About The Author

David A. Mallach currently resides in the Philadelphia, Pennsylvania, area, where he has devoted his entire professional career since 1973 to helping investors develop strategies for income growth and capital appreciation. David has lectured to investors and professional investment advisers in Europe, Scandinavia, the Middle East, South and Central America and the United States.

Chapter 1

TO most of his friends on the West Coast, no one went to Philadelphia willingly. It was one of those cities with a reputation it didn't really deserve. Behind the well-known visible negatives everyone knew about—the run-down buildings, the urban blight, and congestion—there was a pearl to be found by those who really knew Philly. It was a rich, historic city which simply bore the scars of time.

"Miss," said Austin, craning over the two passengers sitting next to him. "Excuse me, Miss." The flight attendant ignored him, pausing only long enough to say, "Please return your seat to its full upright position. We'll be landing in just a few minutes."

Well, that's what Austin wanted to ask her anyway. He couldn't wait to get off that plane. He hated feeling so cramped. The guy next to him took Austin's armrest. Austin crossed his arms tighter and looked out the window. The fact is, this wasn't a voluntary trip back to his hometown. News of his mother's death had been a shock to him, even though he knew she had cancer. He always hated good-byes. He was never good at them, and now he was arriving back home in Philly to say a final good-bye to his mother.

If you're from Philadelphia, you know how the Schuylkill River wends its way through the middle of the city, dividing East from West. He remembered Boathouse Row and the rowing crews that sliced ahead rhythmically at all hours of the day. He hadn't rowed since starting college in California three years earlier. Life was simple back then. What he remembered most about rowing was the pain. He discovered that his own threshold for pain was best first thing in the morning. Fortunately, that's when his crew practiced. Rhythm and pain—that's what he remembered most—everyone focusing on the rhythm, and fighting the pain.

Back then he was focused. He woke up at four-thirty, went to school eight hours a day, and went out with one steady girl. Each girlfriend lasted for about a year and then one thing or another broke them up. His mother was his family. His father had died in a car crash when Austin was five and he didn't remember anything about him. His mom rarely spoke of his dad, and he didn't probe. Life wasn't easy, but Austin always managed to scrape up enough money for saxophone lessons. Music—now that was the real love of his life—that and rowing. That was then. Life was simple. Now, thanks to his musical talent, Stanford University paid for his education while he played in the Stanford Cardinal's Marching Band. He didn't have much money, but he had survival instincts—and they kept telling him, "don't stop playing and everything will turn out all right."

As the plane descended, he put his head back and closed his eyes. His mother's death had caused him to think about his own life. For one thing, he knew he liked to be alone. Life was just easier that way—less complicated. That worried him, because he knew he shouldn't become too isolated from people. His desire to be alone was also pretty confusing. Sure, he often wanted to be alone, but when he was alone, he found he was lonely. Figure that out. His studies at college went very well, but every time a relationship with a girlfriend really developed, he'd find some reason to break it off. That bothered him, too. Why couldn't he build a lasting relationship with just one girl? They were always sexy, and some were wonderful girls any guy would be lucky to have. But it never seemed to last. Was he afraid of getting too close to anyone? Well, at least he knew his weaknesses and would work on them. That's more than a lot of people could say.

But there was one thing in his favor that he liked about

himself—he had been a good son and had returned to spend each Christmas with his mom, even though he sometimes had trouble scraping up the airfare. Now he was glad he had.

But enough of that introspection, he said to himself as the plane landed with a small jolt. He had to face whatever was awaiting him. Things were different now—very different. For one thing, his mother wouldn't be waiting to meet him as she always had done. As he removed his bag from the overhead compartment, he had a feeling and sense that he wasn't just stepping off the airplane but was also stepping into the unknown.

Austin knew he was back in Philadelphia the moment he stepped foot in the airport. To a musician like Austin, every city had its own sound, its own tempo, its own flow. Philly's sound was the march of time. It was straight time. You knew where it was going. Austin liked that about his hometown. It suited his sense of order. And yet, the city held surprises here and there, like a Bach fugue. Philadelphia always had a surprise when you least expected it. He looked forward to that.

The transition from sunny California to a rainy Philly and the mourning and death of his mother had been a little too fast for Austin. His father had remained a mystery—a big unknown. He was too young when the accident happened. As he grew up, his mother had been his family and his anchor, providing the warmth of a home and stability. Now, she too was gone. Austin needed a little time to deal with that before going to his aunt's house where he was to stay.

He jumped into a taxi and gave his aunt's address to the driver.

"Did I miss anything lately?" Austin asked the taxi driver?

"Sure have," replied the driver. "We've got a new mayor. He's building the city up pretty well. Lots of attention."

"No more union strikes?" asked Austin, remembering the garbage collectors' strike. He had left for Palo Alto three years ago, with mountains of uncollected garbage on the streets.

"Didn't say that!" said the cabby, catching Austin's eye in the rear-view mirror. "Philly's still Philly," he laughed.

"Speaking of which, can you take me along Boat House Row?" asked Austin.

"To get to the Northeast? It's way out of the way."

"It's been a while. I like to watch the crew teams working. I'll pay for the extra time." It would be out of the way, but Austin needed the diversion. Anyway, he wasn't ready to arrive at his aunt's house. Not yet. He was too "off beat" and needed to ease into what was ahead. The drive past the old, familiar scenes—the river, the crews practicing—eased his anxiety and helped prepare him for what lay ahead. He watched the straining crews and knew they were at their limit of pain. He was dealing with a different kind of pain. They had theirs. He had his.

Austin was staying with his Aunt Diana in what they call the Northeast—a sort of "second" Philadelphia, separate from Center City or University City, or South Philly. The Northeast was like a world unto itself, and they liked it that way. People there owned their homes, which for the most part were small and standard. Most people in the Northeast worked hard for what they had and took pride in it.

Austin stepped out of the taxi with his sax slung over one shoulder and his Army surplus duffle bag slung over the other. Had his aunt changed much? What would he say? Would her hair be grayer than it was last Christmas? He hadn't really seen much of his aunt over the last three years, being in college and all. How was she reacting to her older sister's death? Hell, he wasn't even sure how he was reacting. What he remembered most about his aunt happened when he was a little kid of about six. She took him to the park where he fell off a swing and broke his arm. To a six-year-old it was the end of the world, but she didn't seem too concerned about it. That didn't seem right to an injured little boy and since then, he'd kept his distance, seeing her only with his mother at Christmas.

"Hi, Aunt Diana." Austin laid his duffle bag down in the foyer.

"Austin, sweetheart, how are you? You look great, honey. How're you doing?"

"I'm OK. I guess, considering. Hey, I smell something good."

"Of course you do. You think I wouldn't make my famous stew for you, honey? Anyway, a few of my friends have been stopping by to spend some time with me since your mom died, so it's nice to have something to serve them."

"Are you OK Aunt Diana?"

"I will be, honey. It takes time, you know. Anyway, it's good to see you," she said brightly. "Why don't you go on up to your room and get settled in."

Austin was up the stairs before she finished her sentence. Aunt Diana hadn't changed much though. Oh, my God, did he hug her? No, he didn't think so.

Leaving his sax and his bag on the bed, Austin went down to the kitchen. The walls had been the same awful yellow for as long as he could remember. "I love your stew, Aunt Diana." He moved up to her, and he hugged her. She was a thin, gaunt woman with her hair in a bun and an intense air about her, completely different from his mom.

"Sit down. I made some coffee." The cream and sugar were already on the table.

Austin took a long sip of coffee and cleared his throat. "So what's going on with the arrangements? By the way, thanks for doing so much." He smiled.

"Oh, Austin, your mother was a good woman." He thought he saw tears in her eyes.

"I know," said Austin. "I hope she was happy."

"How long will you be staying?"

"Only through the funeral and the weekend. I have to get back to classes."

"She was proud of you, you know."

"I hope so. You know, she made me take music lessons. If it weren't for her pushing me, I'd never have gotten that scholarship, let alone have gotten into Stanford to begin with. She was a good mother," Austin said, fighting back the mist in his own eyes.

"She was a survivor, Austin. After your father died, she had a rough time as a single mother, but she pulled through—for you and for herself."

"I know, I know," said Austin while biting his nails.

"I wanted to give her the best send-off we can," said Diana. That's the least I can do for my older sister. I always did what I could for her after your father died, Austin. But your mother pulled away—from me, from everyone. It wasn't my fault."

"Well, we always saw you on holidays," he said brightly, trying to lighten up the mood.

"First, I've made all the funeral arrangements," she said in a businesslike tone. "The service will be held at St. Paul's Church. I hope that's OK with you."

"It's fine. What do you need me to do?"

"Everything's taken care of. But it seems like you're going to be busier than you think."

Austin found this a bit strange. Usually, the bereaved greeted the guests—there shouldn't be too many—and did little else. Emotionally draining, yes, but it shouldn't keep him busy.

"When's the funeral?"

"Saturday afternoon at 2," she replied.

"I have a little money in the bank, and I was happy to put it toward giving your mother a decent funeral. Well, you can imagine my surprise when I got a call from her lawyer regarding her will."

"Will? Mom had a will?" Austin leaned forward.

"More like an estate that needs to be settled, the lawyer said. But that's your business, I guess. That's the first I ever heard of her having any financial matters to speak of. She was a very private person and never told me anything," she said with a sound of hurt in her voice.

"An estate?" He noticed that clicking noise of his nail biting. He had to stop that! He'd done it for years—part of being a nervous kid growing up without much security and no father, he supposed.

"I don't know anything about it, Austin. I guess I'm not entitled to the details. But you have an appointment with a Mr. Clark Parkinson tomorrow. I have his card on the counter somewhere. His office is in Center City. On Walnut Street. I take it he's a very important person. He said the funeral arrangements would all be paid for out of her estate. I don't know any more than that, Austin. No one tells me anything."

Diana got up and tended to her stew in a sort of sullen silence. Austin didn't know what to think about this news. Was his mother rich? Couldn't be. Absolutely couldn't be. His father? No, he was retired from the military when he died and they sure didn't pay well. So where did the "estate" come from? How could that be?

Did he really know them? Not his father of course, but what was there about his mother he never knew?

"Aunt Diana."

"Yes, honey," she said without turning away from the stove.

"Things will be OK," he said, trying to assure himself as much as her.

"We'll see, honey." He could tell her feelings were hurt by being left in the dark, and especially by that unknown attorney jumping in at the last minute to pay for the funeral. What's going on here, he thought.

Austin took a bowl of stew and went back up to his room. What a surprise this was turning out to be! Was it good or bad? He didn't like not knowing what was going on. In fact, he hated it. He'd always been the kind of person who needed to feel secure and understand things, and he understood none of this. This was the first he'd heard of any attorney, of any will, of any estate. Estate? It all sounded so substantial and serious—even a little pompous. Like his aunt, Austin always thought his mother had just enough money to get by. Now this? But Austin was looking forward to meeting the lawyer. He had to admit being excited by all this surprising mystery. What had been going on all his life that he never knew about? Austin wished he could talk to his mother for a long, long time and regretted the many times he could have, but didn't. He couldn't help but thinking—how well did I really know her?

.

Chapter 2

HE arrived downtown about 10 the next morning, heading to the attorney's office. He had spent the night wondering about this will and this surprising turn of events. It wasn't as if he expected some sort of inheritance or something like that. He didn't want that guilt, and it was too late now to reconcile "normal" desires, now that both his parents were dead. No, he just had to know what was going on. How many times had he warned his mother not to ever throw him a surprise party? He had a thing about surprises—he didn't like them. It was the not knowing that bothered him. Well, nothing wrong in having that little hang-up, if you can call it that.

Power and money—that's how the law office felt the moment he walked in. It reminded him of one of those Michael Douglas movies—offices of rich investment bankers or corporate attorneys. The elevator even had wood paneling. This was his mother's lawyer? No attorney here would come cheap. That was for sure. More mystery. More unanswered questions. Austin wondered about an affair. Maybe his mother was having an affair with one of the lawyers. Then he felt guilty about even thinking about it. According to his aunt, she had no personal outside social life. His mother had her volunteer interests here and there, but nothing he would call a steady social life. At least that's what he thought. But who could be sure of anything now? Did she ever date after his father died? It was sort of a "don't ask, don't tell" kind of thing. But now it was time to ask and find out what had been going on all this time.

Austin stepped out of the elevator looking down at his unpolished loafers. He knew he didn't fit in these plush surroundings. The receptionist's desk loomed in front of him.

"May I help you?" asked the receptionist. Austin looked up and stared a moment. She was beautiful and young. Now this was a woman who would date a high-powered lawyer. No hair up in a bun like a widow would wear. No wrinkles, self-confident, ambitious.

"I have an appointment with Mr. Parkinson."

The receptionist looked down at her appointment book. "And you are?"

"Austin Montgomery."

She paused. "You said you had an appointment with Mr. Parkinson?" She thumbed through some pages.

"Yes, I believe so."

"Oh, yes, here you are. Austin Montgomery," she looked up. It was the way she smiled at him that made Austin miss a beat. When a beautiful woman smiles at you, it means she likes you. At least that's what he wanted to believe. He smiled back.

"Please have a seat," she said. Austin was already on his way to the leather couch. She picked up the phone and said something. "Austin, Mr. Parkinson will be right with you." She used his first name. To him, it suggested intimacy.

For a fleeting moment Austin forgot he was there because of his mother's death. He came back to reality and was hit with a sharp pang of guilt, the sort only a mother can inflict on a son, even from the grave. Austin put the receptionist out of his head.

He thumbed through some magazines in the reception area and thought back to his big interview at Stanford. Not his interview with the marching band director. That was a piece of cake. He was a good player, after all, and his background in jazz was icing on the cake, especially since California marching bands are fierce rivals. Their directors value musical ability just like the athletic coaches value speed and strength. And they give good scholarships to get that ability, just like the athletic scholarships. The big interview was with the admissions committee. They surprised him by pressing him on issues beyond the scope of music—politics, current events, history, and aesthetics. They had blindsided him with intense questions. He didn't do well with surprises, and he left thinking he was destined for some community college somewhere. But he passed with flying colors.

College days soon settled into a routine and were pretty much laid back—classes, dinner, a date, chats with his band director or the guys in his weekend jazz band. As a liberal arts major, he'd had it pretty easy.

But sitting here in this plush law office, he fought the intense desire to bite his nails. He picked up *Esquire* instead. Fashion, a piece on owning a dog in the city, an article on retirement planning—are you making the most of your 401(k)? It was impossible to sit up tall on these couches. He was self-conscious sitting in this room with the beautiful receptionist watching him. She was watching him, wasn't she? Did he look like a bird craning its neck? He quickly looked at her, hoping to catch her checking him out. She had forgotten he was even here.

To kill time, Austin started reading something about some popular trend called stock "indexing" and how indexing was a sound way of minimizing risk for an acceptable rate of return. It was all Greek to him. That's when Clark Parkinson breezed into the reception area. Austin looked up at the older man standing in front of him and stood to greet his mother's attorney.

"Austin Montgomery, you do look like your mother." Parkinson had the air of a country doctor whose gentle demeanor could assuage the most serious prognosis.

"Mr. Parkinson," said Austin while extending his hand. "It's a pleasure to meet you."

"Good to meet you too, Austin. Why don't we go on back to my office? Would you care for a cup of coffee?"

"No thank you."

"Are you sure? Denise will get it for you," said Parkinson, gesturing towards the receptionist.

"No thanks."

"We'll be in my office, Denise. Come on, Austin."

It was an office with a view overlooking City Hall, a perfect extension of the reception area, with leather from a hundred cows. Leather and brass—neat and orderly.

"Nice office, Mr. Parkinson." But Austin was overwhelmed with the air of serious solemnity that pervaded everything in the offices.

"I have to admit, Mr. Parkinson," started Austin, "I'm a little confused. I thought my mother was a simple person with, well... limited means and a simple life."

"She was indeed a lady with a simple life, Austin. Simple means, though? We'll see. And, by the way, call me Clark. Believe me, we'll be on quite friendly terms if all goes as planned." He began assembling some papers.

"Is this about an inheritance from my mother?" asked Austin.

Parkinson smiled. "Well..."

"I mean, I really wasn't expecting such a...production regarding my mother. For all I knew, my mother was a woman of modest means, right?" he said, replying to his own question and gesturing emphatically with his hands. He wanted answers. "I mean, it took a scholarship to get me into Stanford, Mr. Parkinson. We didn't have the money. It's been quite a struggle financially. So why all of this?" Austin's furrowed brow announced his confusion. He used to look like that when he was first learning to play sharps and flats.

"Simply put, Austin," Parkinson said, "we're here to read your parents' will. First, let me express my condolences. I've been with them for quite some time, and this is actually a special moment for me—sort of a culmination of a generation. Believe me, the world is a lesser place without them." He immediately locked eyes with Austin. "Your parents left you quite a legacy, my friend."

Austin ran his fingers through his hair. "My father is involved in this?" Now he was really confused. He came looking for answers, but the mystery was deepening. "Parents" meant mother and father. But Austin's father died when he was only five—ages ago. He had never been a factor in Austin's life. Aside from pictures and some stories his mother told him, Austin knew very little about his father. Unlike the other kids he grew up with, Austin had no father to help him grow up, be his buddy or teach him how to hit a ball. At first he'd deeply felt the loss, and then turned his back on it, erasing it from his memory.

"I thought this meeting was to discuss my mother's will," said Austin.

"It is, Austin. You have to understand that your mother was determined to continue where your father left off. So this is about both of them."

"Outside of some stories, I don't know too much about my father's successes or failures," Austin said. "Aside from some pictures, all I really know is that he was in the military and was killed in a car accident. I mean, we mentioned his birthday and stuff, but my mother and I rarely spoke about him."

"Really?" wondered Parkinson.

"Were you and my mother seeing each other or something? Of course, she's free to…."

Parkinson stopped Austin mid-sentence. "Actually, John—that is, your father—and I were roommates in college. I like to think I was his best friend. We were close right up to his death. And as his friend and lawyer, I'm proud to help carry out some of his deepest wishes."

"Wishes?" said Austin. He leaned forward, now even more confused.

"Austin, your father lived a sort of charmed life."

"Yeah, sure. Except that he died when I was a kid. Is that charmed?"

"I stand corrected. What I mean to say is that your father was quite a successful investor, Austin." He smiled, leaned back in his chair, and waited for Austin to crack some sort of emotional gesture. Parkinson would follow from there.

"Really?" That was news. "Was he rich?"

"My boy," chimed Parkinson with outstretched arms, "you are quite the fortunate son. Let's talk about you. You are rich. And as you'll see, you can become even richer thanks to your father."

Austin leaned back in his chair. Things were suddenly very different. "I'm ah…confused. Excuse my language, but what the hell are you talking about?"

Parkinson sighed. "Your mother—well, she was never the same after your father's death. But she was faithful to his wishes. Anyway, regarding the matter at hand, your father also had a serious side when it came to money. He was quite a survivor, always boasted about his ability to land on his feet. We used to call him 'The Cat' at college," Parkinson grinned. "Toward the end of his life, your father began doing very well with investments. In fact, he became very wealthy."

"Did all this money suddenly disappear into thin air when he died?" Austin asked, with a bitter edge to his voice. "You know, I had nothing for college. I've been through some pretty tough times financially. Things haven't been easy." He knew that without hustling for that scholarship, he would've wound up at a community college somewhere, studying and holding down a job. Austin was visibly annoyed. On top of all that, here was a complete stranger who knew his parents far better than he ever did.

"Why didn't my mother ever tell me about my father or about her own money? Didn't she trust me? Why did she keep secrets? Christ, I'm starting to think I don't even know my own mother."

Parkinson put down his pen and neatly stacked the papers in front of him. "Austin," his voice was calm but pointed now, "believe me when I tell you that you'll be quite amazed and, I dare say, pleased by what I have to tell you. But make no mistakes about it: what you've had to do is no different from what your father had to do in order to make his mark on the world. Your mother held up her end of her obligation. She allowed you to work through life by yourself. That's what your father wanted. She did what she had to do."

"I didn't know children were supposed to do everything on their own," Austin said with a biting sarcasm coming from the hurt inside.

"Well, as you'll see, the answer—or rather, their answer—was yes and no," said Parkinson. "Besides, your mother was a quiet woman, and she became withdrawn after your father died. I called her a number of times, but we only had your father's memory in common—not the most pleasant of commonalties, Austin. As far as I can remember, I never saw her out or attending any of the social events your father enjoyed. All I can say is that people handle life's disappointments in different ways."

Austin was, by now, totally confused. After all, he could

hardly believe he was coming to a lawyer at all, let alone coming to settle some sort of grand estate secret. There was nothing about this meeting that was simple or easy to understand. Here he was talking to a complete stranger who knew his parents far better than he ever did.

"Why did they keep secrets from me?" Austin blurted out.

"I don't know, son. Your mother and I sort of lost contact after the accident. Your mother died thinking she did the right thing. And you should be sure of that, too. What is important here is your parents' wishes for you. That's where they really show their love to you. And that's where I enter to fulfill my professional and personal obligations to them. Your mother only did what she had to do, Austin. Don't hold that against her."

Austin replied, "But after all this, I really don't know what to believe anymore." Enough of that. Don't get hung up on the past, Austin said to himself. "OK, they did what they thought was best for me, even if they kept it a secret from me. So, where do we go from here?"

"Please allow me to continue," said Parkinson. "When your father was alive, he set up a special trust for you. It was intended to be a secret until after your mother died, which is why you never knew anything about it until today. It was your father's wish that the trust remain a secret to you, and your mother remained faithful to his wishes."

Austin's eyes lit up at the word trust. "So what's left over from my mother's estate goes to me, right?"

"Actually no," said Parkinson, "Your father's trust was set up for you and only you. Your mother had no say over the assets. While your father was alive, he acted as trustee. After his death, I assumed that responsibility."

"Was my mother rich?"

"Yes, she had her own trust. She has quite an estate of her own, but you're not involved in that. The remainder of her estate will go to breast cancer research, which is only fitting I suppose."

Austin's mouth was agape. "That's amazing," he said, while still trying to figure out what it all meant.

"Let me see if I understand all this. My father made a lot of money through investments. He set up a trust for me, which was to go to me when my mother died. But she had to keep it a secret from me. My mother had her own money, and left it to charity. I'm not involved in that. Is that about it?"

"That's it, Austin. You've got it."

"So pretty much everyone else has had control over my life, and I was kept in the dark?"

"Until today, Austin, yes. But from today things are different."

Parkinson continued. "Now, although this may seem a bit confusing to you, Austin, your father always tried to keep things simple. He had a penchant for order, and his investment philosophy reflected this most of all. He went to great lengths to keep things simple, and this trust is no exception. For example, there's a condition for this trust to be dissolved and for you to get the money."

"What condition?" Austin asked suspiciously and worriedly.

"Well, it's in your own interest."

"More mysteries," Austin said. "OK, what's the condition?" But Parkinson was masterful at drawing out the issue and wouldn't be rushed. Austin could hardly bear the suspense.

"First off," said Parkinson, "let me tell you what will be done immediately—today. No conditions. No strings attached. When you leave here today, Austin, you'll have a check for one million dollars in your pocket." He watched Austin's shocked reaction and said, "Buys a lot of reeds, doesn't it?"

"You're kidding. Come on, is this a joke?"

"It's no joke, Austin. I have a check for one million dollars right here," he said, tapping a folder, "and you leave with it today."

That took Austin's breath away. The sheer size of the amount was staggering.

"Well, how-?" he stammered.

"You're a millionaire, Austin. Thanks to your father." Parkinson folded his hands in his lap. "But-"

"Come on," Austin interjected. "This can't be for real. What's the condition? What do I have to do—be married by midnight? What's the catch? There's always a catch."

"Relax Austin," Parkinson said. "Actually, meeting the condition is up to you. Your father, being a clever man, added this condition to your trust."

"What's the condition?" Austin asked again, this time less angry and with his excitement rising. It was dawning on him that this was for real. This was really happening. A million dollars! A new car, vacations, trips—girls. Yes, lots of girls. He was only 21 after all—a great time to enjoy life.

"There's another five million dollars, plus interest, that you'll receive. Only this time, as I said, there's a condition to receiving the five million. You've got to do something to get the additional five million dollars. The condition is simple. You must prove to me, as trustee, that you have earned 15% a year on the one million dollars I'll be giving you today, for three years." Parkinson sat back in his chair. "There it is," he said with outstretched hands.

Austin forgot about the car, vacations and girls and came crashing down to earth. "Wait. Do I understand there's five million dollars more and all I've got to do is earn some interest?"

"Well, not quite that simple," Parkinson laughed. Suddenly serious, he said, "Austin, this is very important. Let me explain it very carefully and if you don't understand, tell me. Five million dollars is riding on what I'm about to tell you. If you can prove you have legally earned this 15% a year rate of return for 3 years, you'll receive an additional five million dollars."

"And if I can't," asked Austin, "I lose it all?"

"No, no. You keep your million, or whatever's left of it at the time," he laughed. "Lord knows there will be temptations to spend that money imprudently. But you'll forfeit the additional five million. It'll all go to a charity your father has designated."

Austin was stunned. First, he was raised without a father. Now his father was dictating his future with intractable rules. He was giving a gift—and controlling his life—from the grave. But still, Austin was a millionaire! He was numb. This had all been too much to absorb so quickly. He had to get it right.

"OK, let me understand what you're saying, because I don't want to make any mistakes."

"Good idea," said Parkinson.

"I leave here today with one million dollars. Right? It's mine. No strings? "

"Yes," said Parkinson. "Effective today, you're a millionaire.

No conditions."

"Then," continued Austin, "if I can show you that I invested the money to get a 15% return in three years, I will get an additional five million dollars?"

"Plus you get to keep what you earn on that original one million, plus the interest on the five million," added Parkinson.

"Do I need to earn 15% each year?"

"No, but you must average 15% a year. In other words, three years from now you have to prove to me that your one million dollars has grown to $1,520,875. Remember that figure—$1,520,875."

"So the original million is mine no matter what?"

"Yes, unless of course, you lose it trying to earn your 15%. And believe me, you could. By the way, gambling is not applicable here because the money can't be verified. Just as well, believe me. What you'll find is that you can earn, say 5% one year, even lose money, and make 30% another year. Just so long as your one million grows to $1,520,875—an average of 15% per year—over the three years."

"When does the three-year period begin?" asked Austin. "Do I have time to prepare?"

"Take all the time you want," said Parkinson. "But the moment you cash this check for one million dollars, the clock starts ticking." Parkinson opened the file, took out a check, and handed it to Austin. "Here's the check."

Austin stared at the small piece of paper—all those zeros! He was amazed that if he walked across the street to the bank, he could hand someone this little piece of paper and receive in return one million dollars! It seemed completely unreal. What a strange thing for his father to do, thought Austin. It actually seemed so complicated. Was all this necessary? It was almost torturous. In a flash, he had very mixed feelings about his father. Gratitude and resentment—both were at war inside him. Why put that condition—and burden—on him? Why not just give him the money and be done with it?

As if he could read Austin's mind, Parkinson said, "Austin, your father talked it over with me. He wanted to give you not only a gift of money, but also a gift of a challenge and a sort of special education—to learn what he had learned. He set it up so you could take the million and blow it. He wanted you to have that right. But he believed in you—that you'd pass the test. Maybe he even had a premonition that he might not be around by the time you became a young man. I don't know. But this is a gift in a lot more ways than you know, son."

Austin listened. He'd have to sort out his complicated feelings about his father later.

"What sort of documentation do I need to maintain?" asked Austin, getting back to the subject.

"It must all be legal, and on the up-and-up. All investments must be converted into U.S. dollars for calculations. For example, if you want to invest overseas that's perfectly fine, just so long as you convert everything back to dollars for final calculations. I will also need all final documentation audited and verified by a CPA." Parkinson clasped his hands. "Any further questions?"

Austin had a question for every dollar at stake—a million questions. This was a condition and test he simply had not expected. He was afraid and excited at the same time. He—a guy who didn't like surprises—had just had about the biggest surprise anyone could ever have. He'd walked in with curiosity. He'd risen to the heights of joy with the news of the one million dollars and all it would bring. Then he was brought crashing back to earth with the strict condition his father had imposed. Now he was stressed-out, doubtful that he could meet his father's high demands. What a roller-coaster ride this morning had been! One thing he knew for sure, though. This was his big chance—bigger by far than any scholarship.

"What should I do from here? I have no idea where to start," Austin stammered.

"As I said, Austin, if you need time to properly prepare yourself for this challenge—and it is a challenge—take your time. Don't cash that check yet. When you do, the clock starts. There's a great deal at stake."

"I know, Mr. Parkinson. I know." Austin was feeling a level of stress he couldn't control. He was sweating a bit, and he couldn't think very well. "Will you be helping me?"

"Austin, I have to be neutral. I hope you understand that. You have to earn this yourself. That's the point your father had in mind. You have at your fingertips, Austin, the opportunity to become wealthier than you could ever imagine. It happened for your father, and I really believe it can happen for you, too. But just like your father, you have to take this opportunity—an opportunity someone else is giving you—and make it into something which can change your life for the better. You could say that from the grave your father is trying to teach you the lessons he had struggled so hard to learn, but died too soon to teach you."

Austin was still struggling with those strong and complex feelings about his father. He'd just file Parkinson's comment to sort out another time.

"Well, speaking of learning things, what do I do about Stanford?"

"By all means, Austin, get your degree! What's more, you're in store for one hell of a post-graduate education once you cash this check, believe me. Contrary to your father's wishes, Austin, the world is a complicated place. People who would have never even noticed you this morning will go to great lengths to get their share of you this afternoon. People will try to take advantage of you, that much I'll tell you. But if you're like your father, Austin—and I think you may be—you can trust your instincts. Always trust your instincts, especially about people."

"I hope you're right about that, Mr. Parkinson. But to be honest, the first thing that went through my head when the million dawned on me was a new car and girls. Actually, one car and lots of girls."

Parkinson laughed heartily, breaking the tense atmosphere. "I wouldn't recommend starting quite like that. There'll be plenty of time for that, believe me. And you're only 21. Seriously though," he said, "I do have some advice for you. It's from your father. As I said, he had a certain wisdom for simplification. He made a lot of money investing and being a man who loved simplicity he reduced the mysteries of investing to a three-part question—a simple, three-part question."

"Should I write this down?" asked Austin.

"I would," replied Parkinson handing Austin a pad and a pen.

"OK. First question: What should you buy with your

money? That is, what do you invest in?" Austin scribbled it down. "Second Question: When do you sell that investment? At a profit? At a loss? Or at a bigger profit? The third question: What do you do with the proceeds of that sale?"

When Austin finished writing he asked, "Whom do I ask these questions?"

"Ask anyone who claims to be an investment advisor ready to help you. And listen carefully—very carefully—to their answers. Your father did. All kinds of people are out there ready to take your money and risk it. After all, it's your money, not theirs. Use these three questions to screen them—to show you if they have a strategy or are investing by the seat of their pants. That's what your father did. If they can't answer these simple questions to your satisfaction, you have to wonder what they base their investment decisions on. You'll probably find that most investment advisors have no coherent strategy whatsoever and many get by on blind luck. When they invest your money and win, it's their skill. When they lose your money, it's the 'market' or the 'economy' or some such excuse. Frankly, this is the last thing you want, right?"

"Absolutely," replied Austin. "I don't want luck. I want a plan, plain and simple."

"You sound like your father already. Luck should have no place in your investments, Austin. And if you use your father's three questions while interviewing prospective advisors, you'll eventually find someone who can provide you with the strategy and planning you need to get that five million."

"So this is the strategy my father used to become wealthy?"

"Well," replied Parkinson, "let's say it's how he selected people who could help him become wealthy. That's what we're talking about. After all, Austin, you're already rich. Now you're looking for someone to help you become even more successful."

Austin had to trust Parkinson on this. The lawyer looked like he knew what he was talking about. Then it hit Austin. His father was giving him a structured and orderly means of making something of himself. Like everything else about his father, he had to think about that some more.

"How often should we meet?" asked Austin.

"As often as you like," answered Parkinson. "Remember,

though, I can't help you make decisions. You're on your own. But feel free to call me when you want to talk. I recommend that we stay in touch." He handed Austin a business card. "Again, my condolences about your mother, but congratulations all the same." Parkinson stood up and extended his hand.

"We're finished?" said Austin, standing to shake Parkinson's hand.

"I'd love to have lunch with you, but I have other appointments. I'm sure we'll be seeing each other often in the future."

Leaving Clark Parkinson's office was certainly easier than arriving. On his way out, Austin winked at the receptionist. She was on the phone and once again didn't even notice him.

Next time, Austin thought.

Chapter 3

HE grabbed a taxi and headed back to his aunt's house. In his pocket was a small fortune. He could actually do nothing and be a millionaire. He was still stunned by it all. On the ride home, it slowly dawned on him how clever—maybe you could even call it manipulative—his father had been. He'd left him a temptation—take the million and blow it having fun. And he'd left him a test—use it to earn the other five million he had dangled like bait out there in front of him. But to get the five million, he'd set a tough condition and very high hurdle. To get it Austin would have to buckle down, grow up and get serious —and fast. Well, that's what the old man wanted, Austin said to himself, smiling. A temptation and a test! Smart. The old man was really smart, Austin had to admit.

About halfway home, Austin began feeling more manipulated than anything else. He wasn't quite sure why. This whole thing with his father was affecting him more than he knew. For one thing, he hadn't thought about his mother in the last hour and a half. Instead, he was consumed with his million and the five million dangling out there in front of him. He felt guilty about that. Twice during the meeting, he'd thought about asking Parkinson if he could legally break his mother's gift to breast cancer research. And how much money did she have? Now, he was ashamed that he'd even thought of that.

By the time he got home, he'd decided his mother's money was hers to do with what she wanted. No, he'd better focus on the challenge of earning that five million his father was dangling in front of him. To do that, he'd have to be as systematic as possible. The whole point of the condition, as it was becoming clear, was to help him become more systematic and responsible. If he couldn't, he'd forfeit the additional money—and that would be a crushing defeat. Sure, he wanted the money, but above all he wanted to beat the challenge, and pass the test his father was putting him through. Earlier this morning, one million dollars would have been all the money in the world. Now it faded into the background as he focused on the five million—just as his father knew he would. After all, Austin Montgomery was a chip off the old block.

When he arrived at his aunt's, Diana was just setting the table for coffee and cake. Lemon poppy cake was Austin's favorite, so she baked it all morning to cheer him up.

"How did it go?" she asked Austin when he came into the kitchen.

"It was OK. Hey, lemon poppy cake."

"Have a seat. I just took it out of the oven, honey. So it was all right? No great surprises? My friends were telling me that settling an estate can be emotionally draining, not to mention having to show up at an attorney's office. So what did he want? Was there some jewelry or something?"

Austin didn't know how to answer. He loved his aunt, but he knew she was—well, let's face it—a kind of busybody, curious and poking her nose where it didn't belong. His own mother had once told him that. Everyone's business was hers, especially now her nephew's. How would she feel when he told her he was a millionaire? What's more, what would she say when he told her there was nothing for her? No, the less said, the better.

"The meeting went fine," he said. "Did you know that Clark Parkinson was their friend for some time? He was dad's college roommate," he said trying to change the subject.

"Now that you mention it, I do recall your mother

mentioning something like that. He might have called once while I was over at her house or something." She sat down and cut two pieces of cake.

"Did you know my father at all?"

"Yes and no," answered Diana. "He was a nice guy. Treated everyone well. Kept to himself. I assumed he was nice to me because I was his wife's sister. I remember one time he came back from a trip and gave me a beautiful gold bracelet with emeralds. He remembered it was my birthstone. He was like that. He wouldn't talk too much with me, but he knew my birthstone."

"Did mom wear a lot of jewelry?" He took a bite of cake.

"Yes, that's why I asked if the meeting was about her jewelry. Actually, she donated most of it after he died. I guess she felt better giving it to strangers. I never wore that bracelet after that, out of respect. I guess she kept a piece or two for memories, huh?"

"What about bank accounts and stuff," he asked, keeping the questions flowing.

"I don't know, Austin. You'd know better than I would now. You should have asked the lawyer about that. That's important. I do have a box of pictures upstairs, though. There are a bunch with you and your father. I'll give them to you later."

Austin finished his cake and decided he needed to lie down for a bit. What a morning it had been! Everything had changed in just a few hours. He excused himself without saying more about his meeting with Parkinson. "I might be staying a while longer than I expected," he said. "I can do my college assignments from home. They'll understand."

"I'm sure they will, dear," said his aunt.

Austin was fatigued while in the kitchen, but as soon as he was alone in his bedroom, he felt vibrant and excited. Maybe he'd leave school altogether. Why waste time there? No, he had to keep his feet on the ground. He needed the college education, and he'd certainly want a degree from Stanford. It would give him a pedigree when he met other rich people—rich people like him. Rich like him! The thought was overwhelming. What a difference one morning made! He looked at the check to make sure it was still there; that he hadn't dreamed up all this fantastic morning. Those zeros were for real! He fell asleep thinking of all the beautiful resorts around the world he could go in the next three years. And he wouldn't go alone. The "temptation" side of his father's plan was working overtime.

The next day, Saturday, was the day he had to bury his mother. He did his best to push all the previous day's shocking events to the background and focus on saying good-bye to his mother. She'd had the greatest influence on his life, mostly by her example. She'd thrown herself into charity work after his father's death. Not the fund-raisers, which often are fronts for social climbing and making contacts, but the hard, practical work in the hospital. She read books to bed-ridden children. She comforted the lonely—everything practical. Nothing was beneath her. She was a giving, caring woman, and those who came out that rainy Saturday to say good-bye knew and loved her. And more than a little of her character had rubbed off on Austin. He'd gotten his self-reliance, self-drive and caring from her. More than once when facing some dilemma or quandary, he'd find himself asking what his mother would do.

By Monday the funeral was in the past and the challenge of his completely changed life faced Austin. He had a job to do and a test to pass. He felt totally focused, just as if he was rowing again. Now, he had to develop a plan and a strategy. The first thing to do was to figure out when to cash the check. Once he did that, there was no turning back, and time became his enemy. Austin didn't want to rush things. He couldn't afford mistakes. So he decided to do as much fact gathering as he possibly could before starting the countdown.

He knew next to nothing about investing. No one ever taught him about stocks and bonds in school. That was problem number one, he thought. Imagine how many choices there must be that he didn't even know about? Stocks, bonds, starting a business—these things came to mind. Maybe real estate. He was sure people made money in real estate.

Austin got out of bed deciding to spend the day investigating opportunities in the stock market. That seemed like a good place to start. Well, take it one step at a time, he told himself. Start with stocks. Then move on to real estate. After all, it can't be that difficult, he said to himself as he brushed his teeth.

As Austin shaved that morning, he looked at himself in the bathroom mirror. He had what might have been the best sleep of his life. Understandably, he was not the most secure person in the world. He had a nervous stomach, especially when things became disorderly or unpredictable. He liked—no, needed—order in his life. Music attracted him because it is disciplined, orderly. But, being a new millionaire must have soothed him, though. He wasn't nearly as nervous as he thought he'd be. His main worry was blowing his big chance. Not only did he risk losing five million dollars plus interest, he also risked losing the original one million. He showered with a renewed sense of resolve. Today was for stocks. He'd heard people made big money there.

Downstairs, a hearty breakfast awaited him. Diana prepared eggs, bacon, ham, fresh juice and muffins. "It helps keep me busy, Austin. It's really no problem at all. Come on, sit down."

Austin sat down and began to eat heartily. "Do you get a newspaper?" he asked.

"Yes, I get the Philadelphia Inquirer." She handed him the paper. He laid it next to his plate and began thumbing through. "Are you looking through the classifieds already?" she asked him.

"Actually, I'm looking for the business section," he replied.

"I heard on the radio that the job market in Philadelphia is getting tougher and tougher for young people. Are you planning on coming back after you graduate?"

One thing he liked about Diana—she never asked him what he was going to do with his music major. "To tell you the truth, I'm not sure yet," he said. "Actually, I was looking for some information on stocks."

Diana was at the sink and answered without turning around. "Really? That must have been some visit with the lawyer." He could sense she was about to ask another question.

"Have you ever invested in stocks?" asked Austin. He had learned with his aunt to pre-empt her questions with his own.

"Well, Austin, you know I never went in for that, not on my budget. I had a retirement plan at work. Just my nest egg money."

"All these years in school," Austin replied, "you'd think someone would teach us how to invest money. I mean, part of the point of getting an education is to get a good job and make money.

But what do you do with what you save? What then?" Austin came to the vast columns of stock quotes and put the paper down. Diana sat down at the table next to him. "At the risk of sounding stupid, it always seemed so confusing. Nowadays, there are commercials all the time about this company and that company, always attacking each other...this return and that return. With five experts you get six opinions. Economics never interested me. Why do you ask?"

Austin had to decide then and there how to handle telling his aunt about the money he had received. "Well, it seems Dad had quite a lot of money which he left to me, but not to mom. That's why you never knew about it." He felt the tension in the air as Diana cleared his plates.

She was back at the sink. "Really? Is it a lot?"

"Yes it is."

"Did your mother have money, too?"

"It was left to charity. I had nothing to do with it."

"I suppose not. Was breakfast OK?" she asked, struggling to sound disinterested.

"It was great." Austin sensed it was time to leave. He knew his aunt would keep probing and he needed out. He was feeling overwhelmed already. Parkinson was right. You just can't anticipate how people would react to your having money.

"I thought I'd spend the next day or so looking for someone who could help me with investments," he said as he got up to leave.

Diana took a deep breath. "You need a professional, then. Do the right thing, Austin. My friend Carol's brother is always talking about stocks whenever I see him. His name is Jim Burton. Maybe he can help you."

Austin was relieved. This was his exit cue. "Do you have his number?"

"There are a bunch of business cards in the drawer next to the phone. His card should be in there."

Austin called ahead and made an appointment with Jim Burton. He was downtown, like Parkinson. He called a cab and went on his way, leaving his aunt vacuuming the house.

Burton's office was in the Mellon Bank building. The office was not nearly as impressive as Parkinson's, but it was bustling with people Austin assumed were brokers who knew what they were doing. He felt better immediately. Burton came out to greet him.

"Austin, Jim Burton." They shook hands. "I'm sorry to hear about your mother. I met her a couple of times. She was a wonderful woman."

"Thank you, Mr. Burton."

They went back to Burton's office. Austin started right in. "My Aunt Diana thought you might be able to help me with some investments. I inherited some money, but I don't have much experience with investing."

"The issue," said Burton, "is not the amount of money, but knowing what to do with it, Austin. As an accountant, I deal with that every day."

"So you're an accountant," Austin asked, hoping he didn't sound disappointed.

Burton handed Austin a card. "Jim Burton, CPA, Arthur Waterhouse Inc."

Austin wondered how he missed that. His excitement must have blinded him to the obvious. "I'm probably not in the right place then. I thought you were a broker."

"Not me. Your aunt must have thought so because I talk about investments a lot. I hope she didn't say I was another Warren Buffet or something." He laughed, but the joke was lost on Austin. Sensing this, Burton continued. "Not to worry, my friend. I'll be more than happy to refer you to someone else. I'm a good friend with a broker at Washington Investments. His name is Bobby Lane. He's good. He knows what he's doing."

Austin began to feel better. Contacts. That's what he needed. "Is he your broker?"

"No, he's not. He works with some of my clients. I do their tax returns, and I can say they certainly do all right in the market. I'll even call him for you and arrange an appointment." Burton winked at Austin. "If I refer you, he'll take good care of you."

Austin smiled. "Thanks for your help. Sounds like I'm getting somewhere."

"I hope so," replied Burton. "Just keep in mind that, as with most things in life, you get what you pay for." Burton went on to tell Austin that successful advisors usually charge a fee or commission for their advice and guidance.

"So you can almost tell how good an advisor is by the fee they charge?" asked Austin.

Burton smiled. "Sort of, Austin, sort of. You'll find that the fees usually range from 1% to 4%. Commissions usually average about 1 ½%. Some brokers may charge a nominal commission—the so-called 'discount brokers'—but they usually give no advice. They just take your order."

Austin jotted all this down. Burton waited for him to catch up. "Large firms like Washington Investments pride themselves on the advice they provide their clients. Bobby Lane, for example. Bobby will tell you what to buy based on Washington Investments research department's recommendations. It's that simple."

Austin smiled. "Well, let's do it," he told Burton. "And thanks."

Austin hustled across town to Bobby Lane's office. Now he was on the right track. What Burton said about being referred to special people confirmed what Austin suspected since starting Stanford—it's all about whom you know. After all, his high school band instructor was a personal friend with the director of Stanford's marching band. The next thing he knew, Austin was flying out to California for an interview. That contact got him into Stanford. Contacts—that's what makes things happen. With any sort of luck, this Bobby Lane would be the man to show him how to make the money he needed. Those five million dollars seemed closer.

The Washington Investments office was very busy, and Austin felt he had definitely made the right decision coming to see Lane. Phones were ringing constantly; people were moving all around. There was a buzz about the place. The buzz of people making money, Austin thought.

When Bobby Lane walked into the reception area, Austin was immediately struck by the man's height. He had curly brown hair, wore large-framed glasses and a beige suit, that covered the height well. Austin introduced himself, and the two walked back to Lane's office.

"So your mother recently passed away? You have my condolences," said Lane.

"Thank you. I need your help in investing a small amount of money. It's not much," Austin lied, "but I could use your help all the same."

"How much money are we talking about?" said Lane, as he stubbed another cigarette out in the overflowing ashtray. This guy was a chain smoker.

"About $25,000," said Austin, a bit startled by his own lie.

"That sounds like a nice amount to work with," replied Lane. "Especially for a student. Makes you a bit more popular with the girls, huh?" Lane laughed and looked out his office door. "Excuse me a second, Austin." He yelled to his secretary who was sitting outside. "Barb, if Don Bush calls, tell him I'm out, and I said it was all right for him to sell the Banyan shares." He looked at Austin. "He made about four dollars a share today. Thousand shares. Not a bad day's work for him, huh? Where did you say you went to school?"

"I'm a senior at Stanford."

"Stanford's a great school. I played against them while I was at UCLA. Good rivalry. Cute girls, too." The phone rang. "Who is it, Barb?"

"It's your Uncle David."

"Tell him to hold. Excuse me a minute, Austin." He picked up the phone. "Hey, what's going on? Uh-huh? Don't know the stock. What do you hear? OK, just pick up a thousand shares. If it makes a few bucks, we'll sell out, grab the money and run. No problem. I will. Buzz me later." He hung up the phone. "He picks some good ones," he said to Austin. "Barb" he yelled, "Barb, pick up 1000 shares of Innovation for David at the market. Put it in all-or-none so he doesn't get screwed again."

"What's the symbol?" asked Barb.

"INVN, I think."

Austin was excited by all the action. Lane—a big man—was growing larger by the minute. Austin asked, "You played basketball?"

"Yup. God, those were the days, boy. Know what I mean? Fun. Boy, we crushed every team we played my senior year. We almost won the national championship. Can you imagine if that were today? I'd be a freakin' celebrity the way they treat athletes today. We traveled around the world playing ball… London, Bonn, Rome, Tokyo… oh, those Asian women."

Austin enjoyed talking to Bobby Lane. Lane was far more outgoing than Jim Burton. He was a people man—the kind that made great salesmen. And the stories he told and the way he told them conveyed to Austin a sense of enthusiasm and know-how.

"Do you mind if I ask you a question?" said Austin.

"I know," said Bobby. "You want to know how tall I am, don't you?"

"Well," responded Austin, "since you mentioned it. How tall are you?" He blushed a little.

"I'm six feet ten inches tall," said Lane, standing up to give the full effect.

Austin wondered how people as tall as Bobby functioned in a world constructed for shorter people. "Do you mind if I ask you another question? I mean, it's not often that I meet someone seven feet tall."

"Not seven feet tall," replied Bobby. "Six feet, ten inches," he said, sitting back down.

"I'll have to remember that," Austin smiled. "Where do you get your clothes? Do you have them specially made?" asked Austin.

"Well, there are specialty stores that cater to tall men, although I have my suits custom made." He smiled.

"Really? You know, I've always wanted to know," said Austin, "how basketball players take showers when you travel and stay in hotels. And how do you sleep in those short beds?"

Lane guffawed loudly. "You're actually the first person to ask me that," he said. "Believe it or not, most of the hotels we stayed in had long beds for athletes." He smiled. "Service industry. Anything you want. Showers, though, were impossible. Talk about inconvenient. I actually had to get on my knees!" As he said this, he lit up another cigarette.

The phone rang as Austin laughed. "Hey!" said Bobby, "don't take that comment out of context. People thought my knees were red from playing ball, but it was really from moving around on my knees in the shower. Hold on a sec…. Barb?"

"It's Danny Powell."

"Does he want to make a trade?" asked Lane.

"No, just checking in."

"Tell him he's still down on Pioneer Drilling, but we've got an order in to sell at 7 ½. But change it to 7. He should get filled. And tell him I rolled those calls we sold on AOL so he wouldn't lose the stock."

Austin was impressed. This guy had been around. The lingo and terminology were from a world of their own. The fast, sure decisions impressed him. This guy looked good. His suit looked great and his office was pretty big and had the appearance of wealth and success. He must know how to make money for people. But Lane's phone kept ringing, and he seemed to have a lot of clients. Austin wondered how much time Lane would devote to making Austin's 15%. Maybe it had something to do with the fact that Lane thought Austin only had $25,000. Perhaps that was to be expected, thought Austin, but he still didn't have a feel for Lane's thinking or strategy.

At that moment something happened to Austin for the first time in his life. He asked himself, what would his father do? Austin knew he'd probably be asking himself that question many times over the next three years. He had no other road map—no other guidance. It made him feel even more alone and on his own. It was just him—and his father's voice from the past.

Lane interrupted his thoughts. "Do you play ball? You must be popular with the ladies, huh? You'll have one on each arm by the time we're finished, Austin. The market's great. People are printing money. Money gets the chicks, Austin. It's my first rule of investing. Second rule?"

Austin smiled and shrugged his shoulders.

"Rule two," continued Lane. "You can't have enough of either. Right? Right?"

"I guess not," said Austin. And he pretty much believed Bobby on this one.

"Anyway," said Lane, "what should we do here?" The phone rang. "Excuse me...' he looked at his watch then at Austin. "I bet that's Rick Paxin. He always calls about now. Barb... is that Rick Paxin?"

"Yes, Bobby."

Lane picked up the phone. "Rick, talk to me, baby." He

laughed out loud. "You did not. You kill me, man. You really kill me, know that? Anyway, you're up ten on AOL... uh-huh... look, you can't lose if you take profits. We'll buy it back cheaper, I'm sure....what?... nothing goes straight up, Rick. No problem. Let's pick up some Innovation, too. I just this minute heard some good things about it. Hot stock. I can smell them. And I'm also buying High Speed Tech... looks good at first glance. No problem. Hey, advice is what I'm here for." Lane hung up the phone and entered the orders. "OK...Barb, hold my calls for a couple of minutes. Sorry, Austin. I'm all yours." He smiled.

"Well, like I said," responded Austin, "I have no idea what to do with the money. I was thinking about buying a car, but that would be a wasted opportunity. That much I do know."

"True. There's lots of money to be made, Austin."

"I play in a jazz band on the weekends," continued Austin, "so I have spending cash."

"Musicians have it all, huh?" grinned Lane. Austin shrugged. "Well, you won't need the money in the near future, right?"

"Right," answered Austin.

"Have you ever invested before?"

"This is my first time," said Austin.

Lane leaned back in his chair. "There are basically two choices you have when it comes to investing. The first is investing in stocks. The second is investing in bonds. It's that simple, really. Would it help if I described the differences of each? That way you can make your own decision and feel comfortable with what we do. All I want is for you to be satisfied and understand the sort of returns you will get for the risk you're willing to take. This way, we don't have any misunderstandings about returns, right?" Lane smiled.

Finally, thought Austin, we're getting to returns. "Good. Please continue."

Lane held up two hands, one representing stocks and the other representing bonds. He opened his left hand. "Stocks are issued by companies because they need money to continue operating and to grow. People buy the stock; thus, the company is called 'public' or 'publicly traded.' When a company sells stock to investors, the money is used to buy equipment, for example, or hire people. It should raise the sales of a company. The money may also be used to pay debts and so on. Is that clear?"

"Sure," answered Austin.

"Good. So when you buy a stock in a company, you are actually becoming an owner of that company." Lane noticed Austin smiling. "You like that, huh?"

"That I like," replied Austin. And he did. He loved the idea of owning part of a company.

"OK." Bobby opened his other hand. "Another way for a company to raise money in order to grow and expand is by borrowing it, right?"

"Bonds," asked Austin, a little more confused.

"Exactly," said Lane. "If you buy a bond from a company, you're essentially a creditor. This means that the company owes you back your money at some time in the future. Like a loan you are making to the company. Along the way, the company will pay you interest on your loan, just like you pay interest when you borrow money, right?

Austin was ready to talk returns. He wanted to hear about returns. "What kind of money can I make in each?"

"Well, that's the question. The rate you get on a bond depends on how safe the bond is and how long you intend to lend your money to the company."

"Well," said Austin, getting impatient now, "If I buy a $25,000 bond for three years, what can I make?"

"Again, the interest and total return depends on the quality of the paper."

"Paper?"

"Sorry. The quality of the company issuing the bond. You know, some companies, like General Electric, have been around a long time and are quite safe. Others are new companies with little or no track record, and they're much riskier. Accordingly, the best companies will pay you less-"

"Less?" interrupted Austin. "I'd think they'd pay more."

"No. They are safer. That's the appeal, not the interest rate. For example, for a bond maturing in three years—so you get your money back in three years—issued by a top-notch company, you can get about 6% a year."

Austin's heart sank instantly. This would never do. That was not even half of what he needed. "What about riskier bonds?" asked Austin.

"Again, the lesser the quality of the company, the higher the interest rate but the greater the risk."

Austin perked up. Here it comes, he thought. Money in the bank. "What do they pay?"

"With a three-year maturity date, I would say about 10% per year."

Austin's stomach hit the floor again. This was like a roller coaster! The next three years would be excruciating, he thought. "I was hoping to get a better return," said Austin.

"Fine, whatever you're comfortable with. What did you have in mind? You want ten, fifteen, twenty percent?" asked Lane.

"What would I have to do," said Austin, "to earn fifteen percent a year on average?"

"That pretty much rules out bonds, Austin. Even if we went out and found a high-yield bond paying something in that area, the principle may be very volatile. I'm sorry to burst your bubble. We might have to trade some stocks." He smiled. "That's the fun part— where the action is."

"From what I hear, stocks are pretty risky," said Austin. "I don't want to lose the money."

"Well then, you have to understand that potential return is directly related to the risk you are willing to take. Risk more, get more. Risk less, get less. It's that simple. You can't get blood from a stone, Austin. Yes, the stock market has risks. But the returns could be significantly higher than in bonds."

"Tell me about stocks, then," said Austin, becoming more nervous now. "I don't like the way you said could be."

"Well, when you buy a bond, that company agrees to repay your money back on a specific date. This is not the case with stocks, however. At the end of the three years, say, you will get back whatever they're worth at the time."

"They could be worth more or less, then?"

"That's right. But of course, my job is to buy the right stocks so that you make money." Lane smiled.

"Good. What could I earn if we buy the right stocks and

36

avoid the wrong ones?"

"Look," said Lane, "if you make two dollars on a ten-dollar stock, there's twenty percent, man!" He clapped his hands. "Boom! Just like that. It all depends."

"On what?"

"Well, the economy, inflation, interest rates, the general business environment, momentum on a given day. Nowadays, the overseas markets are becoming increasingly important, and this makes the market more volatile."

"Bobby," cried Austin, "you're making me crazy. Please make it simple. Every time I think we're moving ahead, something pops up to destroy it. Look, if all goes well and I buy stocks, what could I earn?"

"You should be able to get your 15%, Austin."

Austin leaned back in his chair and breathed for what seemed like the first time during the entire conversation. He threw his hands up. "OK. That's what I wanted to hear." He felt he could kiss Bobby Lane for saying the magic number.

Lane laughed. "Who knows, Austin? Maybe more."

"More is fine," said Austin. "Just fine. So what do I have to do? I'm ready to start right now. 15% a year."

Lane sighed and rolled his eyes. "Austin, please understand that there are no guarantees. Understand that, because I don't want to have any misunderstandings here. It's possible you'll earn less, though I doubt it."

Austin was biting his nails. "How much less?"

"Anything is possible. None of us has a crystal ball. I wish we did, right? You and I would be on our own private island." He laughed. Austin didn't. "Would you be upset if you only made 3%?"

"Of course I would," said Austin sarcastically. "You just told me that 15% is possible."

"Possible, not guaranteed."

Austin could tell that Lane was growing impatient. "I'm sorry to seem so ignorant. It's just that I have a bet with someone that I could earn 15%. I was hoping it would be easier than you're making it sound."

"I just don't want any misunderstanding, Austin. If it was

that simple, everybody would be rich—not just my clients!" He laughed heartily. "Right?"

"I guess," said Austin.

Perhaps it was Bobby's self-exaggeration, or his laugh. Whatever it was, Austin suddenly remembered the advice Parkinson gave him—his father's advice—the three questions. If Lane answered them satisfactorily, which Austin assumed he would, then Austin would go with him and hope things worked out. If Lane didn't answer the questions satisfactorily, then, well, he'd keep looking. He almost forgot about Parkinson's advice—actually his father's advice.

"Assuming we go ahead with the stocks," said Austin, "what would you recommend I buy with the money?"

"Ah-ha. That's the kind of question I like," said Lane. "Right now, there are two companies I really like. If they come through with what I've heard, Austin, you'll make your 15% and then some, believe me. The first is High Speed Tech, Inc. They make computer chips. Boy, these guys could be the next Intel. I own it myself. Imagine having been in Intel from the get go!"

"Wow," said Austin dreamily.

"The other company is Micro Valve. They make this heart-valve system that is supposed to be state-of-the-art. I hear they could move right past Medtronic."

Austin felt a lot better having finally gotten two specific investments out of Bobby. "My second question is when do I sell these two investments?"

"That's a much harder question. It's hard to say. We don't have a target price. We can shoot for your 15%. If we think it's going higher at that point, we'll hold. We'll play it by ear. I'll call you when it's time to sell. I've got a feel for those things."

Yes, Austin thought, my money, your feel.

Austin was looking for a detailed strategy, but outside of two stocks he couldn't discern a plan. It all seemed so speculative. Already, though, his father's simple wisdom with those three questions was beginning to impress itself upon Austin.

"The last question," said Austin. "When we do finally sell, what would you invest the money in next?"

"What is this, a test?" The questions seemed to increasingly bother Bobby. "Hey, you have to trust me on that. Obviously, we'll have to see what looks good at the time. I can't possibly tell you what stock to be in three months from now or whenever. There's always something hot at the time, Austin—don't worry about it. You don't need to know all that stuff. That's my job. Trust me, OK? First things first. We haven't even bought the first stocks and you're talking about what to buy after we sell them!" He laughed. "You're a funny guy, know that? "

Austin realized that Bobby Lane couldn't answer the questions. At first, Austin couldn't tell because he never asked them of anyone before. But he had a funny feeling about Bobby Lane. Perhaps his father experienced the same troubles. Austin decided to stick to his father's advice for the first time in his life.

Austin looked down at his watch. "Well, thanks for you time, Mr. Lane. I've got to meet my aunt for lunch. You've taught me a great deal about investing. I appreciate it. I'd like to think things over."

Bobby stood up to see Austin off. "Are you sure you don't want to open an account today? The sooner the better. We're pushing some good stocks today and the markets don't wait for anybody, you know. I can have my assistant take care of the paperwork. No problem."

"No thanks," said Austin, "but thank you for your time."

The phone rang…"Bobby Lane speaking…Jimbo! Yes, your timing's perfect. It's all timing, Jim. You're in and out. Sell out and take your profits. We're making money, friend."

By the time Austin got home, he had a splitting headache. He was exhausted, starving, and he felt empty inside from all the adrenaline that flowed through his body during the emotional ups and downs of his conversation with Bobby Lane. Austin knew Lane was not up to the task at hand—but who the hell was? And what if Austin made a mistake and entrusted his future to someone who, in the end, couldn't make him 15%? Or worse—what if he actually lost money? What then? He would be worse off than he was today. If he did nothing, Austin would be a millionaire, guaranteed. But according to Bobby, there were no guarantees in the market, and Austin could lose his money. He felt totally lost. Tomorrow, he decided, he would look into real estate.

Before going to bed, Austin gave his girlfriend Audrey a call. They'd been seeing each other for a few months, and he really liked her. He really hadn't thought much about her these last few days. In fact, he hadn't thought much about anything but the money. Was this the way his life was going to be? He hoped not.

"Hello?"

"Hi, Audrey." He realized he missed her.

"Hi!"

"I miss you," Austin said.

"I miss you too. How's it going? Was the funeral OK?"

"Yes. Tough, though."

"Is everything OK?"

"Yes, just busy, you know." Austin said.

"Yeah, well, take your time. I'll be here when you get back," said Audrey.

"I might have to stay longer than I expected," said Austin.

Audrey wasn't sure quite what to say. She figured just being there as someone to talk to would be the best thing. "No problem. Do what you have to do. Call me anytime you want to talk. Anytime. We'll have a nice dinner when you get back, OK?"

"Definitely," said Austin.

"Anyway," said Audrey, "you haven't missed much. Since you've been gone, the guys have thrown one party after another."

Austin used to think of parties as fun. But lately, they were just more of the same old drinking and hooking up. Well, maybe not all bad at his age, he thought. "I better go. I don't want to run up my aunt's bill."

The next morning was a new day, and Austin felt new enthusiasm. He was sure today would bring some answers. If bonds provided an insufficient return, and stocks were too risky—or at least, if Bobby Lane lacked the sort of strategy his father used— then maybe real estate was the answer. His aunt knew plenty of realtors. He would ask her for another referral. Still, he couldn't rule out investing in the stock market. But what he was going to rule out were investment advisors who couldn't answer those three questions.

Over breakfast, Austin asked his aunt if she knew any realtors. "Why yes," she answered. "Why don't you give my friend

Mary Lou Fox a call?"

"You know you're fattening me up with all these big breakfasts," said Austin, thumbing through the business section of the paper again. He noticed that a stock was up big the day before. Was that one of the companies Bobby Lane mentioned? Did Austin make a mistake and miss the boat like Bobby suggested he would if he didn't hurry up and invest his money?

"Austin…"

"Huh?" He hadn't even heard her speaking to him. "Sorry, I was thinking."

"Lost in the world of high finance, huh?"

Austin smiled. "I wish," he said.

"I was saying that you can find Mary Lou's card in the drawer where you found Jim Burton's. By the way, how did that go?"

"He was very nice," replied Austin. "He's an accountant, though."

"Is he? So he couldn't help you?"

"Well, he referred me to a stockbroker at Washington Investments. But I'm not sure if I want to invest with him yet."

"Is it such a big decision?" asked Diana. "I mean, is there that much money involved? Can't you just buy a mutual fund?" She started clearing the table.

Austin noticed that when she became upset, she busied herself cleaning up even if there was nothing to clean. He certainly didn't want to upset her, but this was his business. His mother had no say over his trust. His dad had made it clear—it was his money to lose or win.

"No," he said, "it definitely isn't that easy."

"Well, what would I know?" said Diana.

"I better call Mary Lou," said Austin as he got up from the table.

Mary Lou Fox worked in the Northeast, not far from Diana's house. Austin walked over. It would give him time to think and prepare. Austin tried, but he simply couldn't help being a bit snappy with Aunt Diana. He felt badly about that and would apologize when he got back. For all his disappointment yesterday, he realized he had learned something after all—his father's advice, passed along by Parkinson, was making more sense all the time. His father gave him a test and a road map to use. Unquestioning people like Aunt Diana were just the sort of people Bobby Lane liked as clients. He would say buy or sell, and they would. They called it "sound investing," whatever that is.

But people like Diana are really just gambling, letting the Bobby Lane's of the world roll the dice for them. That visit shook him up. He couldn't make any sense out of Bobby's buying or selling—there was no rhyme or reason. There should be some strategy or plan in making decisions like those, shouldn't there? He thought so. But what did he know? There had to be a difference between buying and selling stocks—in and out, on one hand—and investing to get his 15% on the other. Somehow, those three questions were the key. He didn't know why they were important—just that they were. He only knew what felt right. The problem so far, though, was that everything just plain felt wrong.

Austin sighed. This was going to take some time. The problem was that school, girls, and his music — it was all falling by the wayside. He was completely obsessed with passing his father's test.

The real estate agency was small. It held about five cubicles, a manager's office and a receptionist. Unlike the Washington Investments office, the phones here rang intermittently, and the brokers were not as impressive looking as Bobby Lane and the others he saw moving about downtown. Austin was immediately concerned, and he made a mental note to buy an expensive suit. So far, to get by in the investment world, appearances seemed to be more important than having a solid plan. Maybe that was just a first impression. He hoped so. Well, he'd have to play the game by the rules.

"Hi," said Austin to the receptionist. "My name is Austin Montgomery. I'm here to see Mary Lou Fox." Austin could feel everyone look up at him. Like fish at feeding time, he thought. He felt more confident today. And this receptionist was certainly a cut below the beauty at Washington Investments.

"Hi. Mary Lou will be with you…"

"Hey!" Austin was startled, but the receptionist just smirked. A woman in red was coming straight at him with her arms outstretched. "Diana never mentioned her nephew looked like you!" She looked him over from head to toe. "It's great to meet you. Your aunt talks about you all the time." She took his hand and walked him into her private office.

"I hope everything she said was good," said Austin, a bit flattered, a bit shocked.

"We'll see," said Mary Lou. "Here, sit in my favorite chair." She winked at Austin. "It's seen a lot of action."

Austin hesitated before sitting in the chair.

"Oh, don't worry," said Mary Lou. "The memories are dirty, but the fabric's clean," she said laughing. "Come on, sit down."

Austin sat down, and began thinking about this crazy lady in red and her chair. "I need your help," he said.

"That's what I like to hear. Tell me…"she goaded him on with her hand. "Tell it to me. Not too fast now." She winked again. "You college boys are always going too fast."

Austin smiled. He enjoyed the attention Mary Lou was giving him. She'd be interesting to have around at a party, he thought. A little old for the college crowd, but he knew what they said about experienced, older women.

"Well," said Austin, "I have some money from my mother's estate, and I'd like to consider real estate as an investment option." There, he said it. He practiced it the entire way over.

"So you want to be the next Donald Trump, huh? Who knows, maybe we should date?" She laughed out loud. "You're blushing." Austin put his head down and laughed. "Hey, Betty," cried Mary Lou to the receptionist through the open door, "what's the count?"

The receptionist checked her watch. "Two-and-a-half minutes flat."

Mary Lou fired her mock finger gun and blew into the smoking barrel. "Made ya blush in near-record time." And she was right. Austin was beet red, but smiling all the same. "I haven't lost a step," Mary Lou said. "Haven't lost a step, have I Betty?"

"Not a step," said Betty.

"Anyway," said Mary Lou, "take the Don. He made gazillions investing in real estate, Austin. Think about amounts of money you can't even think about. But you got to start somewhere."

"Exactly what I was hoping to hear," said Austin.

"I like it," Mary Lou said. "Now, what's your price range?" The question flowed out of her without pause.

"I have about $25,000," replied Austin.

Most sales people would lose spirit right about here. But not Mary Lou. She sensed this boy was holding out on her. And no man could hold out on her forever. "That's all, big boy? That's not even enough for a down payment. Been spending too much on the girls? Take it from me. If you want the real women, you got to have a house," she winked. "It's a sign. You know what they say... the size of a man's real estate... yeah!"

"How much do I need?" continued Austin.

"Is there such a thing as big enough? Oh! You mean money?" They both laughed. "I'd say at least $100,000 for starters. You're talking investment property, right? So that would get you a small apartment complex. If you put down a hundred grand, you could pick up a complex selling for about $500,000, no problem."

Austin raised his eyebrows. "So all I need to put down is 20% of the purchase price?" He quickly imagined a five million dollar apartment complex.

"My, and you're smart, too," joked Mary Lou. "I have something in mind available right now, although there's a bid in. But we should be able to get it. Let's go take a look." She opened her drawer, shuffled some keys, and glanced at him from the corner of her eye.

"Wait a minute," cautioned Austin. "You're going a mile a minute here. We just started." Mary Lou closed her desk drawer with a rattle. "I really only came to ask you some preliminary questions, and you're trying to sell me an apartment building for half a million dollars."

"Sorry, sonny. I thought you were ready to roll. Most people don't come to a realtor unless they're serious buyers. Unfortunately, we don't get paid by the hour for consultations." She laughed. "Boy, how I wish. What about that, Betty?"

"Ha! Wouldn't that be nice," answered Betty while answering a call.

Austin was visibly embarrassed. "I'm not saying I'm not

interested. I just want to understand things a bit first."

Mary Lou sat back in her chair. "Well, ask away," she said and threw her hands up.

"First off, if I were to buy an apartment building like the one you have in mind..."

Ah-ha! Mary Lou knew he was holding out on her. He's got more than $25,000, she thought. "Or even larger if you like, Austin," she prompted. "Remember the rule in real estate is, 'The Bigger the Better.'"

"Well, say something pretty big. What would the return be after three years?"

"You should be able to make about 20% a year."

"Really?"

"Assuming you're handy. Can you do your own electrical and plumbing work, for example?" she asked.

Austin was startled. "Why, no!"

"Hmmm... we'd probably have to manage the place for you. Say about 7% in fees and associated costs, plus a vacancy rate of about 5%. Then if we can sell it-"

Austin blinked sharply. "What do you mean, if we can sell it?"

"Well, obviously, you can make quite a bit if we can sell it three years from now. But of course, that depends on the real estate market at the time, right?"

"And I have to pay someone to do repairs and-"

"And manage it," she added. "This way, you don't have to lose sleep when tenants refuse to pay rent or something. Believe me, it's worth the peace and quiet. You can hire us to do it."

"What other expenses are there?" asked Austin. He saw his profits dwindle by the minute.

"There's insurance and any legal fees you might incur. That sort of stuff."

"Is there anything left over for me?"

Mary Lou laughed. "Don't forget the write-offs you get, Austin. Really, most people who buy investment real estate do the work themselves. But someone like you, someone with some money to spend, ought to have a building of some size and with that goes certain fixed costs."

"Will I make 15% a year?"

Mary Lou shrugged, bored now with the kid's fixation on percents. "Who knows, Austin? Maybe." Her phone rang. "Hello, Mary Lou Fox..."

Austin was thinking about the three questions. Actually, Mary Lou answered the first question, what to buy—an apartment building. There was no answer for the second question aside from whenever someone will buy it. The third question—that would be a nightmare trying to discuss with her. Austin felt his head spinning. Here we go again, he thought, remembering yesterday.

"Well, big boy, what do you say? Shall we take a look?" She arched her eyebrows. "These things don't stay around too long."

"But I thought you said the real estate market was rather slow?" pressed Austin.

"For mediocre properties," responded Mary Lou without missing a beat. "Not preferred properties like this one. We're talking a whole different game here, Austin. I thought you understood that?"

Austin shrugged. "But-"

"If it's even still available. I haven't checked the listings today. When I said I didn't know what you'd make percentage-wise, I just didn't want to mislead you. After all, a friend referred you to me. How would that look? You'll make your money, Austin, believe me."

Austin felt like he was breaking up with this woman even though he just met her. He decided to follow his time-honored tactic of blaming himself for the entire misunderstanding. This way, he could just go his own way with no strings attached. After all, he'd done it enough times with girlfriends—just take the responsibility and walk away.

"I'm sorry if I gave you the wrong impression, Mary Lou. Like I said, I'm kind of new at this, so I may be taking up your time inappropriately. It's my fault, really. I'd better just go. And...."

Mary Lou held up her hand and silenced Austin immediately. She would be damned if she was going to let this kid give her the old "it's my fault" shove off! "Impressions don't mean a thing to me, Austin. Actions mean something. Give me a man who can make a decision on his feet without asking everyone else for approval—that's a real leader. Am I right, Betty?"

"MacArthur didn't ask for permission," said Betty, following her cue to the "T."

Austin looked confused. "Didn't MacArthur get fired by the President?"

"Isn't he smart, Betty? Of course he was, Austin. Obviously the President was a bigger stud! Come on, you got to work with me here, kid. Too many men are just boys these days, I guess. Too book smart! Believe me." She blew some hair out of her face.

Austin certainly did not believe her. What he did believe was that Parkinson was right—people would pretty much tell him anything in order to get what he had, and this woman didn't even know how much money he had! He stood up from his chair, "I want to thank you for your time, Mary Lou, " he said. "I'll tell my aunt you said hi."

"Austin!" she said abruptly. He was startled to attention. "There are a couple of buildings for sale nearby. Nothing too grandiose. And the fact is, Austin, you can't possibly assess the potential returns without at least seeing something. I'm surprised at you!" She already had the keys in her hand.

Austin scratched his head. "I guess you're right," he said.

"All I'm saying, Austin, is that you can't make an... informed decision without knowing what the heck you're talking about, right?"

Well, thought Austin, she's right. After all, the whole point was to learn something about real estate so that he could make an informed decision. "I guess so," he said.

Mary Lou grinned. She would be damned if this kid was going to get away without at least a viewing or two! "Good. Let's go."

They rode over in Mary Lou's green Ford Taurus. Austin commented on the new-car smell. "That's the best part of buying a new car," said Mary Lou. "I got it a couple of months ago. The dealer's a friend of mine. Ex-boyfriend. If you're in the market for a new car, let me know. He'll take care of you."

"I'll keep that in mind," said Austin, wondering who in the world would date Mary Lou Fox.

"I'm a full-service broker," she quipped as she pulled the car up to the curb.

They got out and stood before a four-story apartment building. Like the rest of the buildings on the block, this one had dirty-brown siding and cracks running along the concrete steps. The front lawn – what little there was – was also brown, a favorite rest stop for passing dogs.

"This wonderful little property has six units and should net you about $35,000 a year," said Mary Lou as she fumbled with the front lock.

"Should?" asked Austin.

"Depends on the insurance costs and so on."

"So I have to pay insurance, too?"

"No, no," replied Mary Lou while opening the ground-floor apartment. "You can always just wait for a tenant to sue you," she said sarcastically.

"Ah-ha." Austin imagined a drunk college student like one of his buddies at school taking one last swig before throwing himself down a full flight of stairs.

"This apartment is empty right now, but you could get $500 a month."

"How long has it been empty?" asked Austin.

"Oh, not too long I don't suppose. Put an ad in the local papers, and you should have no problem renting it out."

Austin looked around the musty living room. Aside from the numerous fly corpses adorning the windowsills, the place smelled like an old sweatshirt in bad need of a washing. And he swore he could hear things scurrying around in the walls. He grew suspicious. "Why doesn't the present owner do that?" he asked.

"Dead," said Mary Lou. "I think this was his apartment. That's how this neighborhood is. Once you rent a place, you can almost assume they'll be tenants for life. They'll die here. You can almost count on it." She opened the fridge and closed it quickly. "This apartment is indicative of the others. There's a couple of two-bedrooms also. They rent for $950."

"Can we see them?"

"No. I couldn't get the occupants on the phone."

"Maybe they're dead," said Austin.

"The others are like this one, though. And you can always

raise the rents and bring in your own tenants. You might actually prefer to do that."

"Why?" asked Austin, thinking it better to take the bird in hand.

"Well, who knows who they are, you know. You'd rather bring in tenants you know are reliable." Loud, hacking coughing emanated from the second-floor apartment where someone was listening to a foreign-language radio much too loud. It sounded like whoever was coughing had a pair of dice lose in his lungs. Mary Lou tried to laugh it off. "Sounds like there might be an opening soon!"

"What's down there?" asked Austin, gesturing to a heavy door reading, "Tenants Only".

"That, I believe, is the basement. There's a washer-dryer down there, but I think it's on the fritz. Make them use the coin-op down the street. An old boyfriend of mine used to own coin-ops. Very lucrative."

Austin opened the door and peeked down, half expecting to be attacked by starving rats. "It stinks down there," he said and closed the door abruptly.

"It's probably the garbage. The landlord is responsible for putting out the garbage every Monday. If you keep the garbage on the sidewalk all week, you'll get a summons," replied Mary Lou.

"So I'll be a garbage man, too," said Austin examining the shaky banister on the steps to the second floor.

"Like I said," replied Mary Lou, "it helps if you can do the minor repairs like that banister on your own. Helps make ends meet."

They went back out to the street. Austin was getting a headache. What a mistake he had made letting her push him into coming here! He should have followed his instincts the minute they said leave. Suddenly, even bonds looked attractive.

"The price is right, Austin. They're asking $300,000, but I can get it for less," she said casually. "Interest rates will probably be around 8%."

"I also have to pay interest?"

"Of course. But you get the write-offs on the interest as well as on the money you put into maintenance and so on."

"So I won't even make 10%!"

"Austin, hon, you've got to start somewhere. And just think, Austin… you'll be a landlord!"

Yes, Austin thought, and a plumber, electrician, fixer-upper and rent collector. No thanks, he said to himself. He thanked her for her time and she dropped him off on the main street where he could get a cup of coffee and a ride downtown.

CHAPTER 4

OVER a cup of coffee he thought about his first two days as an investor. Yesterday went nowhere, and what a waste of time this day had been so far! Austin had thought real estate might be an alternative to stocks and bonds. But if Mary Lou Fox was any indication, real estate simply wouldn't do. Also, Mary Lou herself bothered Austin. Everything was flippant and off the top of her head. Making money was serious business and should be treated seriously, he believed. His instinct said run, so he was back where he started.

He was taking a break to read the paper and thinking, what next, when he came across a full-page ad for Brigadoon Mutual Funds. From the ad, it sounded like there was a difference between stocks—the only thing Bobby talked about—and mutual funds. Maybe he should look into them. If, as they boasted, Brigadoon was the largest fund company in the world, chances were it was also the best. The logic followed. And one of its funds was up 37% and another up 42 %. That's it, Austin thought. That's what I need. Why hadn't Bobby Lane told him about mutual funds?

Brigadoon was located downtown, and Austin went straight to see them. First, he stopped at the local magazine store and picked up a periodical called Mutual Fund Investing: A Guide to Managing Your Own Wealth. On the train downtown, he read it. It was very interesting. He already knew there were basically two types of mutual funds—stock funds and bond funds. Remembering what Bobby Lane said about bonds, Austin immediately skipped that section. He concentrated on stock mutual funds. From what he gathered, they were more consistent and safer than individual stocks, or so the magazine suggested—something about "spreading the risk." And some mutual funds were up over 100%! That hit him like a thunderbolt. And it had to be true. They couldn't print it if it weren't true. After the real estate fiasco, he felt like he'd found a life raft in a stormy sea.

He headed to Brigadoon's office feeling good, certain he was getting close to his answer. Austin checked in with the receptionist, asking to meet with one of their representatives. He could hardly contain his enthusiasm—up 37%, up 42%. That was for him! The receptionist seemed unimpressed. "Please have a seat, and I'll call someone for you."

Austin sat down and read more about Index funds. There was that term again. After about 20 minutes, Austin asked the receptionist how much longer he would have to wait. "I'm sorry," she said. "All of our representatives are busy at the moment. The next available representative will be with you as soon as one is free."

This woman sounded like one of those recordings you hear on hold. Instead of feeling special, like he did at Washington Investments, he felt like he was back at college registration. It was very impersonal—fight your way to the front as best you can. To his delight, however, the representative who glided into the waiting area was bright and energetic. And she was cute—very cute. Austin's mood changed immediately. He noticed right off the bat how young she was. She had to be right out of college. A welcome change, thought Austin, after his experience with Mary Lou Fox.

"My name is Cathy Devin. It's nice to meet you." She looked Austin squarely in the eyes and smiled.

"Hi, I'm Austin Montgomery," he said as they shook hands. Things were certainly starting off in the right direction. "Well," he said, "I was beginning to think nobody loved me." She smiled back.

"What do you mean?"

"I've been waiting here for 20 minutes at least."

"Well, it's my job to love you today, Mr. Montgomery. Come on back and we can talk."

They went into a room with a round table, a few chairs, and no windows. "Is this your office?" asked Austin.

"No. This is the conference room. I don't rate an office yet—just a cubicle. It's more private here," she said as she shut the door.

"Most people here look young, like you," he said.

"Brigadoon likes to hire young, aggressive people right out of college. Keeps the blood fresh, know what I mean?" She smiled at him again and took out a pen and pad. "So how can we help you today, Mr. Montgomery?"

"Call me Austin. You make me sound like an old man. Really, I'm probably about your age."

"Good," she said. "Then we should have a lot in common. So what are you looking to do?"

Austin was more careful this time. "I have some money." But he couldn't help boasting a bit in front of this girl. "Let's just say that if I get good returns, there could be more. Quite a lot more."

"OK. What's your definition of a good return?" She made a note or two on her pre-printed questionnaire. "Once we know your expectations, we can match you up with a suitable mutual fund portfolio." She looked up and smiled as if to say, it's that easy! "Here at Brigadoon, we have one of the largest selections of mutual funds available under one name. Whatever you're looking for, there's a Brigadoon fund to match."

Austin found this reassuring. What a welcome change from earlier today. And it seemed particularly suited to his needs. "I'm hoping to average 15% a year over the next three years. By then I'll have graduated."

"Oh? From where?"

"Stanford," he said nonchalantly.

"Really? Great. I graduated from the University of Pennsylvania. Will you be coming back to Philly after graduation?"

"If there's something—or someone—to come back for."

Cathy smiled. "What's your major?"

"Liberal Arts. I'm a musician."

"A musician, huh? Not the type to take home to mother. What do you play?"

"The sax."

"Like Bill Clinton," she said. "Definitely not the type to take home to mother."

Austin was about to make a cigar joke but thought better of it. He didn't want to blow his chances, because he was already interested in her. And she could hold the key to the right mutual fund to build his million to $1.5 million and change. That's what I'm here for, he reminded himself.

"I must say, Austin, you've got your sights set pretty high."

Austin was feeling playful. "Why, are you that special?"

She laughed. "I was referring to your 15%. I'm harder to get."

"Seriously, 15% a year is a healthy gain." She asked Austin a series of questions about his investment experience, net worth, and so on. He answered everything in full detail, except his net worth. He found the entire thing a neat way to be introduced. She finished with his local address. "So then you won't be too far from Center City tonight?" she prompted.

"If you're around, I can find a way," he said.

"Good," she said. "If you're free, drop by. We'll get a bite to eat. It's not everyday I meet interesting young guys from Stanford. Now, where were we?"

"We were going to talk about choosing mutual funds," said Austin.

Cathy pushed some sales literature in front of Austin. "As I said, we have over 50 mutual funds to choose from. Each differs in some way. They range from very aggressive to very conservative. Again, it really depends on your objectives."

Austin responded quickly. "15% a year on average—do you consider that very aggressive?"

"It really depends. When the market is good, you should make that, no problem."

"What happens when the market is bad?" asked Austin, remembering his conversation with Bobby Lane.

"The value will decline. Really, most of our funds go up and down with the market. If the market's up or down, so is your investment."

Austin figured it was time to ask the three questions. "For starters, Cathy, which mutual funds do you recommend I invest in? Where should I put my money?"

Cathy handed Austin a catalogue of mutual funds. They were all Brigadoon funds. "Well, I'm not permitted to make specific investment recommendations." She shrugged and smiled.

Austin was a bit surprised. "You mean I have to make my own investments decisions?"

Cathy nodded. "Yes. It's your money and your choice. I'll gladly help you review your choices, but we're not licensed to give investment advice."

Austin was now shocked. "You can't give advice? That's amazing. So your clients get no ongoing investment advice from you?"

"None at all. We do meet with them regularly, however, to review their portfolios. We just can't make any specific recommendations."

"How do people like me know what funds to choose, then?" asked Austin, confused again—a condition which was becoming normal to him over the past two days.

Cathy pointed at the fund guide. "We provide ample historical data on each fund we manage."

"So I end up picking last year's best funds?"

"Or you can use the last five, ten, or, where applicable, fifteen year histories. That's what most people do?"

"Is that reliable?"

"It's as good as you're going to get. But you'd be surprised how many people do exactly that. We get thousands of phone calls every day from people wanting to know what the top-performing funds in the past are. Take a guess how many phone calls we get a day."

Austin shrugged his shoulders. "I don't know...say a thousand?"

Cathy laughed. "Ha! Guess again. And don't think so small. We average 25,000 calls every day! And the number of clients increases every year. We're getting new money at the rate of over

$100 million a month. Can you believe that?"

"That's incredible," said Austin. He was truly impressed and felt like he'd been missing out on something huge. He felt stupid. "You must have a great sales force or something."

Cathy laughed. "Wrong again. As you just found out, we have no active sales force like the brokerage firms do. We get most of our clients from advertising. For example, how did you find us? And don't tell me you followed me up here from the street," she laughed.

Austin threw up his hands. "You caught me. No, I saw an ad in the newspaper."

"See what I mean?" said Cathy. "You came to me! We do spend a tremendous amount of money on advertising, 800 numbers and stuff like that."

Austin thumbed through the brochure of mutual funds. "It looks like you have a lot of choices here."

"Something for everyone," beamed Cathy.

"There's international, bond, stock—too many choices for me to tell the difference on my own. How am I supposed to know?" asked Austin, feeling a bit overwhelmed again.

"We can review them in more detail, maybe over dinner," she said.

Austin returned to his three questions. "You're on," Austin said. "But let me ask you another question Cathy. I understand that you can't tell me what to buy. But assuming I invest my money with you, can you at least tell me when to sell?"

Cathy laughed. "Sorry, Charley. You've got to make all those decisions on your own. Anyway, don't you want to be the one in charge? Most men like that."

"Well," said Austin, "if it were my jazz band, then I'd like to be in charge. But I'm not an expert in investing. That's why I'm here. If I could do it on my own, I wouldn't be here. I guess, then, that if I did sell a fund, you couldn't tell me how to re-invest the money?"

"Only to describe our menu of funds. But don't worry, Austin. Let the portfolio manager do the work for you. In a mutual fund, you've got a pro working for you. What could be better than that? Just buy his fund."

"Ah-ha," said Austin. "So, which fund should I buy?" he quipped, raising a finger to emphasize his dilemma.

"That's for you to decide Austin, after we determine your investment goals, risk profile, and so on. All our portfolio managers are outstanding, although some are clearly better than others."

Austin jumped on this opportunity. "Excellent. Which funds are those?"

Cathy smiled. "All the performance numbers are in that brochure I gave you. But I'm not allowed to say that one manager is 'better' than the others." She made quote marks around "better."

"It's easier than it sounds," she said.

"Is it?" Given the last two days, Austin felt it was anything but easy. It was damned confusing. Cathy was beginning to sound like Mary Lou Fox—buy today, worry tomorrow. The problem was, Austin couldn't afford to learn by trial and error. The errors would kill him. He had to anticipate the mistakes and avoid them. That's what Parkinson was talking about. That would be the difference between $1 million and $5 million.

"You're questions are good, though, Austin," she said, her voice bringing him back to the present. "They show you have some understanding about the problems facing investors today. But like I said, let a professional do the work for you. Let the mutual fund managers earn their keep."

"I'm beginning to think that my questions are only leading to more questions. I'm getting really confused," said Austin. And he was. For his part, he felt trapped in an endless circle of question-and-no-answer.

"Did you think of these questions on your own, or did you get them from somewhere? It sounds like you've been thinking about this stuff in advance," said Cathy.

Austin thought things over for a second or two. He felt confident in one thing now—he could at least verbalize what it was he was looking for in an investment advisor. "Well, there's a rule I have about investing. If someone giving investment advice cannot tell me what to buy, when to sell, and what to do with the proceeds after I sell, then I have to keep looking."

"No wonder you keep asking me what funds to buy," Cathy said. "I'm sorry I can't be more specific. But anyway, we'll see what we can hammer out tonight over dinner. How's 6:30 sound?"

"Sounds great," Austin said and took her address and phone number. He was happy that he'd at least salvaged something from meeting Cathy.

He said goodbye to Cathy and left with an armload of information on the various mutual funds. How on earth, he wondered, could he tell one from the other? Why not just invest in the ones with the biggest returns and be done with it?

It sounded good. He was very tempted, but his father's three questions kept coming back. He was given them for a reason. Did he dare ignore them? The mutual funds sounded good, and he could just pass his job over to a pro and let him earn the 15% a year. It sounded easy. In fact, it sounded far too easy—and that worried Austin. Why's it so easy? What am I missing here? If something sounds too good to be true, it usually is. And those three questions—mutual funds could answer none of them. He left more confused than ever.

Socially, the meeting was promising, but that's about all. Austin was overwhelmed by what was turning out to be a world of salesmen rather than advisors. Bobby Lane was really selling, not advising. So was Mary Lou Fox. So, too, was Cathy in a way. Austin decided to get some lunch and try to sort things out. He turned into a bustling diner, grabbed a stool at the counter and ordered the tuna special and a Coke.

OK, he thought. Time to review what I know. For one, people got rich investing. His dad did. He knew the three questions somehow held the key, but no one was interested in them, or could even answer them. He sure as hell didn't know what he was doing. His search was failing and he was getting nowhere. For the first time, he didn't know what to do next. He was running out of nexts.

Yet, there had to be thousands of people like him—well, maybe not with a million dollar check in their pockets-who had the same questions, the same need to invest and who were getting the same sales pitches. Take this Cathy at Brigadoon—here was one of the most successful investment companies in the country, but no one could offer any advice. You might as well shop blind at a supermarket, Austin thought.

Looking through the mutual fund brochure Cathy gave him,

Austin found out that he could invest in 25 stock mutual funds, 33 bond funds, and about 20 funds that had a combination of both. Not to mention the assorted other "specialty" funds like real estate trusts and so on. All Austin could wonder was how in the world do people make a knowledgeable investment decision with so many choices? Are all these funds really that different? And if so, how was someone like him supposed to make the right choices?

The one bright spot so far was his dinner with Cathy. He needed some diversion, some fun. Not only had he been dealing with the death of his mother, there was also Parkinson's discussion about Austin's father, news of millions in inheritance, the contingencies as a trust, a myriad of investment advisors, stocks, bonds, options, mutual funds, brokers, real estate agents, order takers—it was enough to make a grown man cry. And at times these last two days, Austin thought he might. Then there was the question of graduation. When would he return to school? What if he didn't find the right investment strategy in the near future? Simple. He'd fail the test and lose the five million.

With his head spinning, Austin thought about just cashing his check and calling it a day. Why not just take the million dollars and be done with it. He could do a lot with the million—have a hell of a good time and still put money aside for the future. So, why kill himself—and risk his million—to meet his father's condition? At least he had the million. If he tried for the five million and chose the wrong investment he could lose that million and be broke again! Admit it, he could wind up with nothing! That nightmare scenario was always in the back of his mind and made him break out in a sweat. A bird in the hand is worth five in the bush, he thought, over and over.

To calm himself down, Austin reminded himself of the two things he knew for sure, and they made life seem a hell of a lot better. First, he was definitely a millionaire—so how bad could things really be? Well, pretty bad, if he lost it all chasing that other five million! He knew he needed to keep things in perspective. It was then, between bites of his bland tuna melt smothered with too much mayo, that Austin realized something for the first time—for the past few days, he'd been completely obsessed with the thought of money. And his search for investments and advisors only made things worse. It was pulling him in deeper each day. It wasn't even the money that consumed him. No, it was the thought of more money. Money wasn't everything, and he sure didn't want to spend the rest of his life chasing it, as he had the last two days. There are a lot of other good things in life. And, anyway, how much is enough? The second thing he knew for sure was that he had a date that night with a very cute girl. That translated into fun. Just plain, old-fashioned fun. Boy, how he could use some fun about now. But having fun wasn't the only thing on his mind. This evening, in addition to having a good time with Cathy, Austin wanted her to teach him everything she knew about mutual funds. He caught himself. Oh my God, he thought, what the hell's happening to me? I'm dating a pretty girl, and all I'm doing is thinking about mutual funds. I've got to get all this over—and soon.

Austin finished his lunch, and felt rather refreshed having thought things out a bit. On his way out of the diner, he noticed the First American Investors office directly across the street. First American was, according to an ad he read in the paper, the largest financial services firm in the US—bigger even than Washington Investors. First American boasted of offices around the globe. There were six offices in the San Francisco area alone. Moreover, their selective hiring practices made their investment advisors among the best in the world. The firm's proximity to the Bay Area would make things easy if Austin decided to finish out his senior year. Austin thought he might as well stop in.

Austin approached the receptionist's desk. Introducing himself became rote now. "Hello, my name is Austin Montgomery, and I would like to talk with someone about investing some money."

"Certainly. Do you have an advisor in the office?" asked the receptionist.

"No, I don't," replied Austin. "Do I have to have an advisor first?"

She smiled. "Of course not. Please take a seat, and I'll call someone to meet with you," she said with the charm and caring of a kindly grandmother.

Austin found the office quite impressive. It certainly lived up to the firm's reputation—an image of size, strength, and security.

The artwork, he noticed, depicted colonial settings. Being a Philadelphian, Austin appreciated the sense of history, order, and rootedness these images portrayed—he had learned the term "rootedness" in his Modern Cultures, Modern Times class. The chairs had fine fabric and were a welcome change from Mary Lou's infamous seat of passion. There was lots of oak and brass around the reception area, too.

Austin was just beginning to feel comfortable when a young man appeared in front of him. "Mr. Montgomery?" he asked professionally. "My name is Harrison Langford III. It's a pleasure to meet you."

Austin stood and they shook hands. "Good to meet you, too," he replied. "I'd like to talk to you about investing some money. Do you have time to see me? I know I don't have an appointment."

"Sure," said Harrison. "Follow me back to my desk."

Austin was becoming familiar with the routine of introductions. Harrison said "desk" not office, so Austin assumed he was relatively new to the business. This in itself was not a bad thing, so long as the firm provided its young people with the necessary support, guidance, and insights needed to navigate the markets. Harrison's desk was rather neat and tidy. He didn't have much space in his cube, but things seemed to be in order. There was a little marker board next to Harrison's computer screen, which read, "Tomorrow is Another Day." Harrison's desk was one of many situated in the middle of a large room. There were partitions separating each desk, but you could easily see the other brokers' heads as well as hear their conversations. All the brokers in the cubicles were on the phone talking over each other.

Hello, can I speak to Mr. or Mrs. Stanley... Our fees are comparable...I think we should plan everything very carefully...risk-to-reward...scenario...dollar-cost-average every month... asset allocation is the best way to go... we take a long-term planning approach here at First American... having a clearly delineated strategy is what we preach here, sir...

Some people might be afraid of being a walk-in—in other words, just popping up in a brokerage office and asking to be assigned to someone for advice. The problem, some might fear, is that they will be assigned to any Tom, Dick, or Harry, or the "New Kid on the Block" who is in dire need of accounts. But in fact walk-ins are commonplace at brokerage offices. The advantage of being a walk-in with a firm like First American, however, far outweighed the drawbacks. To begin with, First American had a reputation for hiring only the best and the brightest, especially where its young advisors were concerned. It was common for First American to hire young people as advisors. Those who were actually hired represented some of the country's brightest prospects, all of whom had to undergo a rigorous multi-year training program and apprenticeship. Indeed, First American was renowned for its training program, and its young advisors entered the world of investments armed with a wide variety of expertise.

"Please have a seat," said Harrison. "How can I help you?"

"Well, I've recently received a small sum of money from my mother. She passed away and left me about $25,000. I need your advice on what to do with it."

"Not a problem," said Harrison. "How old are you?"

"I'm 21."

"Are you married?"

"No," said Austin. "But I have a date tonight."

"Good luck," replied Harrison. "Just so you know, these types of questions help us to know our client, as they say. It's very important that we clearly outline your long-term investment needs so that we may devise an appropriate strategy for you. This will be done through careful asset allocation—financial planning."

"Please go ahead." Austin found this procedure so different from his experience with Bobby Lane he was genuinely interested in what Harrison had to say. It seemed clear. Young as he was, Harrison seemed to be invoking the methods of First American. This was comforting and Austin was right about Harrison—he was substantially different from Bobby Lane. For Harrison, the brokerage business represented far more than trading stocks. It represented security and peace of mind. He worked for First American, and saw himself as a trusted advisor who worked with his clients to achieve long-term financial success.

"Well, here at First American," started Harrison, "we generally look at investing for the long-term. That is to say, we place a very heavy emphasis on a planning-based approach to investing. This way, we can centralize all your present investment needs and build a sort of base from which to approach your future needs."

Austin was curious. "Can you give me an example?"

"Sure. For example, right now you have $25,000 to invest. We'll do an in-depth financial plan that will guide our investment decisions and create a retirement and savings plan for you. It's totally customized, you see."

Austin nodded. He was envisioning all his "future needs." "Please continue."

"Well, the financial plan will show us your so-called 'dream scenario' and give us a sense of what asset allocation is needed to get you there. Suppose you want to retire at 50 worth a million bucks."

"Or more," chimed in Austin.

Harrison laughed. "Yes, of course! Or more! The financial plan will lay out everything we need to do to get there." Harrison was among the leaders in his office when it came to doing financial plans, despite his limited time in the profession. As a result, Harrison's clients felt comfortable that their ship was always pointed in the right direction. Having a financial plan, felt Harrison, was like having a compass in your ship. If you have one, you always know where you are headed. If you don't, you will most likely drift with the winds, heading wherever they might blow today.

"So this plan selects investments and things like that?"

"No, no," said Harrison. "I make the investment decisions. The financial plan doesn't actually make any specific recommendations where investments are concerned."

This surprised Austin. "Really?" Austin was thinking that this plan would be something like a pre-packaged investment program, something soup-to-nuts, which really involved the advisor only minimally.

In fact, Austin couldn't be further from the truth. First American provided its advisors with a vast array of tools to draw upon. It all depended on the client's needs. And whatever those needs, First American had the appropriate advice and aids. Harrison was proud of this and drew strength from it.

Sensing a problem, Harrison elaborated some more. "Understand, the planning process is intended to provide us with some tools to use. Remember," he smiled. "I'm the investment advisor. It is my job to sift through the data, look through these markets, and help you realize your dreams. You're 21, right?"

"You got it."

"Well, I suppose a house is in your future plans, maybe your first big purchase?"

Austin always dreamed about having a custom house built. Would Harrison help him get it? "That would be a good bet."

"So then, we will figure in a house purchase in your financial plan. You see, we'll have a savings and investment goal!"

Austin was getting caught up a bit now. "How about building my own house?"

"Yes, all the better, but all the more need for a clearly delineated plan, right? Moreover, you need to begin an IRA savings plan as well as centralize all your assets in one single account whereby you run your checking, your investments, your charge card and even your online shopping right through the one, single account—I mean, that's efficiency."

First American had recently moved into the credit card and online shopping arena as a means of consolidating and simplifying its clients' lives. It was First American's intent to become a hub—a center of life—for its clients. Harrison was a golden boy in his office, because he believed in this vision and brought it to life time and time again with each new client he took on.

This was tremendously different from what Austin heard heretofore. He thought for a moment. "You know, I like the idea of knowing what my money will be worth at such-and-such a time. It helps me-"

"Plan things?"

They both laughed. "Yes, precisely," said Austin. "So this plan will tell us how much my $25,000 will be worth when I'm ready for a house, or ready to get married, or ready to retire?"

Harrison nodded. "Sure, we just input different rates of return and from there we decide how to allocate your money now and into the future."

Austin grimaced. Something didn't quite make sense. "But what if we actually get a different rate of return?"

"You mean like higher?" responded Harrison.

"Or lower," answered Austin.

"That will simply change the numbers."

Austin winced. "But then where does that get us?"

"Austin, planning is a matter of continual fine tuning. Your portfolio is like an engine. It runs fine for a while, then needs to be tuned up, runs fine again, and so on. The planning process never ends, you see. Plus, we factor in your mortgage though First American, your credit cards, even your life insurance, and the next thing you know, you have a personal bank at your disposal."

Now obviously, $25,000 wasn't the sort of estate that raised immediate insurance and tax needs. But growing with the client was what Harrison, and First American, represented. At First American—and particularly with Harrison—building wealth was a process above all, like building the pyramids, and required methodical planning. It required a strategy.

Nevertheless, Austin was getting jumpy. "If I give you my money, what will you buy?" asked Austin.

"Remember, first we do the plan. When it comes back…"

"About how long does that take?"

"Oh, about three weeks. When it comes back, we'll have an asset allocation for you."

Austin grimaced again. "Can you describe that for me?"

Harrison took some papers out of his desk. There were charts of the S&P 500 historical returns, charts of growth versus value investing, pie charts outlining small-cap, mid-cap, large-cap, international. The options seemed endless. They really did. Austin was a little overwhelmed. And to some extent, that was Harrison's intent. Building an investment plan was nothing to scoff at. It was Harrison's career, after all, and he took great pride in First American's premier planning resources.

The main point was explicit—do not lose money for your wealthy clients! Of course, this meant diversifying your client sufficiently enough so as to never lose a large amount in any one investment.

"Austin," he said, "it can all seem overwhelming. But don't worry, that's exactly why we do a financial plan."

Austin cocked his head. "But isn't that a little like a self-fulfilling prophecy?"

Harrison nodded. "Perhaps, but that's business. Look, the whole point is to take extra precautions so as not to get hurt by any one investment going bad. Remember, investing entails risk. There will always be something that goes down in your portfolio."

"Yes," said Austin. "I'm glad to hear you say that. But still, I'm not very comfortable losing my money."

Harrison laughed. "Nobody is, Austin. Nobody is. That's why we diversify your assets, especially as you acquire more and more. We may start you out with some large-cap growth, but also large-cap value. Also, we may give you some U.S. stock mutual funds, but also put some money into an international fund. See, not losing a lot of money is infinitely more important than making a lot of money."

Austin didn't like the sound of this. He wasn't sure why exactly. Perhaps it was Harrison's emphasis on protecting money over growing money. More importantly, Austin had serious time constraints to reckon with. The obvious question remained.

"OK, Harrison, suppose we do the financial plan as you recommend. Then we pick mutual funds as you chose them. The question remains: how do you choose them?"

Harrison cocked his head. "Ah, that is the question all right." He took out some more papers. They were mutual-fund sales sheets. "Never fear. That's the beauty of working with First American. We offer some 350 different mutual funds from just about all the fund families." He leaned closer to Austin. "To be honest, I rarely do First American funds. There are some others which look great right now."

"But how do you choose them? What do you buy with my money?"

"Well, after we get your financial plan back, complete with allocation models, we enroll you in a great fee-based program which enables you to buy different funds. The program is called

Fund Monitor. They take your allocation model and come back with some funds that would be appropriate for you."

Austin shook his head. "I see. So you buy what they tell you to buy?"

Harrison nodded. "Sure. They know better than we do, right? And what's better, when it's time to sell they notify us, and we swap into the fund they recommend as a suitable replacement. It's a beautiful thing!"

"So they tell you when to sell, too?"

Harrison smiled widely. "Yup! You got it. First American Investors assumes responsibility for all the investment recommendations. They are privy to things that you and I simply aren't."

Well, there it was. Harrison answered Austin's three questions. But still, there was the matter of time constraints. "What about time?" asked Austin.

"Well," replied Harrison, "that's what we call your 'time horizon.'"

"What's our time horizon? I mean, everything you've said so far sounds great. It really does. But I have some serious time constraints."

Harrison nodded. "I see. I'm glad you told me, because I have to understand your expectations, especially where time is concerned. The problem is, Austin, that we can't rush things. Sure, your portfolio might go up at first. But it might go down as well. My job is to ensure that your investments go up steadily over time. So again, it might take time. It usually does, Austin."

This was not exactly what Austin wanted to hear. He wanted to press Harrison a bit, because he did like most everything he heard. It was just this issue of time. But of course, that's precisely the issue when it comes to many investors. What is a reasonable time frame? What sort of growth should one expect from an advisor? Yes, some strategies move faster than others and provide superior returns over any time frame. But is this always appropriate for all investors? These were the questions running through Austin, so he voiced them. He flat out asked Harrison for his opinion.

"The problem," responded Harrison, "is that there is no one answer to these questions, Austin. And I don't mean to talk around you."

"Why is there no answer?"

"Because it all depends on the individual investor. I can choose you more aggressive mutual funds; I can choose you more conservative funds. The point is the strategy has to be appropriate for you. Apparently, you can handle a great deal of volatility or you wouldn't be talking about being so aggressive. But short-term swings can set you back for a while, and you might find yourself down just when you need your money."

Austin nodded. "Yes, yes. I understand. But how long is a reasonable time frame to outperform the market?"

Harrison shook his head. "I don't know, Austin. I don't have a crystal ball. And most funds don't outperform the market, you know."

Austin was once again disappointed with his potential advisor. But that was First American's approach to investing—slow growth, no big losses, average returns happen. That's why there are averages.

And so Austin left the meeting feeling empty still. He wanted superior returns within a couple of years. He understood the risk involved, but still hadn't heard someone who could propose to him a suitable investment discipline for achieving his goal.

"OK," said Austin curtly and rose to leave.

On his way out, Austin stopped by the receptionist's desk. "Excuse me," he said. "When I came in a little while ago, you introduced me to Harrison Langford III."

"Yes! Good, isn't he?"

"Actually, if I wanted to speak to someone with more experience, what would I have to do?"

The receptionist was taken aback. "I suppose you can talk to Mr. Hall, the manager."

"Will Harrison get in some sort of trouble?" asked Austin.

"I don't know. Unfortunately, though, Mr. Hall isn't in today."

Austin headed for a nearby diner with his head spinning—a pretty common sensation these days. He sat at the counter and ordered a cup of coffee and apple pie. It was about three in the afternoon and he was getting nowhere—absolutely nowhere. One thing was for sure, though. If he wanted experienced help, Austin would have to ask for it. Otherwise, he'd just keep getting the rookie of the day like Harrison. Austin neither liked nor disliked Harrison. For all Austin knew, Harrison was the average broker. But the guy had no idea about investing and didn't even hide it.

Another dead-end meeting. He'd almost had enough of all this. Why not just settle for the million? That's not chicken feed, he thought. I can have some fun with part of it and put the rest in the bank. That's a lot better than losing it all while trying to get the 5 million. Well, old dad of mine, Austin thought, you've really put me on the spot!

It wasn't just an emotional outburst after yet another confusing meeting. By now, Austin was clearly moving in the direction of not looking for other advisors. He was deathly afraid of losing the million he had, while trying to make the other five million. Give it to guys like Bobby or Harrison III? No way. He'd keep the million. How difficult was it to understand the gobbledygook—and that's all he had had these last days! He knew greed often led to grief, so better just take what he had, be content and move on in life. The choice was firmly shaping up in his mind.

While finishing his coffee, Austin decided to read over the two prospectuses Harrison gave him, out of curiosity. The amount of fine print was staggering and said little Austin could understand. No wonder things were so confusing. Here were the mutual fund companies themselves explaining their investments in such a convoluted way, Austin wondered if anyone could make heads or tails of it. He was in over his head and sharks like Harrison were out there swimming around ready to take his money and say, "Trust me and go away."

"What do you think?" asked a distinguished looking man sipping his coffee on the stool next to Austin. "Pretty confusing, aren't they?" he said, as he nodded towards the prospectuses. They both laughed.

"Sorry, I couldn't help but notice. Hi, I'm Johnny Long."

"Nice to meet you, Austin Montgomery."

"Well, Austin, if you can read and understand all that stuff, you're going to make the boys who wrote it unhappy."

"What do you mean?"

"Well, I'm in the business, and I don't know one in a

hundred who can understand all that stuff. Legally, they have to give it to you, but they'd fall over backwards if they knew you read it, much less understood it."

Austin swiveled around to get a better look at his neighbor. He was tall, slim, about 55 and had a distinguished, confident air about him. The graying at the temples framed a chiseled, lined face. He was well dressed and obviously successful. Austin was interested. Did he say something about being in the business? Maybe he knew something that could be helpful. Come on—a financial conference in a diner? Not likely, but hey, nothing to lose.

"What do you think?" asked Austin.

"Oh, it looks OK. Nothing great. First American is really pushing it. It's a new fund of theirs, so they want money in it as quickly as possible."

"I never thought of it like that," said Austin. "I just figured the company liked Latin America as an investment."

The stranger laughed. "Sure they like it. And if it works out, they'll like it even more. But they'll make money on it no matter what happens—up or down. 'Caveat emptor,' my friend."

Austin never understood how the mutual fund companies made their money. "You mean in commissions and stuff?" The man laughed again. "You have to excuse me," continued Austin. "I'm kind of new at this."

"No, no problem at all. In fact, you're right. Investors are rarely told how mutual fund companies make their money." He smiled, "unless, of course, you have your magnifying glass and can find the expense breakdown in that prospectus there. Good luck."

"So in addition to commissions, there are other fees?" This, Austin never knew, but it was crucial to making a decent return—and he had to make that 15%.

"In addition to any commissions you may or may not pay—'no-load' funds are commission free, for example you will always pay a management fee."

Austin was surprised. He really never thought of it this way. "Even Brigadoon?"

"Sure. What'd you think? They're in business for free? Any idea how much a full-page ad in the New York Times costs? Part of your profit every year goes to the mutual fund company, without exception—win, lose or draw."

"So this'll affect my returns?"

"Sure. Whatever you think you made at the end of the year, you really made more. The mutual fund company takes their cut off the top. Likewise, if you lose money in a given year—and you can—you really lost less before fees. However, don't fall into the trap of thinking that free advice is worth taking. Quite often, you get what you pay for. Many times, if you pay nothing in commission, you get nothing in terms of service and advice. So commissions shouldn't be your concern. Returns should."

More decisions. More complexities. The caffeine and the anxiety of these last few days were making him sweat. "Would this Latin America fund, for example, be worth the fee?" asked Austin.

"I really don't know what would make this fund look great. Maybe someone who sells a lot of mutual funds could tell you. To be honest, I don't like mutual funds that much. Oh, they have their place. That's for sure. They're good for some investors, I suppose. They're OK, as an alternative or small part of your portfolio. But I would much rather invest in individual stocks, or better put, in a select group of stocks that meet my criteria."

"But doesn't the mutual fund manager do the same thing?"

The man put his hands up. "Well sure. But as I said, I have my own criteria over which I have control and determination. You have no way of knowing what's going on in your mutual fund as it happens. You're not supposed to know. In fact," he laughed, "in some cases, I'd be surprised if the fund manager knows!"

"That's exactly what this girl at Brigadoon told me. Only she made it sound like an advantage to have no role in the decision-making. Just leave it to the pros, she said."

The man turned and looked Austin right in the eye. "Me, I prefer to put together the portfolio for my clients, not give the money over to someone I don't know."

This man was confident, and Austin could sense it immediately. He seemed different from the others, and very certain of his criteria, whatever that was. Call it a gut feeling. "I like that," said Austin. "Do you work for an investment firm?"

"Yes. I'm at First American Investors across the street."

Austin's excitement grew. He liked the reputation of the firm—nothing wrong with it. He just wanted someone other than Harrison, who could answer the three questions. "I was just up there talking to Harrison Langford."

"New guy, but very connected," said the man. Austin nodded. "To tell you the truth, the new guys come and go so fast I lose track. But I know Harrison. Everyone knows Harrison." The way he said it didn't sound complimentary.

"I really wanted someone with a proven track record. This money's important to me."

"Well, finding the right guy—that's the trick in our business. Money's been around since society began. Nothing's really going to change. Nothing much has changed since the invention of fire—no time to go into that now. The problem with most young brokers is that they try to beat a system that's both ancient and unbeatable, which is why it's ancient! You can't beat capitalism, because it's the principle upon which our society is founded. And you can't beat the market. Instead, you work with the market! Once you understand that, you have the key to success."

Austin shrugged. "Just seemed to me that Harrison had no clue what he was doing—just doing what he was told."

"Well, there's a lot of that going around," Johnny said cryptically.

"How long have you been working for them?" Austin asked.

"Oh, about 23 years," replied Johnny. "Which is probably longer than you've been alive. Right?"

"You're right about that. I'm still in college. I'm a senior at Stanford."

"Very nice. And then what?"

Austin wasn't quite prepared for the bluntness of this question. Most people he met were impressed with the fact that he went to Stanford. "I'm a musician, but of course it's hard to make a living in that. Anyway, the more I learn about the investment world, the more interesting it looks. But it's sure full of confusion and inside terminology—haze and smoke and gobbledygook. If someone ever learned to explain it logically, a lot of people like me would beat a path to their door. At least that's how it seems to me...but what do I know?"

"Interesting observation," Johnny said and turned to take a closer look at Austin. Good material here, he thought. The kid's observations of the business were right on, Johnny thought. This guy gets it. He's like a blank blackboard to write on—nothing to unlearn. No bad habits to break. Interesting.

"I suppose you think First American is a great company?" Austin asked, interrupting Johnny's appraisal of the young man next to him.

"I wouldn't be there for 23 years otherwise. You couldn't find a better place to work in retail brokerage. Most importantly, we have the best research on Wall Street," he said proudly. "We have great trade executions and at least a thousand other good things. So if you're seriously thinking about getting into the business after college, maybe we should talk some time."

"I still have one more year to go at school. Do you think you'll remember me?"

"Believe me, if you're cut out for the business, you'll make sure I remember you. Make yourself necessary and unforgettable— valuable and visible—Austin, and you'll go places. Very simple, really."

The waitress dropped both checks on the counter in front of them. Austin scooped them both up without thinking twice. "This one's on me," he said.

Johnny smiled. "There you go. That's the way to people's hearts."

"Anyway," said Austin, "you can get it next time."

"Look at that, setting me up for a next time, too. A cup of coffee sometime in the future with Austin Montgomery. See, I remember you already."

"I was thinking more like Le Bec Fin."

Johnny laughed. "That's an expensive cup of coffee. Maybe you're cut out for this business after all!"

"If I go into the business, I hope my incompetence isn't what turns out to be the most memorable."

"Austin, believe me when I tell you everyone starts out in brokerage completely incompetent. By the way, what instrument do you play?"

"The sax."

"Did you just pick up a saxophone one day and begin playing like Clarence Clemens? Of course not. It takes time. First you start by playing individual notes, then scales. Believe me I know. My son is learning to play the piano. Later you play songs, although it might take a while to recognize them!" They both laughed. "Finally, you become a composer. You create your own music."

"You're right," said Austin. "I know what you mean. What level are you?"

"Me? I'm a virtuoso, one of the best in the business. And I mean that. It took me a long time and a lot of mistakes. But now I know my business. I know how to invest money. I'm a composer—an investment composer."

Austin recognized the opportunity and seized it. This man might—just might—turn out to provide the answers Austin was looking for. At least he would provide better insight than Harrison or Cathy. But would someone like Johnny Long—obviously a successful, wealthy, established money manager—be interested in Austin and his paltry $25,000? Austin was still cautious and would keep quiet about the $1 million.

"Do you mind if I ask you a question about investing?" Austin asked.

"No. Go right ahead," answered Johnny.

Austin was surprised how weird he felt lying to Johnny Long, even though he just met the man. There was something about him which commanded both respect and honesty. But wait a minute—he'd talked to others who also seemed good at first and it didn't work out. So, better safe than sorry.

"I recently inherited some money. Not much. Just a little," he lied, "and I don't know what to do with it. I've done a little studying and a little research on my own." He gestured towards the prospectuses on the counter and shrugged. "For all the questions I've asked so-called professional advisors, I'm only more confused. Would you consider opening an account for me?" Might as well hit him between the eyes up-front. He could ask his three questions later.

Johnny raised an eyebrow. "Well, that depends," he said. "Obviously, I've been in this business a long time. I'm fortunate enough to be able to pick and choose the clients with whom I work."

"It's not very much money," Austin lied again, feeling more deceitful this time.

Johnny smiled. "I'll tell you something, Austin. It's not really the money any more. True, part of my job involves growing the assets I have under my management. But at this point in my career, Austin, I'm more interested in the client."

Austin was intrigued. "It must be wonderful to be so happy in your work after so many years."

"To be honest, Austin, I only take on a new client if I find him or her interesting. The best clients, Austin, are those who are compatible with me and my style of investing. Otherwise, we're just not right for each other. Not a problem. I just don't have to worry about client problems any more. It's a privilege I've earned."

This was an important moment for Austin. At 3 in the afternoon while having coffee in a diner, he'd make the plunge and try to get the help of this man who could quite possibly help him make that five million dollars—or lose his million trying. No preparation, little forethought; that's how it happens sometimes. It was happenstance, fate, luck—whatever you want to call it. A crucial part of life, Austin knew, was an ability to recognize and seize the few important opportunities in life as they arose. That was going to be the premise for his senior thesis. As a musician, he knew that when the right melody comes to you, you've got to build it into a crescendo.

"Well, what about me?" said Austin. "Do you feel I am… compatible with you and your style of investment?" Austin realized he didn't even know what Johnny's investment philosophy was! But there was something about the man. "Trust your instincts," he remembered. Austin had to trust himself sometime.

Johnny loved to be solicited for advice and complimented for his insights. Call it ego or whatever, but what successful man didn't?

"What do you have in mind, Austin?"

Austin decided to up the ante. If he told Johnny he had only $25,000, it might put him off. "I have $100,000 to invest. I know it's not much, but it's important to me. At my age, I feel it could really provide for my future. I know it's a small account for you, and...."

Johnny held up his hand. "Austin, like I said, I'm more concerned with who you are than with how much money you have. You remind me of myself when I was in college. I appreciate your honesty. In fact, I admire it. I like you, or I wouldn't still be sitting here and certainly would never have asked you to come see me after graduation. This business is already too full of dishonest salesmen. The key is honesty and trust." Johnny really believed that. Not a day passed that he didn't say it to someone. "Tell me more about why you need my help."

Austin responded. "I inherited some money as part of a trust. In order for me to get the money, though, I've got to average 15% growth a year over three years. The second rule is that the investments must be legal and the returns certified by an independent accountant. That's it."

"What happens after this is accomplished? If we're able to get these returns, and everything is accredited, what then? What will you get?"

Austin paused a moment. "I'll get an additional $500,000."

"That's a challenge," said Johnny. "That's what I like about it. At this point in my career, that's the kind of thing I'm interested in. I love challenges."

" I just don't know what to do."

"Well," said Johnny, "You know one thing."

"What's that?"

"Me." Johnny stood up and fixed his tie. "I've got to go, Austin, but I believe I can help you. Come and see me tomorrow. We'll talk in more detail then. Until then," and he left, leaving Austin sitting on his seat.

Austin headed home to get ready for his date with Cathy. To his surprise, he found himself too preoccupied with his talk with Johnny Long to think much about his date. Money before girls— now that was earthshaking! He surprised himself, being far more excited about his meeting with Johnny the next morning than he was in scoring with Cathy tonight. Austin wondered if this was a sign of things to come. Would he spend the next three years interested only in making more and more money? He hoped not. He knew people who were obsessed with money and very few were really happy. That's not for me, he thought. Oh, well, he'd go with the flow, at least for the time being.

What really stuck with Austin was how much he trusted this man he met in a diner. This was no salesman. He was clearly first-rate and exuded confidence and honesty. Austin had no idea what his strategy was. He had faith in the man. If the man was good, his strategy would be good.

If Johnny Long could provide the answers to his three questions, this stranger from the diner would be his man—a man who could make or break Austin. But he still had to answer those three questions. If he did... well, that's tomorrow. This is now. Austin forced those thoughts from his mind and rejoined the real world of a 21 year old. Cathy filled his thoughts. Women could be just as confusing and unpredictable as investing. But there were sometimes good "returns." With women, you never could tell.

Chapter 5

CATHY lived in a high rise near the Philadelphia Art Museum, a popular haunt for young University of Pennsylvania grads. Like the campus, the Museum District provided a nice blend of culture and nightlife. There was even a doorman, and this made an impression on Austin. Finance, he thought with a smile, was definitely a career path he had to look at!

After calling up to Cathy's apartment, the doorman directed Austin toward the elevator. When Austin stepped off on the twentieth floor, he saw Cathy standing in an open doorway down the hall to his left. He greeted her with open arms.

"Cathy! Long time no see." They hugged.

"So are you rich yet, Austin? I certainly hope you haven't ruled us out yet."

He stepped inside. "That depends on who the 'us' is," he said.

"Why Brigadoon and me, sweetie." She closed the door behind him. "This is my apartment. Welcome into the lair of an older woman," she said smiling.

"Older woman?" Austin asked.

"Yes, I'm 24. You're only 21—a baby. It's OK, I have no

principles," she laughed.

She took Austin by the hand and led him inside. "It's a two-bedroom. I live with my friend Clare from school. Have a seat while I get us a glass of wine."

Austin sat on the cream couch. "Sure thing," he said. Cathy's place was nicer than his aunt's. It even had a view of the Schuylkill River. Cathy had some framed posters on the walls, a nice television, a dining area with a table and place mats, wall-to-wall carpeting without beer stains, nothing like Audrey's place at college where he and his band hung out. Audrey—a flash of guilt. Well, don't think about her, just for the night. Austin made himself comfortable on the plush couch. He could get used to this, he thought.

Cathy returned with two glasses of Chardonnay. She placed them on coasters and sat down next to Austin. "Please excuse the mess," she said. "We've only been here about six months, and we haven't gotten everything fixed up quite the way we want it."

"Really? Looks good to me."

Cathy laughed. "Men. Sometimes I think men could live out of a Chinese take-out container."

Austin laughed. "Well, to me, it'd be like a studio apartment in New York."

"How romantic,"she said while handing Austin his glass. "A toast."

"A toast."

"To making money," she said. "Something we're both interested in."

"I'll drink to that," said Austin.

They clinked glasses and took a sip. "Come see the view of the river," Cathy beckoned. She took him by the hand and led him over to the large window. They stood next to each other and watched a few crew teams row. "You know," she said, "I just love to watch the crew teams work out. It seems so effortless."

Austin took a sip of wine. "I used to row, you know. In high school. There's a lot of effort in what they're doing."

"Really? A jock, huh?"

Austin blushed. "Well, now I'm a musician. You've heard about them, so watch out."

"Uh-oh. You must love Philly. You've got the river and a great musical tradition, huh?"

Austin nodded. "This town's very interesting. I'm beginning to see things in a whole new light this trip."

"I gathered from our talk today that you've been meeting some interesting people these days," said Cathy.

Austin took another sip and nodded. "Yes. But to tell you the truth, my head is kind of spinning."

Cathy took a seat at the cocktail table and gestured for Austin to sit down on the couch. "Well then, what can I do to put your mind at ease a little? I gather our talk earlier wasn't as helpful as you had hoped."

Austin sat down. "How do you mean?"

"Well, to tell you the truth, we get so many people who want to invest their money with us...."

"I know. I was surprised. What a job—people calling or coming in and giving you their money to invest. I'm thinking of looking into a job like that after college."

Cathy sipped her wine. "Austin, we get a lot of people asking important questions. It's their money, their life-savings, but we aren't really allowed to give advice. It's kind of depressing for me."

"It is?"

"Yeah, because I like to do things, not just sit around and write out deposit slips."

Austin saw her point and said, "I guess that's why I play music. I always feel like I'm creating something."

"OK, I know I have to start somewhere," Cathy said, "and I know our mutual funds inside and out. But I'm not really learning as much as I'd like, given my educational background. There are investment advisors at Brigadoon who do give investment advice like any broker does, but they've got a lot more experience than I have. You have to pay for those services just like you would with a broker, so they don't get too much business. And you have to have at least a million dollars to invest."

"Well, that leaves me out," he lied. "You should hear what people say about my future when I tell them I'm a music major." They both laughed. "Hey! I'm not that much of a lost cause, believe me!" protested Austin.

"Oh, that old 'believe me' line, huh? I've heard that before."

The wine was getting to Austin a bit, and he stretched his bravado a bit. "Let's just say that I could have some business to throw your way."

Cathy called his bluff. "Right, you said you had $25,000 to invest."

Austin raised his eyebrows. "I might have more, we'll see."

"Yes, we will."

Austin put his glass down and continued. "I'd like to hear a little more from you about mutual funds. That is, if you don't mind."

"Hey, what's a date for, right?" She smiled. Cathy didn't work on commission, so she really did intend to answer Austin's questions as truthfully as she could. "Ask away, Austin. I only wish they'd let me answer questions in the office."

"Can you explain again what a mutual fund is? Please keep it simple. I'm a musician." They laughed.

"OK," said Cathy. "A mutual fund is an investment where you give your money to someone else to manage."

"You're not picking the investments, right?"

Cathy shook this off. "At Brigadoon, no. But that has its advantages. For example, you might like talking to me on a regular basis, right?" she asked smiling. "But you might not want me actually picking your investments. Instead, you add your money to other people's money so that a mutual fund manager can pool it all and invest it."

"Can you give me an example?"

"Sure. Let's say that you have a thousand dollars to invest. I also have a thousand dollars. Neither one of us really knows what to do with our money because we're not investment experts."

"So we give it to a mutual fund manager, right?"

"Right. When you buy a mutual fund, you're giving a mutual fund manager your money to invest for you. The mutual fund will buy different stocks with your money."

Ah-ha, thought Austin. "How do they decide which stocks to buy? That's the question."

"That depends on what they're buying at the time you send your money in. There are different mutual funds that buy different sorts of stocks, like growth, value, tech, and so on."

"Yeah" said Austin. "But how do they decide on what to buy, and how do they decide when to sell?"

Cathy had no idea how to answer this question. She considered getting more wine. Then she realized she didn't really care because no matter what, she got paid her salary. She decided to press on with what she wanted to say from the start, moving right past Austin's objection. "Wait, let me finish. We'll get to that. OK, now let's suppose there are a hundred people with a thousand dollars each to invest in this mutual fund. The mutual fund will take the $100,000 and invest it in stocks they think will appreciate in value, see? The manager thinks the stocks will go up. They're the professionals, right?"

"But there's no guarantee?" objected Austin, forgetting about his three questions.

"No, but they usually go up over time. That's why I gave you that book of historical returns. If the fund is worth $100,000, then each of those one hundred people has an investment worth one thousand dollars."

"Right," said Austin.

"If the fund is good and it goes up to $150,000, then each of those one hundred people's money has gone up from $1,000 to $1,500."

"So basically," said Austin, "people who invest in mutual funds don't really have the time or the knowledge to manage their own money?"

"That's the idea. And also because mutual funds own many different stocks and the money is spread out over many different companies, so the risk is spread over a lot of companies. There's safety in numbers, right?"

"But would you say that advisors who sell mutual funds don't really have the time or the knowledge to invest the money themselves? I hope that doesn't sound rude."

Cathy was wounded a bit, but she was used to hearing it from friends of hers who were brokers. "That's true Austin, although there is a certain knack to picking good mutual funds."

"But I thought you said you couldn't give investment advice?"

"True. But still, picking mutual funds isn't as easy as you think."

"I can imagine," said Austin in an attempt to appease this girl with whom he hoped to have a very good evening. "I could never do your job. So mutual funds are safer, then?" He smiled and leaned towards her to get in good again. "They are usually diversified, yes? How many different stocks are there in an average fund?"

Cathy got up to refill their wineglasses. She spoke to Austin through the kitchen pass-through window. "That depends on the size of the fund. Do you want some cheese?"

Austin had better eat, he thought. Another glass of wine without food could make him blow the entire evening. "That would be perfect, Cath." She might respond well to the pet name, he thought. He wanted to get the conversation over with and get on to dinner and whatever came later. But he had his priorities—information.

Cathy poured the wine and quickly remembered why she hated her job—they did not teach her enough to defend herself. She absolutely hated that, both as a woman and an Ivy Leaguer. "If it's a big fund, there could be as many as five hundred different companies in the mutual fund. So your thousand dollars is spread out over all those investments." Another drink for her—that's what she needed. Cathy came back into the room all smiles. "Here you go, Austin."

"Thanks."

She sat back down on the couch.

"Is that really safer?" he asked. "All those companies. Is more really better?"

Now things were moving into her comfort zone. No more testy, challenging questions.

"It's not better, it's safer. You have to understand the difference. If you have all your eggs in one or two baskets and you drop them you're in big trouble—bigger, at least, than you would be if you had your eggs in one hundred baskets and dropped three of them, right?"

They sipped their wine for a moment and thought things over. Austin excused himself and went to the bathroom to collect himself.

"Wow," he said when he came out.

"What?" she asked, genuinely curious about what could have impressed Austin so much about her bathroom.

"Nothing," he said. "Your bathroom smells so nice. I think I might enjoy a woman's touch." He winked at her.

"Nothing's for free, my sweet."

Austin didn't get it. He was too concerned with this thing about safety in numbers—diversification. "You know, he said, I see your point about diversification being safer. Can we say the same thing about profit, though?"

"How do you mean?" asked Cathy.

"Well, I'm probably missing something. If you own so many stocks and if some go down a lot you won't really get hurt, isn't it also true that if some go up a lot, you won't really make a lot of money either?"

"So you think they sort of offset each other?" asked Cathy.

"Well, that's how it Seems to me, but what do I know?"

Cathy mulled this over quickly. "I guess you're right. But most people who invest in mutual funds are more concerned with safety than they are with returns. You hope that the mutual fund manager will generate profits overall, but people are really much more concerned with not losing their money."

"Can you really lose all your money?"

"Not really," said Cathy. "But they think so, especially the older clients."

"It seems to me," asserted Austin again, "that profits and loses could offset each other."

Cathy shook her head. "Austin, mutual funds are not savings accounts. They're designed to appreciate over time. A good manager—and you will find them using the historical returns I gave you—will make you money over time while minimizing risk. That's really all I can tell you. Mutual funds have been around for some time, and they are immensely popular. There must be a good reason."

"Minimizing risk? Risks vary, right?"

"Each fund has a different risk level. The broad-based funds will hold many different positions in many different sectors of the economy like airlines, technology, food, retail, you know, stuff like that. And then there are funds that focus on a particular sector like a tech fund or something."

"Is finding out the value of your investment as simple as dividing the total value of the fund among the investors?"

"More or less," said Cathy. "The proper terminology for the value of the fund divided by the shares all the investors own is called the net asset value or NAV. You can follow it in the papers, too."

"Good!" said Austin, trying to lighten the atmosphere.

"Yeah. That way, you can see if the fund is going up or down."

By the fourth glass of wine, Austin was still asking questions. Cathy was now feeling beyond caring about this or that mutual fund—my God, they were just mutual funds! "You know, Austin, you ask too many questions. Look, just study the five-year returns and use it as a barometer. None of us has a crystal ball, Austin. If we did, you and I could head for our private island and have a lot more fun than all these questions."

That was it. Warning signals! Cathy had had enough of the questions. Even a little drunk, Austin heard the alarm bells ringing. Suddenly, Cathy began to look sexy again, just like she did when he first laid eyes on her. "I know. You're right—absolutely right."

"I thought you musicians were action-oriented. I hope you can make music as well as you ask questions." She smirked at Austin and got up. I'm going to change for dinner." She blew him a kiss and walked into her bedroom. "Oh, and I'll take another glass of wine, please, Austin. Just bring it in the bedroom."

Austin went into the kitchen and opened a new bottle of wine. The thought of Cathy changing in the bedroom started Austin thinking about something he hadn't thought about in some time—sex.

"Austin!"

"Huh? Oh, coming." He pulled the cork with a pop.

"I think you've gone a bit deaf from hearing yourself talk all evening."

Austin laughed and realized he was drunk. Now, he hoped he could get this money thing wrapped up for the night and get into that bedroom. The drink made him a little reckless and he had another question. "You know, Cath, everyone is always talking about funds which do well and funds which do not. How do you measure what's good or not good?"

He poured two sloppy glasses of wine and re-corked the bottle. He could hear Cathy mimicking him in the bedroom.

Oh no, Cathy thought, more questions. What's it going to take to get this guy off his questions?

"The S&P 500, Austin," she said wearily. "People use the S&P 500 as the index measure."

"But that's an index fund," said Austin. "An unmanaged investment."

She was mimicking him again. "Just find the funds that beat the index and bring me my wine, baby. Wine!"

Austin delivered the glasses to Cathy's bedroom. He glided into the bedroom and held a glass in each hand. She had changed, all right. She was now wearing a skirt and a cut-off cotton sweater. Cathy's baby-blue toe nail polish caught Austin's eye like a shiner lures a hungry bass.

"You look great," said Austin. "Now that's how a sweater was meant to fit."

He took a sip of wine and looked her over. Cathy liked this sudden change in attitude. She certainly didn't invite him over to be grilled about mutual funds. She invited him over to blow off a little steam and that was that. Call it a perk of her job. She met a lot of eligible bachelors in her job. They had some money and were looking to her for answers. She liked the way they fastened on every word she said, and she could handpick her personal favorites. If she wasn't seriously involved with one guy, she'd pick and chose. She was now between guys and in walked Austin. No man she had chosen—and make no mistake, she did the choosing—had yet resisted the sweater that broke a thousand hearts. Clearly, Austin wasn't going to be the first, if he'd just stop with those damned questions!

"So did you learn anything tonight?" she asked, taking her wine and giving Austin a whiff of her perfume.

"Teach me more, teacher," Austin said.

"Well, sit down on the bed and watch me finish changing. That should clear your head of those questions. Go ahead. Sit down."

Austin did as he was told, and Cathy continued primping just to be watched. She'd be damned if Austin was going to get the best of her before dinner! Anyway, she had a way of getting men to do what she wanted.

"Hey," said Austin, "do you..."

Cathy held up her hand and cut him off mid-sentence. "Did I give you permission to speak?" She turned around and held her arched foot out for Austin's inspection. "How do you like my nail polish? Baby blue, my favorite."

"Love it," said Austin, staring at her foot poised right in front of him.

"Even more than your measly $25,000?" Cathy pouted.

Austin's eyes began to travel up Cathy's leg—from her foot, up past her ankle, over her knee, onto her thigh.

He slid his hand along her calf.

Cathy pulled her leg away abruptly and blew Austin a kiss. "So where are you taking me to dinner, my sweet? I'm tired of talking about investments. I'm hungry and I want another drink."

"Huh? Oh? Wherever you want."

Cathy moved up against Austin who was still sitting on her bed. "Good. Let's go to Le Bec Fin." She took him by the hand and led him out the door.

He didn't flinch, thought Cathy. Maybe he's rich. The choice of restaurants was a test, sort of. Austin could get used to this kind of attention. Maybe he should tell her about the million. That would sure impress her.

Austin got ready to leave Cathy's shortly before dawn. The sun was rising in the East, so the Schuylkill River and the museum were aglow with a burning orange light. The view from Cathy's window was marvelous. They watched it together. For the first time since he landed in Philly, Austin stopped to think about something other than money or death. What a relief!

Cathy put her arm around him. He'd had a fantastic night, like never before. Cathy was a passionate, experienced lover and took him to the moon and back. Before all that, they'd had champagne, exquisite French food such as he'd never had before, and had taken a horse-and-buggy ride around Old City. But afterward, while watching the sunrise on a new day, he knew he'd made a mistake sleeping with Cathy. Nothing about it felt right. At least, not since he sobered up. By then, of course, it was too late. Mistake made and Audrey didn't even know. She was back in California, probably fast asleep and dreaming of him.

"What are you thinking about?" asked Cathy. "You're a lot more quiet now." She chuckled.

"Just thinking."

She pinched his ass. "Well don't think too much, buddy. It paralyses you. Anyway, one thing I learned about life during my senior year—it happens. Live it a little."

"I guess."

It doesn't take much of a hint for an insightful woman to see the truth. "I had a great time, Austin. Thank you so much. Time to sleep now. You're welcome to stay, but I'm guessing you feel like leaving." She kissed him good-bye. "Give me a call anytime, hon. You know where to find me."

Out on the sidewalk, Austin was awash in the beautiful orange hue of the sunrise. Another day was starting, perhaps the most important day of his life. He had his meeting with Johnny Long to look forward to. But he still felt guilty about Audrey.

Chapter 6

"HELLO, Mr. Montgomery. Johnny told me to expect you sometime this morning."

Johnny Long's personal assistant, Moira, showed Austin to a seat in a reception area outside his office. Austin passed Harrison in his cubicle on the way towards Johnny's office. They stared at each other, neither saying a word. When Harrison saw Austin with Moira he did a double take.

Johnny was very well known within the firm for handling only large amounts of money for highly select clients the world over. Some were Middle Eastern sheiks and businessmen. Harrison knew that. This guy from Stanford sure didn't have that kind of money—or did he?

"Austin! It's good to see you again," Johnny said. "See, I remembered your name after all this time."

Austin rose to greet Johnny. "Yes, it has been a long 24 hours."

Johnny raised an eyebrow. "Has it indeed? You do seem a little worn out. Well it's time for work now. Come on into my office."

Austin took a seat at the table in Johnny's office. The view was as breathtaking as that from Cathy's apartment. And Johnny's office was almost as big as Cathy's living room! "Thanks for making me feel so important. I hope I'm not wasting too much of your time."

"Just wait," said Johnny. "The steak's as good as the sizzle." Moira brought in two cups of coffee and told Johnny she'd hold his calls, as she did every time Johnny was meeting with a client. Remembering Bobby Lane and the frequent interruptions, Austin immediately picked up on this. "Thanks for your attention."

Johnny took a seat at the table with Austin. "Let me start by reintroducing myself. As you know, I've been employed by First American Investors for over twenty years. Always doing the same thing. That is to say, I've always managed money. I am a money manager. Is that clear?"

"Yup."

"Good. Let's get down to basics, because I'm sure that if you've been shopping around for a financial advisor as you told me you have, there must be a million things running through your head. Forget them all for the moment, OK?"

Austin welcomed this. "Sure thing."

"First of all, First American Investors has one of the largest and best research departments in the business." Pointing to the back of a research book, he said, "These are the analysts who do the actual research and number crunching on companies. I'm not an analyst. Nor do I get involved in the day-to-day operations of this office. That's for the office manager to do. I stress these distinctions because I want you to know that I spend all my time managing my clients' money. Thus, I am a money manager. Is that clear?"

Austin was right with Johnny. Things were crisp and clear. "Got ya."

"OK. You mentioned to me yesterday over coffee that you needed to get 15% on your money. As I understand it, if this can be done, you'll then receive a substantial amount of additional funds. The trustee of your father's estate must approve audited statements. Am I right so far?"

Austin nodded. "You got it down in half the time it took me. Remember, though, I have three years during which I must average

15%. If I document this return, I get more money. But if I fail to get these returns, I keep only what's left of the original money after the three years. The remainder of the trust goes to charity."

"I gather," said Johnny, "that you're not quite in the philanthropic stage of your life yet?"

"Exactly," said Austin. "I want that extra money, Mr. Long. It's sort of a test my father put in front of me."

"I think I understand, Austin and you're in luck. You've got me."

"So you use some sort of special strategy that other people don't use?" Austin asked.

Johnny smiled. "Yes and no, Austin. Yes, over the past twenty years I've developed an investment strategy that's successful beyond most clients' dreams. And no, I'm not the only one who uses the Strategy."

The way he said "the Strategy" made an impression on Austin. The Strategy—that suggested thought, planning, a system, order. The word implied there was some kind of rational, coherent plan at work—not like all the vagueness of the others he'd talked to.

"Is your strategy well known?"

Johnny grinned. "Right now, the Strategy is circulated throughout the entire firm worldwide. By my estimates, thousands of financial advisors throughout the world use my strategy."

Austin was very impressed, but he was still thinking of those three questions and determined he wouldn't jump in unless they were answered. They were still his road map and he'd be damned if he'd decide anything without hearing those answers.

"It might not sound like much to you just yet, but it literally took years to develop this strategy. Hundreds of hours of painstaking research and back-testing went into developing it, and countless hours of work by interns—and God knows what else."

"So you've basically been using the Strategy for your entire career?"

"Nope. I started like the rest of the young guys—clueless! Only I had no Johnny Long to follow. I will say that since starting the Strategy many years ago, I and many financial consultants in the firm have found the performance to be nothing short of outstanding."

"Wow. You've got me interested."

Johnny held up a hand. "Let me explain the details before you go chomping at the bit, Austin. I prefer to be very detailed with my clients, so bear with me a minute."

"Don't worry about me," Austin said. "This is all new to me, so keep going."

"First," continued Johnny, "we must agree on a game plan. I'll explain the risks and rewards of my strategy to you. If you find this to be what you're looking for, we'll begin investing your money right away." Johnny sensed some hesitation on Austin's part.

Austin felt both excited and rushed. He still had a nagging doubt. Could he trust Johnny?

"I'm sorry, but are we moving too fast? Like I said, Austin, I'm a money manager. I invest people's money. If you like my strategy—and I think you will—I'm going to invest it for you. That's how it goes. I know you're new at this, but some things you'll just have to trust me on, Austin. This is a team effort, you and I. I mean that. You need my strategy and I need your trust."

"OK. Go on."

"I will. And believe me, if nothing else, you'll learn a lot about investing, no matter what you decide to do. OK, step one. A sound investment strategy must have three components to be successful. The first component, of course, is knowing what stocks to buy with your money. Right?"

Austin nodded. "Yes, that makes sense."

Johnny smiled. "You say that as if every broker you talk to knew what they're buying and why, Austin."

Austin thought back for a moment. "I guess they do."

"OK, so the first rule of investing is knowing what stocks to buy. The second component is knowing when to sell."

This was the first time Austin heard a financial advisor mention that—even in response to Austin's direct question.

"I want to stress this, Austin. Don't take it lightly. Knowing when to sell is fundamental to making a lot of money in the stock market. Yet—and I've been in this business a long time, Austin," Johnny said, lightly pounded the table for emphasis—"people just don't seem to understand how important it is to have a firmly established method for selling a stock. Do you understand that?"

"I understand that you think it's important, but I'm not sure why."

"You will, Austin. For the time being, you'll have to take my word for it. It's the key. Which brings me to the third component—knowing what to do with your money after you sell a stock. It only follows that if selling a stock is the guiding principle of the Strategy, knowing where to reinvest the money is a close second. Right?"

Austin was speechless. What Johnny had just outlined directly answered Austin's three questions, and Austin hadn't even asked them! His father had given him these questions as a road map to go along with the test—the tools to earn that five million. And now Johnny was answering them before he'd even asked them! This was incredible. His instincts and what Johnny had just said told him this was the man for him. Follow and trust this man. OK, decision made. He'd go for the five million his father had dangled in front of him. He'd go for it—invest his million with this man—and risk the million to make the five million.

With that decision made, Austin felt a huge burden lift from his shoulders. He was so relieved he just sat there saying nothing, with a big smile on his face. Oh, he'd be careful, for sure. He was no plunger. He'd start with the $100,000—then add more slowly. But the bridge was crossed. The decision, which had been tormenting him, was made. Yes, he'd go for the full five million.

"Austin, I notice you're quiet. Don't worry; I've seen this before. It's a light bulb turning on. All my clients experience it at one time or another. The smarter clients, shall we say, see it sooner than others. You're right up there with the best, Austin."

Austin snapped out of his haze. "It sounds very good, Mr. Long. I have one question, though."

"Sure. That's what you're here for."

"This might sound strange," said Austin, "but where did you learn these rules for investing?"

Johnny held his hands up. "That, Austin, is the question of my life. After all, it's not everyday that someone presents you with the goose that laid the golden egg."

"That was aimed at me, right?"

"Sure, Austin. This is your goose I'm handing to you. Don't underestimate that. As for me, I learned these rules from a man I met while vacationing in the Caribbean—a very wise man."

"I like it. It almost has musical overtones to it."

Johnny smiled. "Well, now you're with me, Austin. Take this gem of shared wisdom, and run with it. Just like I did."

"I will, Mr. Long, I will."

"OK, here's the story. I was scuba diving in the Caribbean with a group of people. I used to dive a lot—very relaxing. As you may know, each person pairs up with a buddy. I was told to pair up with this stranger. I'd never met him before but we were paired up and he looked like he knew what he was doing. If you know the history of the Caribbean islands, you'll know that there are many wrecks to dive. Lot's of fabulous diving, but risky."

"Well," chimed Austin, "risk and reward are related, right?"

"Now you're learning. So my buddy decided he wanted to go into the wreck we were diving on. I signaled that I didn't think it was a good idea. You know, underwater, the environment is totally different. It's easy to underestimate a situation and get yourself into trouble fast."

"I can imagine."

"Yes, but he goes in anyway. Of course, he didn't come out for what seemed like an hour. Probably, it was only ten minutes. But like I said, underwater, even time moves against you."

Austin shrugged. "I wouldn't know, Mr. Long. I've never scuba dived before."

"Well," replied Johnny, "there's a parallel here to what you and I'll be doing. Let me finish my story. So I have to go look for this guy. I had to go into the wreck, which is exactly what I didn't want to do in the first place. I searched the front of the ship first. I couldn't find him."

"Was it scary? You've dived a lot, though, right?"

"Yes, I'm pretty experienced. I used to teach scuba. But like I said, underwater, you never know what will happen. You always have to be prepared for the worst. The second you start guessing, or start doing things without thinking, or take the unpredictability for granted, that's when you end up in deep trouble."

"I can relate," agreed Austin. "I hate unpredictability, except, of course, when I'm playing jazz. But even then, there are notes, scales, you know. There's still an order of things."

"Good!" said Johnny. "Anyway, so I was searching the front of the ship, and nothing. I worked my way toward the back of the ship, and there he was, all tangled up in rope hanging from the ceiling."

"Was he dead?"

"He would have been, and soon, if I hadn't found him. He'd never have gotten out. I worked hard and finally got him loose and we surfaced."

"My God, he owed his life to you."

"He thanked me profusely when we got ashore. He offered to buy me dinner and I accepted. He was an interesting guy, too. During dinner he had some wonderful stories to tell. He'd really been around. Military and all that."

"I can imagine."

"I remember he was a cognac drinker."

"You have a memory like an elephant."

"Well, I remember, because in the bar after dinner, he ordered Louis XIV. Even back then, it was $85 a snifter. If you've ever had a sip of this cognac, you don't forget it."

"I wouldn't either. 85 bucks a snifter!"

"Anyway, I knew this man was wealthy. At the time, I was new in the investing business, and like any new guy, I knew next to nothing about investing. We got around to talking about investing. OK, I'll be frank about it—I admit I was looking for new clients."

"Even though you knew nothing about investing!" joked Austin.

"Yes!" They both laughed.

"So one thing led to the next, and he said—I remember exactly—'Johnny, I've learned something about investing I want to share with you. Take it as a token of my gratitude. You saved my life. I want to tell you something which I hope will make as much difference in your life as it has in mine.' That's what he said."

"I can see why you'd remember that."

Johnny grew quiet. "He shared his investment strategy with me that night, Austin—the Strategy. It's the same insight I'm sharing with you today, and the same I've shared with some of the most successful brokers in this firm, not to mention with some of the wealthiest people in the world."

"So he gave you those three rules?"

"Yes. Always know what to buy, when to sell, and how to reinvest the money. Never, he said, invest a penny of your own or someone else's money unless this can be determined in advance—beforehand."

"Wow. You must've been grateful."

"To say the least. I didn't sleep a wink that night. All I could think about was how I was going to redesign my entire view of investing overnight. What would I tell my existing clients? What would I tell my new clients? What stocks would I buy? Most of all, how do I go about finding the answers to those questions? The questions were the key, of course, but I still had to figure out how to find the answers to those questions. I came back knowing the questions to ask and it changed my life. But where would I find the answers? The questions without the answers meant little. That was the big challenge—how to find those answers."

"What was his name? Was he famous?"

Johnny shook his head. "You know, that's the funny thing. I remember what cognac we drank and the three rules he gave me. But I can't for the life of me remember his name. I wonder if I ever even knew his last name. Maybe Roberts or something. Sorry to say, I don't know. Call it a youthful oversight."

"It was just fate," said Austin.

"Like a Wagner opera," replied Johnny. "Some things are just meant to happen. I really believe that."

Austin was beginning to think he'd stepped into the twilight zone. What if Johnny was talking about Austin's own father? No, that was too far-fetched. No way. Too many unknowns. But still—there were those same three questions. Anyway, it didn't matter. Like Johnny said, some things are just meant to happen.

"You make it sound as if it happened yesterday, Mr. Long."

"It did, Austin. It happened yesterday, and it'll happen again today, and tomorrow, and so on."

Austin was confused. "I don't understand. What are you saying?"

Johnny laughed. "I'm being figurative. To tell you the truth, I don't know how I first told the diving story. But over time, I've come to tell it as a story which illustrates the stock market."

"You mentioned something about that."

"It's true. Think about it. At the risk of sounding trite, diving is a journey into the unknown—just like diving into the market."

"Well," said Austin, "people weren't meant to breathe underwater."

"Sure. And as any experienced diver will tell you, you must be prepared for the unknown. You've got to know and follow the rules. Otherwise, you'll get into serious trouble. Same with the market. Diving is unpredictable. That's why I love it. It's a rush. The sea is ancient and nothing I do is going to change that. Likewise, capitalism—the free, uncontrolled marketplace—has been around since the beginning of recorded time. The stock market is like the sea we're diving in. It might seem like a controlled environment sometimes, but it's no safe place to be without knowing what you're doing. And you've got to know. It's not good enough to leave it to someone else. Right?"

"I think so."

"You'd better believe it. The pros say, 'leave it to the pros. Trust us the way you trust your doctor.' That argument sways millions of people. But there's a hell of a big difference between a doctor you know who has a proven, standard procedure for dealing with your specific problem and an investment advisor without any discipline or strategy. And that's most of them. You'd better know something about it yourself. And you know, I think most people want to know more about how their money can grow. I really believe that. People aren't stupid and they're not sheep. They want to know." Johnny went on, "That's why I'm explaining my strategy to you. I could just say, 'trust me and good-bye,' but I think you want to know how the Strategy works—how you'll make money. Am I right?"

"Damned right!" Austin exclaimed.

"OK. So I came back from that trip determined to find a way to get the answers to those three questions. And it didn't drop out of a tree! As I said, it took years of effort. I spent countless hours of research pouring over thousands of analysts' reports looking for a pattern—a way to answer those questions. When I thought I saw patterns that would answer those questions, I back-tested them to prove them out. Then I had interns checking and double and triple checking everything.

"And in the end—after all the years and research—I discovered how to answer those three questions. It's a simple rule— no, make that an 'immutable law'—of investing. I've proven it out over many years since. It's changed my life and made profits for my clients. Thousands of other brokers are using it, too. Why? Because it works. I call it simply the Strategy. And don't forget, that's why I usually handle only the largest accounts of some of the wealthiest people in the world. We're not talking theory here, my friend.

"But we can't go too fast," Johnny continued. "We can't cover it all in one visit. You can only absorb so much at a time. So let's take it one step at a time, OK? First, let's just talk in general," Johnny went on. "The first thing you need to know is that on a day-to-day basis, the stock market follows no rules. None. Zip. That much I can assure you."

"But I hear people all the time talking about what to do. They seem to know," Austin countered.

"I repeat, Austin, from day to day there are no rules. There's no predicting the market on a day- to- day basis. Get it out of your head. That's guessing, gambling—and anyone trying to figure out the day-to-day changes in the market is doing just that—guessing. Nothing more. Sometimes, of course, they guess right. But it's still guessing—and very often they guess wrong.

"Why? Well, the day-to-day market is driven by a thousand and one factors—that day's news, good or bad economic figures, interest rates, labor costs, rumors, an economist's comments, a politician's statement, trade figures, and most of all by human psychology. And tell me, who can figure that out? That's what moves the day-to-day market. And you're going to figure it out? Good luck! You'll need it. But over the long-term the market does follow a rule—well more like an immutable law. Over the long-term—that is, for investors—the market follows one rule and one rule only, and that's what those three questions led me to discover." Johnny waited, building the moment. "Do you want to know what that one rule is?"

"Yes, of course!"

Johnny smiled. He loved to draw this moment out. "Good. Now let me tell you first what it isn't. Most people are preoccupied with the daily price of their investments. And that's good, right?"

"Right" said Austin.

"Totally wrong. You're off on a wild-goose chase already— not the golden-goose chase." Austin grimaced. "I never look at the price of a stock to decide when to buy or sell."

"You don't?" Austin was astonished. What a difference with someone like Bobby Lane who was preoccupied with every little price change. They shot up and down, dragging Bobby up and down with them, whip-lashing and driving him to chain-smoking. He lived—and often died—on that day's prices.

"But, aren't prices what it's all about? I mean, buy when the price is low and sell when the price is high. Isn't that it?"

"Austin, knowing what moves prices is more important than the prices themselves. They'll change daily, but what moves them never changes. The fact is the price of a stock is just a 'reflection' of what investors expect the company to do in the future. A share price today is a kind of 'advance look' at what investors expect in the future."

"So then, the current price of a stock isn't true?"

"What's true? Save it for the classroom. This is the market we're talking about. OK, look at it this way—have you ever tried to spear a fish in water?"

"No, not since living with Eskimos a few winters ago," Austin joked. They both laughed. "But I know what you mean."

"OK. The fish isn't really where it appears to be, right?"

"Right."

"Well then, the price of a stock has the same sort of misleading appearance. Today's stock price reflects what investors think the profits of the company will be about two years into the future. Got it?"

"Yes...well, I think so."

"Let's say a company suddenly loses their largest client who cancels their orders and leaves. The stock price of that company will fall because investors believe the company will earn less money in the future. All other information, past or present, I don't care about. It's all irrelevant. Why? Because it's already in the price. Only what happens in the future counts. Do you understand that? That's very important for you to get."

"But how come information about what's happening today is unimportant? They have entire television networks dedicated to stock market news. They've got information coming out their ears...well mouths," Austin said.

"It's all marketing, Austin. It's all a show, entertainment. They make their money selling time. They get paid more if they've got higher ratings and more 'eye-balls'—viewers. Drama sells, hype sells, a crisis—real or hyped-up—sells. Tension sells, short sound bites sell. 'Airplane lands safely,' doesn't sell. 'Airplane crashes,' does. They need drama, suspense, and tension to get those ratings up. So heaven help anyone making investment decisions based on those TV 'shows.' But what the hell, a hundred million Americans are involved in the stock market today. It's America's newest spectator sport, and where you've got that many people, you're going to see everything done—and I mean everything—to capture that audience and feed them anything that sells. It's all 'noise,' Austin. You don't need it and no serious investor does."

"I never thought of it that way."

"OK, back to what I was saying. If something is already known about a company, it's already reflected in the stock price. Done deal. There's no beating the market unless you guess lucky— or unless you have secret, inside information the public doesn't know yet. And that's illegal. I don't do that. People who pick their own stocks, Austin—including brokers—think they're unlucky when they lose money. But what they don't understand is how very lucky they are when they make money! The strategy I use is based on the only reason stocks move up and down. And if they don't base their decisions on that, they're guessing. An educated guess, maybe—but still guessing."

"So what I hear you saying is that the present stock price of a company reflects opinions about that company's future, right?"

"You've got it." The kid is learning fast, Johnny thought. No bad investing habits to get rid of. Go slowly with him—he might be the one.

"OK. Then if there's new information about the future, like reduced estimated earnings, say, the price of the stock will go down?"

"Absolutely. Because there's 'new' bad news about future earnings."

"I'm with you so far," said Austin. "So what you're saying, then, is that if the future looks like it's going to change, then the stock price will adjust to the change— up or down?"

"Right," Johnny said.

"Well, what about a company that may have done well in the past or may have, say, raised its profits or dividends or something for the last, I don't know, ten years straight? Look at that great record. Isn't that a company to buy?"

"I'm not impressed. I know this sounds harsh but in the market, what's past is past. The future Austin is the only thing that matters."

"Only the future? Austin was beginning to find this all a bit cryptic. "How come everybody I ever met said we couldn't predict the future? No one I knows has a crystal ball. Do you?"

Johnny laughed. He'd heard these questions a thousand times before. "Looking back, Austin is like believing that the fish in the water is really where it seems to be. But if you want to spear the fish, you must aim not where it appears to be, but where it will be. The radar in an airplane is used to help the pilot look ahead. Pilots want to see what they are flying into—not what they flew through fifteen minutes ago. Look, Wall Street is littered with companies that were successful in the past but could no longer compete. You have to recognize when a company with a great record of success in the past is no longer competitive and aggressive. It'll start to lose market share and, most importantly…"

"Profits will decrease," interjected Austin.

"Exactly, Austin. You're learning. So what's that tell you?"

"Well, I guess…never use the past or even the present to make today's investment decisions. Am I close? "

"Close? That's it. It's simple, Austin, but millions of people, including brokers, make that mistake every day."

"So you look only at the future—into the crystal ball—and predict future earnings?"

Johnny shook his head. "No, no way. That's what the analysts are for. They deal only with the future—only what's ahead. First American has the leading team of analysts on Wall Street. Each one specializes in just a few companies. They often know a company as well—or maybe even better—than the guys running it. They're paid to know that company inside and out and predict its future. They're my 'crystal ball,' if you want to call it that. They do all the research and number crunching on each stock—and I guess you could say, forecast the future."

"So these analysts give you your information and research."

"Sure. Otherwise, I'd be like everyone else—guessing." Johnny laughed confidently. "Austin, understand something. I don't claim to be a genius, or especially smart, but I know how to use what's available—those analysts' reports. It's the only way Austin—the only way—to systematically answer those three questions. And remember, that's what this is all about—a way to answer those three questions. The analysts have the answers."

"Can you give me an example?"

"Sure. Let's say you're a trustee for a large trust department of a bank. Your job in the trust department is to manage one billion dollars in pension-fund money. You decide to invest five percent in the healthcare industry. You have, say, $50 million to invest in a variety of drug and health-related companies. Let's say you want to buy up to ten companies in that industry. That would be about $5 million in each company, more or less."

Austin smiled. "What a job! Throwing all that money around."

Johnny held up a hand. "Ah… but, Austin, which companies do you pick?"

"Hmmm…"

"Yes, hmm. Remember, the only thing at stake is your job, your reputation, your kids' college tuition, the food on your table, the beach house, and the mortgage—everything. It's all riding on your making the right decisions. Still want that job, Austin?"

"There's not much room for error in finance, is there?" asked Austin. This wasn't some kind of game. He'd have to think twice about investing as a career.

"None. Like the stock market, Austin, the financial services business is unforgiving. But, hey, it's just another one of life's 'risk-to-reward' situations—like choosing a college, choosing girlfriends and a lot of other things. Except in this business if you lose, you lose fast. There's no business like this one, Austin. But it can bite a hunk out of you—and your clients—if you don't know what you're doing."

"So what would I do if I had that money to invest for the bank?" Austin asked.

"Well, just as with me, you need an expert's advice. There are approximately one thousand healthcare related stocks out there for you to choose from. Instead of choosing yourself—after all, you're no analyst—you call an analyst at, say, First American Investors who specializes in that particular market, and ask him or her to develop a list of health-care stocks that are expected to increase earnings twenty percent in the next twelve months."

"They predict that? What companies will grow profits at what rate per year?"

"Yes, they do," answered Johnny. "An analyst's research will predict the growth rate for a company out a couple of years. Obviously, some companies will grow faster than others."

"If I worked for that trust department," said Austin, "why wouldn't I just buy the companies on the analyst's list whose earnings are going to increase the most? Sounds pretty simple to me."

"Good question. Let's look at it from the context of the Strategy. As I said earlier, today's stock prices reflect all the news now in print. If one company is expected to grow faster than another, that expectation is already in the stock price. OK, imagine that there are two investors—let's say you and Charley. I suggest Charley buy stock in ABC Company. By the end of the year, ABC's profits are forecast by the analyst to grow by $10 million, or 10% more than last year.

I suggest you buy stock in XYZ Company. Analysts predict that by the end of this year the profits of XYZ will grow $100 million—or 100% higher than they did last year. Clearly, XYZ makes more money and is a better investment, don't you agree? "

"Sure! Thanks for putting me into it. It's a sure winner."

Johnny smiled. "OK. Let's say Charley buys the ABC stock

and you buy XYZ stock. Its now three months later. I call Charley and say that our analyst has just increased ABC's earnings estimates from $10 million to $12 million. I also call you and tell you that our analysts decreased earnings estimates for XYZ. Our analyst now feels that a profit of $100 million is no longer possible. Instead, he lowers his estimates to $90 million."

"OK," Austin said, "my company is making $10 million less—only $90 million. But we're still making more than the measly $12 million Charley's company is making. I've still got the best company. $90 million is a hell of a lot more than $12 million."

"OK, your company still is expected to increase its earnings some 90%. Not too shabby. But let's see how the stock price reacts to this news. You think you're still ahead of Charley. No way. Would it surprise you that Charley just heard good news, and you just heard bad news?"

"How could that be?" Austin asked. "My company's profits are still expected to be up 90% and Charley's are going to be up only 12%?"

Johnny ignored his question and said, "Now another three months go by...."

"So now it's half a year after buying the stock?" Austin interjected.

"Yeah. Its half a year later, and I call Charley and tell him the analysts have raised the earnings estimates a second time—from $12 million to $15 million. He feels good about the news, of course. But I also call you to tell you that the analyst's estimates for XYZ Company have been reduced again, say from $90 million to $80 million. Your company's profits are expected to grow to $80 million and Charley's only to $15 million."

"So what happens at the end of the year?" asked Austin.

"OK. So at the end of the year Charley's company earned $15 million dollars for the year. Your company earned $80 million for the year. OK, 80% increase is a lot more than 15%. So, tell me, which investor—you or Charley—made the most money in the stock market that year?"

Johnny paused, awaiting Austin's answer. Austin didn't want to show his confusion and hesitated, so Johnny jumped in and said, "Charley made more than you did. His stock soared. Yours took a dive—and you know why? Charley's company made more money than expected. The analyst raised his estimates upward twice—from $10 to $12 million and up to $15 million. So, his stock shot up in value. It always does. Remember that immutable law? Now, your company, my friend, was expected to grow by 100%. The analyst twice changed his forecast downwards to 'only' 80%. Oh, your company made more money—a lot more money—but that's not the point. Your stock dropped for one simple reason—your company earned less than expected. Charley's stock soared. And why? His company earned more than was expected.

"The message here, Austin, is not how much the company is expected to earn. You expected and got the biggest earnings, but your stock went down. Why? And if you get this Austin, you'll make money in the stock market—a lot of money. It's not the earnings that count. It's the change in the estimates of earnings. The analysts changed Charley's earnings estimates upwards. They changed your estimates downwards. His stock soared. Your stock dropped. Here's why—it's the changes in earnings estimates after you buy that pulls your stocks up or down."

"But..." Austin started to ask.

"Let me finish this point. I can't tell you how important it is. When you buy, everything known about the company way off into the future is already priced in. So it's the changes in estimated earnings after you buy—up or down—that pulls the stock price up or down. You could call it a 'financial law of gravity'. It always happens—sooner or later."

Austin took all this in with some difficulty. "You mean that's it? It's so simple."

"Well, that's not all there is to the Strategy, of course. But it's the foundation. Austin, most great truths are simple—so simple that people overlook or choose to ignore them." Johnny was emphatic now. He knew what he knew, and he knew he was right.

"So then a company has to earn money?"

"Oh, no," replied Johnny. "A company can have their losses continually grow smaller and it's considered the same as an increase in earnings. Look at many new companies. They've never made a penny, but their shares are up because their losses grow smaller and smaller. Earnings estimate changes are the key, not profits as such. Never forget that."

"Wow. That's amazing. I mean, I don't know exactly what you're talking about, of course, but the logic follows. If changes in estimated earnings dictate how a stock moves, then knowing what those changes are predicted to be let's you predict which way the stock will go. Is that right? "

"That's it, Austin. But what's most amazing to me is that very few people know how to utilize this information. That's why most guys will always buy stocks or mutual funds randomly— guessing, hot tips, instinct and feel. And I'll always manage money. There's a big difference. I know how to use the firm's amazing research—and it's truly amazing, Austin. I'll tell you that."

Remembering his conversation with Cathy, Austin asked, "But don't mutual-fund managers do this type of research, Mr. Long?"

"Perhaps they do," replied Johnny. "Who knows how they pick a stock? You're never told that. More importantly, how do we know when to sell a particular mutual fund? Answer that for me. Remember my first rule—if I don't know when to sell the investment, in this case a mutual fund, how can it possibly be a disciplined investment strategy? Never forget those three questions Austin. And the second question is the most important—when to sell."

"So," Austin asked, "that's why the stocks in a particular mutual fund aren't really the issue, even though that's all you ever hear about."

"Right! They could be very good stocks, chosen very well. Who knows? That's not the issue for me. I'm a money manager. But how on earth can I call myself a money manager if I don't have a proven strategy for when to sell any investment? I couldn't be. I'd be conning people—mostly myself."

"Austin, investing is a serious business. You're talking about people's nest-eggs, their life savings—their hopes and dreams. How could I ever take that on without having a proven set of rules and laws that's stood the test of time?"

"Laws?" Austin asked.

"Yes, laws, Austin. You know, like the law of gravity. If you don't have laws for investing, you're not investing. You're guessing. OK, you're a musician. Do you play music without following some fundamental rules?"

Austin thought for a moment. "I guess not, because there are always keys."

"Keys, good example."

"Although in some experimental composition the rule may become that there are not rules at all."

Johnny held up his hand. "That's not of interest to me, Austin. That's how you bankrupt people. I'm a money manager, not a guesser. It's OK for some of your music, but not for investing."

Johnny went on, "Laws of justice may be relative—a man might be guilty or innocent. Laws of gravity, however, are not. If you drop something, it'll fall. I know that for certain. Some things fall faster than others do, true. But everything falls when dropped. Right?"

"Right."

"Likewise, if the analyst continually reduces his earnings estimates, the stock will fall. Some stocks may fall faster than others. But they'll all eventually fall and won't rise again without some sort of lift. Right? "

"Right."

"So why on earth would I attempt to experiment with an immutable law—and that's what this is, Austin. I couldn't care less if someone wants to argue against the law of gravity. If I drop a rock on his foot, he'll scream in pain." They both laughed.

"Results, Austin. Results. The proof of the pudding is in the eating and my clients are eating well—very well."

"Can we take a break," Austin asked. He had to go to the bathroom.

"Sure, I need to make a few phone calls. We'll have coffee and wrap this up as soon as we can."

Austin really needed time to think more than he needed to use the bathroom. His head was spinning. He sensed that what he'd heard here today would take weeks, months to really sink in. But the Strategy agreed with his own need for order, discipline and harmony—the very traits that made him a good musician.

Austin apologized for taking so much time, but Johnny said, "Hey, it's an investment. I expect to get some returns—and not just your account."

Johnny had been impressed with how well Austin had absorbed all this so far. The great thing was he had nothing to forget, nothing to unlearn. This kid was a clean blackboard—and Johnny was writing on it.

If things work out.... Johnny thought. Well, we'll see.

Moira brought them more coffee, and they continued talking about what other brokers did with people's money. Austin realized many just didn't know any better. That, or they really didn't care, so long as they got paid. But with Johnny's strategy, it seemed like everybody won.

OK, enough talk, Austin thought. I want to win, too. I want to win that five million. For the first time, he really believed he could. And he was convinced Johnny Long was the man for him. "So how do we begin with my money?" he asked. "We've talked about things in general, but I've still got this money to invest. I need to make that 15%. Where do we start?"

Johnny liked those kinds of questions. "Simple," he said. "First we have to buy. Whenever one of our analysts raises earnings estimates two times within a six-month period, that stock goes on my list of recommendations."

Austin was surprised by the simplicity. "That's it?"

"That's it?" scoffed Johnny. "We cover thousands of stocks. Thousands, Austin. Plus, the strategy has been back-tested for years. Remember, our analysts do a tremendous amount of work developing those accurate earnings estimates, which, by the way, we base everything on. On top of that, my team does a tremendous amount of work reviewing and systematizing all these changes."

Austin felt a bit embarrassed. "Sorry, Mr. Long."

"Not a problem. Hey, what would you know about it, right? What's really important is whether or not the Strategy works. This much I can tell you—if the earnings estimate for a stock has been raised at least twice within a six-month period, there's greater than a fifty-fifty chance that the analysts will raise estimates again—and that's when the stock will go up."

"So, if I follow you right, after the second increase, you can buy the stock. Then, if there are more increases, I'll make money?"

"That's it. You own the stock before subsequent good news

comes out. Remember, stock prices are not pushed up by news you already know. They're pulled up later by new information coming out after you bought."

"It's not predicting the future..."

"An impossibility," chimed Johnny.

"Right. But it's giving you pretty good odds for future good news."

"Exceptional odds, Austin. Remember, greater than fifty-fifty. We have to look for positive news after we buy the stock. That's why we only buy stocks that have had two or more increases within a six-month period. They're very likely to have more."

Austin was feeling more confident now. Not only was he beginning to see the rationale behind Johnny's investment strategy, he was beginning to recognize the stark professional differences between someone like Johnny and someone like Harrison or Bobby Lane. What a difference!

"Tell me, " prompted Austin. "Does it matter what industries we invest in?"

"This might sound strange, but it doesn't matter what industries we start with. If an analyst raises his estimates two times within a six-month period, I recommend the stock. Any industry is part of the capitalist machine. As such, earnings are the prime mover, Austin. Don't get bogged down in the hype about this or that stock or sector. Old news is no news where the market is concerned. For that reason, it doesn't matter what price we pay for the stock. The current market price of a stock is always fairly valued in light of all the news that's known about it. We're looking forward."

"It doesn't matter what price you pay? How do you know if you're getting a bargain?"

"Austin, I just told you a stock is always at a fair value when you buy it. We're looking at those new earnings estimate increases after you buy it. That's what counts."

"Is that why," continued Austin, "you were concerned with when to sell a stock? Well, when?"

Johnny nodded. "That's the important part. You understand now why we buy a stock. So how do we decide when to sell the stock? The two are related. We bought the stock because there were two earnings increases within six months. Similarly, we'll sell that stock whenever there is an earnings estimate decrease of any kind. When the analyst reduces his estimates, I'll recommend that we sell the stock."

"Right then and there, even though it might do OK in the future?"

Hopefully, before the second or third decrease, Austin. Otherwise, you're not following the entire premise about earnings growth. We recommend selling the stock after the first earnings estimate reduction."

"You don't wait for two reductions, then?"

"Why? Things can only get worse from there. Let me give you an example. Whenever I hire a research assistant to work for me, I'll tell him or her to research all the companies that have declined in value from, say, fifty dollars a share to five dollars a share. Now, that's a big decline. I also ask my researcher to note what all the companies have in common. The answer is simple—when the stock was selling for fifty dollars a share, the company was profitable. On the contrary, when the stock was selling for five dollars a share, the company was losing money. The important point is that by the time the stock was down to five dollars, four years might have passed—years you would have been waiting for the stock to recover. But if you were using the analyst's research properly, do you think you'd have seen the analysts raising or lowering earnings estimates?"

Austin thought a moment. "Lowering."

"That's right. He would've lowered his estimates, probably many times. Let's assume you bought that stock for fifty dollars and you still own it at five dollars. Were there times you could have sold that stock and cut your losses to a minimum, then moved on to reinvest that money in a stock whose earnings were growing?" Johnny waited for Austin to answer.

"Yes."

"Yes? The correct answer is 'of course.' That's what they call opportunity costs—the cost of not doing something. In the case I just mentioned, the analyst probably lowered his estimates ten to fifteen times, Austin! Listen to me," he leaned forward, "Opportunity costs will kill you. Keep that in mind, because it'll come up again and again while discussing the Strategy."

"So then, a stock will decline every time an analyst lowers his estimates. But then why do some stocks move back up after bad news?" asked Austin.

Johnny shook his head. "I didn't say that, Austin. I said that if you continue to own a stock and the estimates are continually lowered, the stock price would probably decline. Many times an estimate is lowered, and I sell the stock for my clients and you know what—there are no more earnings estimate reductions. Sometimes I'll sell a stock at a small loss, and the stock will actually go up in value because there was only the one reduction. But the point I'm trying to make is that if you don't sell the stock within a reasonable time after the first reduction, and there are many more reductions to follow, you'll lose more money than you could've made moving into another stock which has just had two earnings estimate increases."

All this talk of losing money and stocks going down was making Austin a bit queasy. What he wanted to hear was talk of making money and meeting his father's test and getting that five million. He hoped this conversation with Johnny Long wasn't going to end up like all the others—warnings about risk and possible returns. He wanted to cut to the chase.

"What happens, Mr. Long, if I've got a big profit? You know the terms of my trust. What if I'm up a lot of money on a stock? Why not sell it, claim my 15% and be home free? Why not bail out as soon as I have what I need?"

"You only sell a stock when the estimates are lowered, Austin—never before. And you'll notice that with this strategy, a few of the stocks you own will be big winners for you. That's the normal progression here. The weeding out process of selling your losers is the cornerstone of the strategy. By selling only the stocks that have estimate reductions, your portfolio will come to consist of many profitable investments by the end of that third year."

"Weeding out," said Austin. "You know, none of the people I've spoken with have ever mentioned anything like weeding out, or even mentioned earnings or analysts. Are you that different?"

Johnny shrugged, although he knew the answer quite well. At his stage of life, though, he enjoyed a bit of humility. "All I can say, Austin, is that these are the fundamentals of growth investing I'm teaching you today. Why more brokers don't invest money like this I really can't say."

"Even here at First American Investors?"

"Well no, because like I said, there are probably thousands of financial advisors in the firm who follow my strategy and watch for changes in earnings estimates."

"How do they follow it so closely?"

"My list of stocks is available on the firm's computer system—at least for now. Some people would like to change that," Johnny said cryptically.

Austin was genuinely impressed. "So you're something like the First American investment guru. Amazing. Really, I must be the luckiest guy, Mr. Long."

Johnny smiled. This was why he enjoyed every day of his job. He enjoyed helping people. "Austin, I'm no guru. I'm not even a particularly intelligent guy. I just figured out a way of systematically bringing First American Investor's leading research to my clients and how to answer those three questions."

"So weeding out, huh?" said Austin.

"Weeding out, Austin. It's the guiding principle of life. Always has been."

"So it's your goal to build a portfolio of only winning stocks? That'd be great."

"Austin, don't get too carried away. There's no such thing as a perfect portfolio. The point is to keep working toward the ideal portfolio, weeding out the losers. The main thing, Austin, is to never sell your winners too soon. That's the greatest loss of all!" he exclaimed, thumping the table with his hand. "The beauty of the strategy is that it creates a systematic way of avoiding the greatest mistake of all—selling a big winner too soon."

"That makes sense," said Austin.

"It should," said Johnny. "In my experiences, the biggest mistake investors—or brokers for that matter—make is selling their winners too early and holding their losers too long."

"You know," said Austin, "from the conversations I've had with different so-called advisors, I can imagine that happening very easily."

"I think it happens because people look at the price of the stock as a means of determining whether or not they should sell a stock. But like I've explained to you, that's exactly what not to do."

"How do you explain that to people who have been investing that way their entire lives?" Another good question, Johnny thought. He knew you could tell a lot about a person by the questions they ask—and Austin was asking the right ones.

"Let's see," said Johnny, pondering a fresh example to illustrate his point. "Suppose you and I go to a baseball game and the score at the end of the sixth inning is five to one. Tell me what the score will be at the end of the next inning without looking at the lineup."

"I could only guess. But isn't that always the case?"

"Sure. But it's foolish to just guess the score without more information. You need to know who's going to bat, who's pitching, and other things like that. Still, most people only look at the score or the price of a stock and try to predict the future based on that alone. Learn what pulls the price of stocks up or down and keep your eye on that information. That'll let you predict the score—the future price of the stock—better than anything else."

"It's no wonder people lose money in the stock market."

"The sad fact is, people don't know an opportunity when they see one," Johnny said.

"I wouldn't recognize it if it hit me in the face," admitted Austin.

"But you know enough to hire me and listen to me. That's the difference. If you hadn't met me, quite by chance I might add, you'd still be thinking that a stock price is all you need to know to make an informed decision. Prices alone are so misleading. A new Mercedes costs $70,000. You know two things about this car—the car and the price of the car. A bargain price for that car would be $50,000. If a friend of yours was being transferred out of the country and had to sell that car, and he'd accept $40,000, you'd see a bargain, right?"

"You bet," Austin replied.

"But if you saw a Ford Mustang at $40,000, you'd know in a flash that was not worth it."

"So what's the relationship to stocks?"

"When you buy a stock based on prices, you can wind up paying $40,000 for a Mustang, thinking you are getting a Mercedes. You really don't know the difference between the two. The price doesn't tell you. So don't look at prices. Look at what drives prices up or down—future estimated earnings. Look at those. They'll tell you if you're paying $40,000 for a Mercedes or $40,000 for a Mustang."

"So, with increasing estimated earnings I'll be looking at a Mercedes stock. And it'll keep going up?"

"Well, over the long term, yes. But we live in a volatile world. Stock prices go down for three reasons. The first is overall stock market declines. The tide lowers the water level for all the boats. If this happens, your portfolio will decline in value also—until the general decline is over. The second reason is because you may have a large concentration in a certain industry that's in decline. The third reason stocks decline is poor fundamentals—weak underlying earnings—with the company. Using my strategy, I've pretty much eliminated the third reason. Under the Strategy you'd have bought stocks in different industries—diversifying, we call it—and you would've sold the stock long before serious problems developed. So, your stocks would go down only in a general market decline—and they always pass."

"When the stocks in your portfolio go down, you aren't worried?" asked Austin in amazement.

"No. Because general market declines come and go and the stocks I own have strong earnings underlying their prices. I know that—apart from temporary market or sector volatility—the stocks will continue to go up over the long term. And we're talking long-term, Austin—many years. It could take that long for the Strategy to fully engage and overcome temporary market declines."

"OK, now, for the third question," Austin asked. "When the time comes to sell one of the stocks, what do you do with the money?"

"You simply replace it with a new stock on the list you do not already own. Or sometimes I might suggest you buy more of a stock you already own. Especially if I think it is a strong bargain."

"Because the earnings are still strong?"

"That's right," agreed Johnny. "If a stock in the Strategy

declines more than thirty percent from its high and we're still increasing our estimates, I'll take advantage of short-term weakness by recommending clients buy more of that stock."

"Because you know about the earnings?"

"Because I know that earnings are still strong or even increasing, by our analyst's figures. As I said, that's why stocks appreciate in value. Does that answer everything, Austin?"

Austin's head was spinning with all the new information. There remained one or two logistical problems. "How many stocks should I own?"

"You should have between ten and fifteen different stocks in as many industries as possible. Are we ready to start? I can immediately recommend a selection of twelve stocks for your new portfolio." Johnny looked Austin directly in the eye as if to say this is your one and only chance, young man. "Do you want me to open an account, Austin?"

Austin knew that he had to pass his father's test and win that five million. He knew there wasn't a ghost of a chance doing it on his own—or for that matter, with the other "experts" he'd talked to.

"Yes," he answered. "What information do you need from me?"

"Moira will take down your address and other personal information. For my part, I'll buy and sell the stocks in your account as the Strategy demands. I'll always notify you beforehand. Do you understand that?"

"No problem," said Austin. "But can you at least tell me what you're going to buy at the outset. I'm kind of excited."

"Certainly," said Johnny. "I'll buy you the stocks on this sheet. I prepared it before you arrived." He handed Austin a piece of paper.

Name	Cost	Shares	Value
Toll Brothers	20	400	$8,300
Best Buy	55	150	$8,300
Cisco	15	550	$8,300
Home Depot	42	200	$8,300
MidAtlantic Medical	30	275	$8,300
Johnson & Johnson	55	150	$8,300
Intel	30	275	$8,300
Tidewater	42	200	$8,300
Argosy	30	275	$8,300
United Healthcare	76	110	$8,300
Alliant	55	150	$8,300
Office Depot	20	400	$8,300

Austin studied the list of names. He recognized some of the companies; others, he'd never heard of. For example, he knew Office Depot from the stores near Stanford. He also knew Intel.

"Mr. Long, do you think investing in Cisco is wise? I mean they are in the high tech business. Aren't they in a lot of trouble with all the tech problems?"

Johnny stared at Austin for a moment. Time and again, he had to endure clients' objections to his investment decisions as if the hour Johnny just spent explaining the Strategy had never occurred.

"Austin, what did I just spend an hour explaining? Didn't I say that every one of the stocks I selected are currently undergoing an increase in earnings?"

Austin felt foolish, but pressed on like only the foolish can. "So you think it is a good investment?"

"Austin, I don't care about the particular company—what it is, what it does. Aside from diversifying into different sectors, all I care about is that this or that stock has had its earnings estimates increased twice within a six-month period. I'm not concerned with the name of the company just like I'm not concerned with the price of the stock. I'm only concerned with earnings estimates and with diversification."

"But don't you care about the underlying business and stuff like that?" pressed Austin.

"My first responsibility as a money manager is to interpret First American's research and make it available to my clients in an understandable discipline. Our research department follows Cisco, and we believe the company will earn more this year than we projected last month."

"In other words," said Austin, "their earnings estimates are increasing?"

"Right," agreed Johnny. "Things are looking good for the company. That's my first responsibility to my clients—to make that information available in an investment strategy. I know they're in the tech business. And unless the client has any particular problems with investing in this sector, I'd neither approve nor disapprove of what they're doing."

What a striking contrast to academic life at Stanford! "You know, a lot of people back at school would find you totally offensive."

Johnny laughed. "Ah, the scorn of academics may be the price I pay, Austin." He held out his hands and gestured around his large office, replete with original paintings from his business trips to Paris, sculpture from his clients at the art academy in Florence, and photos of the pyramids sent from his clients in Egypt. "But I suffer in silence. T'is my lot, I suppose."

Austin found Johnny's sarcasm a refreshing change from the sometimes claustrophobic intellectual environment at school. "So you try to remain objective?"

"Of course I do. It's an absolute must. But the important point here is not to fall in love with a particular company. That's what concerns me. The problem is falling in love with a stock you should sell. Like staying in a bad relationship far too long because you're blind to the hazards."

Austin thought of Audrey and Cathy, and all the others. "In stocks as in life, huh Mr. Long."

"Maybe, Austin. That's not my concern either, though. I'm not a philosopher. I'm just a money manager for First American Investors. All I know is if you start taking sides with stocks, it'll be difficult to make an objective decision later. Remember, there'll always come a day when you'll have to sell that stock. Am I making sense?"

Austin thought of Cathy and Audrey. "Absolutely." He especially thought of Audrey. She was waiting for him to return to her and to school. He was going to have a hard time telling her he wanted to be unencumbered after graduation. It would be time to move on. He didn't want to hurt her feelings and certainly didn't want to raise her own expectations, but he just wasn't ready to get married yet. He'd have to be honest and tell her when he got back. It was only fair.

"Do you ever feel like you're being very cold about what you do?" Austin asked. "What if one of the companies is bad? I mean, let's say I'm religious and I don't want to invest in companies that make weapons. Or I don't like liquor companies. How do you get past that?"

"You don't have to do anything you really don't want to, Austin. There are enough selections on my buy list so that a client may exercise some degree of choice. You'll probably hear me say this a number of times in the future—one of the beauties of the Strategy is that it gives you a great deal of flexibility."

This was not the sort of answer Austin was looking for. "Well, I don't want to invest in a company that is in the tech sector." Johnny handed Austin a second piece of paper. This time, Cisco was replaced with FEDEX.

"What's FEDEX?" asked Austin.

"Federal Express," answered Johnny.

"Is that a wise choice, Mr. Long? I hear that the airline business is in trouble, too."

Johnny stared at Austin for a second or two. "Austin, you're starting to sound like other investors, to put it mildly. Like the baseball game analogy, you're making certain assumptions about the future without knowing anything. Or I should say, you are ignoring what we do know about every single company on my list."

"Well..."

Johnny interrupted Austin almost immediately. "I don't know how many times an analyst is going to change his mind about the earnings of any of these companies. I thought we'd already covered that. We hitch our wagon for the ride until the horse stops pulling. That's it."

"Well, I wasn't sure."

Johnny was getting irritated now. "Let me tell you something. First, if you buy FEDEX today and the analyst raises his earnings projections eight more times over the next two years, you'll see the stock price go up in value. Second, if this doesn't work, I don't know what does. That's all I can say. If the estimates are reduced, we sell and move on."

Johnny was confident, perhaps to the point of being arrogant. But he knew what he knew. He wasn't exaggerating when he said if the Strategy doesn't work, he doesn't know what else does. He was that sure of it—and this feeling of relative security is no easy achievement in the world of finance. Brokers like Bobby Lane figuratively suffered every price movement, precisely because they had no idea why they were buying and selling stocks. People said about guys like Bobby Lane, "stocks are in his blood." In one way, it was literally true. But it's got more to do with the enormous amount of cholesterol he consumes at lunch when the market is getting hit hard. The ulcers, the bypasses, the drinking binges, too many steak dinners, the antacid in the candy dish—these are marks of distinction for the "stock jockey"—the brokers like Bobby Lane who have virtually no idea of why they do what they do. Bobby's clients, like a codependent romantic married to a drug addict, can only be worse for the wear.

Austin began to waver. "OK. I guess you should put Cisco back on the list. OK, do that."

Johnny shook his head. "Austin, am I speaking Greek? I just said it doesn't matter whether we include FEDEX or Cisco. The list is fine as it is."

Austin handed the list back to Johnny and waited. For what, he didn't know.

"Austin," said Johnny.

"Yes, Mr. Long."

"Now is the time you thank me."

"Thank you, Mr. Long?"

"Yes, Austin. After all, you're going to be a very wealthy young man when I'm through with you. Your dad would be proud of you."

"Yes, I do thank you Mr. Long. I know I'm lucky to have you. Thank you. And let's hope things go well."

Johnny shook his head and instructed Austin to see Moira about filling out the account paperwork. "And Austin..."

"Yes, Mr. Long."

"Call me Johnny."

Johnny stood up from the conference table and patted his belly. "Well, I'm hungry."

Austin agreed. "All this talk about making money is making me hungry."

Johnny smiled. "Stay hungry, Austin." He called out to Moira, "Make reservations at the Balzac Club please." He looked at Austin. "I hope you like French food."

"I've never been to the Balzac Club. Is it nice?"

"Nice? It's one of the best. The food is as good as the ambiance. That's the trick to finding a really good restaurant."

"Boy," said Austin; "you have a system for everything, don't you?"

Johnny patted Austin on the shoulder. "Its called maturity, Austin. You'll grow into it yourself one day. I'm certain of it. Come on, we'll walk over. It's only a few blocks away."

"Mr. Long, uh, Johnny, do you take all small-time clients like me to a fancy restaurant?"

"No, Austin, there's something I want to talk to you about."

When they arrived at the Balzac Club, the maitre'd' recognized Johnny Long at once. They were seated at Johnny's usual table near the window. The view of the city was fabulous. Austin took it all in as he sat down. Once again, it seemed to him that there was no end to Johnny's prestige.

"This is a great place, Johnny," said Austin.

"It sure is. It's one of my favorites. Do you see the ceiling?"

Austin looked up. "Yes, what about it?"

"Watch this." Johnny nodded to the maitre'd'. At that moment, the ceiling began to open up, letting in a rush of cool air and revealing the sky above. The maitre'd' closed the ceiling again. Austin was speechless. "And the food is even better. Like I said, only Jacque's Dover Sole rivals the ambiance. Worth every penny."

Austin was delighted almost to the point of being horrified.

"Do you eat like this every day? Excuse me for asking, but I can see making a habit of this."

Johnny noticed how impressed Austin was. This was exactly the impression Johnny wanted made—not as he would with a wealthy prospect, but rather as he would with his son. "Now Austin," said Johnny, "I don't want you to think that life like this is easy to come by. I know we've been discussing fame and fortune all morning, but you've got a long way to go and have to stay focused."

The point seemed lost on Austin. "Uh-huh."

"I mean that, Austin. Making money and even living well requires a lot of self-discipline. It might seem to you that money comes easily after our discussion, but it can be lost even easier. Remember that, and you'll understand another benefit of the Strategy. I take nothing lightly."

Something in Johnny's tone made Austin think. Perhaps it was Johnny's fatherly tone—a tone Austin hadn't heard much growing up. It was almost as if Johnny had been in his shoes once himself. "I'm beginning to realize that, Johnny. I really am."

Johnny was satisfied with this response. "Good. Now about that Dover Sole." He lifted up his glass for a toast. Austin followed suit. "You know, Austin, it's not every day that I get a challenge like this. You're quite fortunate to have an opportunity like this." Austin smiled and Johnny pressed on. "Your father must have been a pretty clever man, if I do say so myself!"

Austin nodded in agreement and was once again amazed at Johnny's perspicacity. He thought to himself, my father sure knew how to catch me. He knew I'd go for the five million. I just wish I'd had time to know him before he died.

"Do you have a girlfriend?" asked Johnny.

"As a matter of fact I do. Her name is Audrey. She's back at school. She's a brilliant musician and after almost two years, I'm still amazed how smart she is. I miss her a lot. You should hear her play the piano."

"Perhaps some day I will." The job offer he was going to make to Austin at lunch was, at least in his mind, such an incredible opportunity it never occurred to him that a young man like Austin would even consider turning it down. That was Johnny—he had a gift for convincing people that they should follow him in his every endeavor.

The waiter interrupted them to take their order. Austin was a bit taken that there were no prices on the menu. Johnny laid Austin's misgivings to rest by telling him to order anything he wanted, again recommending the sole. Once they ordered, Johnny started in again with Audrey.

"Why do you want to know about my girlfriend?" asked Austin.

"Oh, no particular reason. I was just wondering if she'll be joining you when you come to work for me."

"Are you offering me a job after college?" asked Austin, incredulous. How had he missed that?

"For about the third time, Austin," he laughed. "You've just been so involved in all this, you haven't heard me. Look, you've only got one year of school left, but you've got three more years to go to earn the rest of the money. I assumed you might want to work for me when you graduate. I could use your help. I'll pay you something like $25,000 to start."

Without Austin's knowing it, Johnny had been carefully sizing him up all morning—watching his reactions, judging how quickly he picked up things, listening to his questions. Austin didn't know it, but he was "on trial." And he thought he was evaluating Johnny! It was more the other way around. And Johnny liked what he saw. Austin was sharp and open. He got the points quickly. He had nothing to unlearn—no bad investing habits to get rid of. The discipline, logic and love of order and harmony—the very things that got him into music—were the traits needed in this work. He could mold this kid.

"Austin, you know I don't make snap decisions. But in your case, I'm doing so. I need an assistant to understudy me, do the research and learn the Strategy. I could get a thousand and one young brokers, but they'd all have to unlearn everything. I'd rather start with someone who knows nothing and has nothing to unlearn. No bad habits to break. I know the traits needed in this strategy— and I think you have them. Anyway, you need to stay close to me for another three years."

Austin had been thinking about concentrating on his musical

career. The money would allow him to do that. He didn't know quite what to say to Johnny and stammered, "Ah… what would I be doing for you?"

"You'd be doing research, what else? Start at the bottom. You learn quickly and have a good head on your shoulders." Austin didn't reply. "Unless I'm wrong," joked Johnny.

Austin laughed. "No, no. You just caught me by surprise. I guess I'd have to think about it."

"Good," said Johnny. "It looks like I have a new employee. By the way, I'd appreciate it if you would take a few finance courses during your last year. It would come in handy."

Austin choked on his champagne. "Aren't you getting a little ahead of me? I only said that I was interested. I mean, I'd be a fool to just turn you down, but I still have to think about it."

Johnny shook his head mockingly. "Austin, Austin…don't mistake the cart for the horse, and the horse for the cart. Let me tell you what should come, in what order. Trust me when I say that you really have no idea how lucky you are."

Austin put down his salad fork. "How so?"

Johnny ate some salad and gave the appearance of profound thought. "Because my investment method is very special. In time, I'll teach you to do what I do." Austin stared blankly. "Do you understand Austin? It's one thing for you to simply fork over your money for me to manage. But it's quite another actually to learn how to do it yourself and then go on to manage other people's money yourself! Do you understand what I'm offering you?"

"Like the guy whose life you saved? He repaid you by giving you his investment method—those three questions."

"Bingo."

"Well, I'll probably take you up on your offer, Johnny. I just need a little time to think about it."

Johnny shook his head and laughed. "Sure, Austin. Take your time. Mull it over. No rush. No rush."

The waiter arrived with their entrees. The luxurious fragrance of Jacque's specialty wafted across their table. The heavy odor of the good life filled Austin's nose, coated his palate, and whetted his desire to live as well—just as Johnny had hoped.

Johnny sought to pile it on a bit more. "Picture yourself

dining like this with a client, someone whose wealth you'll manage, someone whose dreams you will help make come true, Austin. That, too, is the beauty of the Strategy. Oh, you'll earn every bite, my friend. The easier it looks, the harder it is, believe me. That's what clients don't understand."

Austin swallowed a bite of velvety fish. "Since I'm a client, at least right now, I might as well sound like one. You bought me what—twelve different stocks today. But to be honest, I don't recognize many of them. Couldn't you buy me stocks I've heard of?"

Johnny took a sip of champagne. "Are they in the Strategy and can I diversify your portfolio well enough?"

Austin shrugged. "Um...take a company like General Electric."

"It's not in the Strategy right now. It might be, but it isn't at the moment."

"So you couldn't add it?"

"I could, but I won't. Have you ever heard of Alliant?"

"No."

"Well then, the fact that you haven't heard of one of the most successful stocks in recent years—one that has been in the Strategy for almost as long—proves my point. You have to stay with the Strategy. There are no favorites. Just stocks that meet the standards."

Austin felt embarrassed. "Sorry."

"Your skin will thicken, believe me. Comes with the territory, like a tortoise and his shell." Johnny laughed. "Don't worry, Austin. Some day you may be sitting where I am and you can crack the jokes."

They chatted about Johnny's family for a while, then about Austin's mother. When the crème brulee arrived, Austin returned to the big question. Anyway, after his third glass of champagne, he was feeling emboldened. "Johnny, I appreciate the job offer, but I want you to be honest about it—do you think we can make that fifteen percent a year? Can it really be done?"

Johnny grinned. "Austin, not only will you make the fifteen percent, but you'll understand how it was done. That's the real reward here!"

"That's great," Austin exclaimed. "That's really great! I'm always hearing about this or that stock going way up and making people rich. All those stories are out there and they make it sound easy. I'd love to be part of that."

Johnny knew Austin was a novice. That's partly why Johnny wanted him to work for him. But so too were the thousands of hacks out there, blindly trading stocks with no rhyme or reason. They boast about their stock prowess, mocking professionals like Johnny Long. And yet you never really hear how much they lose, as if they never lost. Like someone who loses their shirt at a casino— they'll always tell you they're doing all right, just fine, kickin' ass. When they win, it's their skill. When they lose, it's the "damned market."

Johnny couldn't help snapping at Austin. It was for his own good anyway. "Look, so many people calling themselves 'investors' are just guessing. Do you understand that? And what's worse is how they keep pressing their luck by pouring more good money—usually someone else's—after bad. They think they're gurus because they picked the right stocks and sold them for some small profit. It makes me laugh, it really does."

"But if they can make a lot of small profits, what's wrong with that? It adds up."

Johnny put down his spoon in the middle of his crème brulee, which was quite unusual for him. "What's wrong with that? Austin, it's guessing!"

Austin stared blankly. "Look," Johnny continued, "successful investing is more than just making small profits. Think about the Strategy, Austin. As important as it is to know what to buy, what rule is equally important?"

Austin thought for a moment. "Knowing when to sell?"

"Of course. Knowing when to sell. As soon as there are earnings estimate reductions, right?"

"Right."

"Because most investors make one crucial mistake in common—they sell their winners too soon and they keep their losers too long. Now, you asked me about your fifteen percent. Could you earn it? If you want to average your fifteen percent, you have to know that one or two stocks will appreciate in value five to ten times your original investment. Simple. If you have a portfolio of about fifteen stocks we buy because their earnings are going up, only one or two will go up five or ten times."

"Only one or two?" Austin never thought about this before. "Is that bad?"

Johnny laughed. "No, not at all. Remember, we're weeding out and selling our losers. I was about to say that most people would never have those kinds of gains. Once a stock goes up a little, most investors sell it. It's called 'profit-taking'. Sounds good. Who doesn't want to take profits? But it can be the worst mistake you make. Or they hold a mediocre stock forever and miss out on opportunities elsewhere. Worse are those who hold their losers thinking they'll come back some day. Problem is, because they had no sound reason for buying them to begin with, they usually continue going down. How on earth can you know what to do if you don't have a sound underlying strategy for buying and, more importantly, selling?"

"So taking your profits by selling one of those big winners too soon is a real danger? They make a few bucks, but sell it before it can become a really big winner for them? I think I get what you're saying."

"That's what happens when they pick a stock solely based on price. They sell it on price, too. They don't look at what actually makes that price move up and down—and may continue making that price move up. And up. And up. Now that's what really matters."

"And if a stock happens to go up a lot, they could get fooled into selling too soon?" Austin asked.

"Yes. And it keeps going up. They've lost out. They're not keeping their winners and selling their losers—the way the Strategy does. They're doing the opposite—selling their winners and holding onto the losers, hoping they'll go back up. Buying and selling based on price is a great way to lose money," Johnny said. "You know, most stocks fluctuate between thirty and one hundred percent over the course of a year. Now imagine what people must go through just trying to decide whether to buy or sell—or when!"

And Johnny's colleagues warned him he'd better watch out that his clients didn't move their accounts to an on-line trading firm.

Thousands of investors were doing that and a lot of brokers were scared. That warning made Johnny laugh inwardly. No matter how long these brokers had been in the business, no matter how long they knew about Johnny's strategy and how successful it had been, they never seemed to use it. Sure, they were in danger of losing clients to on-line trading. After all, the clients could guess on-line as well as their brokers off-line. But Johnny's strategy made him an invaluable asset to his clients.

"And that, Austin, is yet another benefit of the Strategy."

"You've lost me, Johnny. One minute, you're talking about stocks going up, the next minute you're talking about stocks going down. Now you're talking about becoming obsolete."

Johnny held up his hand. "Austin, you need to learn how to find the continuity in things. There are only two things you need to know about becoming an advisor. First, the Strategy. Second, use the Strategy to distinguish yourself and your clients from the myriad of clueless people calling themselves 'investors' and 'advisors'," Johnny said, pointing at Austin for emphasis. "And maybe a third rule is that stock prices move up and down normally. Knowing why is the important thing."

Austin nodded. "I guess that's the synthesis of the first two, as a musician would see it."

"And if you look in the paper," Johnny continued, "you'll notice that the year's high and low can be as much as one-hundred percent apart. Most investors see their portfolios going down for a while and automatically assume there's something wrong. Worse yet, they try to time these fluctuations and end up missing the boat. That's what kills their performance. We've talked about not buying on price—and never try timing. Who can time the day-to-day market? If you understand that, you'll be well ahead of the game."

"So there's not always something to worry about when a stock goes down? That's just when I'd start worrying!"

"The market moves as a matter of course. It's what I call the stock market inhaling and exhaling—taking air in and letting it out. It happens. It's natural—even good—but it panics a lot of people. What investors should look at are only the projected earnings of a company. If the company's profits keep growing, the stock price will follow in time, especially if profits are higher than expected."

"That'd be a nice surprise. I'm beginning to understand what you're trying to teach me. It does make sense, doesn't it?"

Johnny laughed. "What did you think? I was making all this up?"

Austin laughed.

"Now, I take it a step further and try to select stocks that I believe will grow faster than expected. That's the hard part. That's where our analysts come in. The analysts are crucial to the Strategy. Without their research, the Strategy wouldn't exist. But without me, their research would never be utilized by our clients to its fullest extent. Am I making myself clear?"

"Yes. Use the research to buy stocks before the positive news comes out."

"Now you're catching on," lauded Johnny.

"Seeing how haphazardly most people invest their money, the Strategy seems simple."

"No one ever said investing is hard. That perception is a result of the huge marketing engine that has come to drive this business. Small-Cap, Mid-Cap, Value, P/E, Beta, the mutual fund of the day. It all just comes down to one thing—earnings! People complicate things far too much." They both paused while the waiter refilled their coffee.

Austin broke the silence. "So let me see if I've got it. It's all new to me, you know. You basically have three rules. One, have a strategy. Two, have reliable research. Three, be patient. Right?"

Johnny wanted to encourage Austin's eagerness. "Well done."

"Johnny, I've learned more about investing today—and avoided more investing pitfalls and gobbledygook—than I could have ever believed possible. Thank you. I really mean it. Thank you."

"It's my pleasure," Johnny said.

They finished the memorable lunch talking about growing up without a father, college, girlfriends and life, avoiding the unanswered question—would Austin come to work for Johnny?

Afterward, Austin went back to Johnny's office with him to sign the papers for the account and to say good-bye to Moira.

Chapter 7

AUSTIN flew back to Stanford University with a great deal on his mind. He used the long flight to make some decisions. First, he decided to work for Johnny after graduation. He was smart enough to see a good thing when it came along. Most importantly, he decided to really enjoy his last year in college. He had a strong suspicion that working for Johnny after graduation meant his life was going to become a hell of a lot more complicated. If he was going to live life to the fullest this last year, he'd have to feel free to date whomever he wanted. No more of that guilt he felt with Cathy. So, he'd have a talk with Audrey and hoped she'd understand. They were never engaged or very serious, but still, he owed it to her to share what he was feeling.

Austin got a second wind academically as well. As a liberal arts major, it was easy for him to slide from class to class, from subject to subject, clear across the millennia. Aside from his studies in music, which were intense and regimented, Austin's studies tended to lack focus. There had been no guiding theme to his academic life, not to mention his social life, or his life in general. Now there was. For the first time he was focused and not improvising things on a day-to-day basis.

He would follow Johnny's recommendation and take some economic courses to complement his music studies. He was excited about learning and energized. He wanted to learn. Whether or not his newfound enthusiasm would last longer than a plane ride—well, that remained to be seen. But Austin was returning to Stanford motivated.

For the first time, Austin planned for courses outside his major. Of course, having no prior experience in the field, he would be limited to introductory classes in economics. This was Stanford, however, and even so-called "introductory" classes maintained a high degree of intellectual rigor. In fact, the most sought-after classes, introductory or otherwise, often required the professor's prior approval.

In the field of economics, there were several classes offered—so many that Austin thought he'd better call Johnny and ask his advice. If Austin learned anything, it was to trust Johnny Long where matters of finance were concerned.

As expected, Moira answered the call. She was delighted to hear Austin's voice. Everything was fine with her and after a brief hello, she put Austin through to Johnny.

"Yo, Austin. How's it going?"

Austin was thrilled. He was now calling his "own" broker across the country, just like some tycoon. "Hi, Johnny. What's up?"

"You tell me."

First things first. "I thought a lot about what you said, and I'd like to take you up on your offer."

"Excellent." Johnny was not surprised. He usually got what he wanted, people included.

"So I thought I'd prepare by taking some economic courses."

"Like I said, Austin, this is the best job in the world. You'll enjoy it."

He realized he would understudy and work for one of the best. Austin was overwhelmed, but tried to cover it up as best he could. "I'm pretty excited about it, Johnny. I have a problem, though. I'm not sure what courses to take. There are a lot of business courses. Should I take an accounting course, too?"

There was a brief pause. "Actually, Austin, there's a lot more to being a successful money manager than what they teach you in business courses."

Austin frowned. "So what, I should study, physics? Come on,

help me out here."

Johnny laughed. "I can see you still have that Ivy League sarcasm. OK, consider taking courses in mass psychology."

Austin was surprised. "Really?"

"Studying mass psychology will help you understand two things. First, how an individual behaves under different degrees of pressure and stress. That's for sure. You know, managing a person's nest egg can be difficult when the markets go against you. It helps to understand why people become upset and confused about things like the market that they can't control."

"Makes sense. Got it."

"Good. Second, you will learn how a group of people generally act under different conditions."

Austin was again impressed with Johnny's foresight. "Actually, Johnny, one of the most popular courses is Professor Williams' Introduction to Human Behavior. Everybody tries to get in that class."

"Well, there you go," said Johnny, quite pleased with himself.

"The problem is that Professor Williams only admits students after interviewing them personally."

"Well, that makes perfect sense, right. Think about it. His class is a controlled environment for the study of human behavior and interaction. Of course he screens people. Come on, Austin, you need to be tougher than that. Remember, find the continuities."

"Well, he is one of the best, so I hear."

"Then he's perfectly justified in being selective," replied Johnny curtly.

"It'll be difficult."

"The best things are, Austin. Give it a try. You need that class. By the way, I know Bernie Williams. He did some consulting work for the firm. I want you in his class."

"I'll try," said Austin. "Now what else should I take? Anything in finance?"

"Sure. Take a general finance class. If nothing else, you'll be familiar with the terminology before you start with me. Now that I think about it, make sure you take a class in corporate finance, and make sure they teach you how to read a balance sheet. Find an interesting professor, otherwise you're wasting your time. Topics like corporate finance, the role of management, executive compensation and so on will help you understand the Strategy."

Austin jotted this down on a pad. "OK, got it. Accounting, too?"

"Yes, but again, make sure you get an interesting professor. Otherwise, just read a book. Just as well."

"I'll load up on this stuff," said Austin.

"Wait, though. Also take a course or two in religion and other things people talk about. You want to become well-versed in the ways of the world, especially given the sort of people you'll be working with as clients."

"Yeah, I guess that's true. That's what liberal arts is supposed to be about."

"You'll meet all types of people in your new profession. Learn to understand that people are different. Who knows, someday I may send you to Saudi Arabia to talk to some of my clients. I may send you to Mississippi. I've got clients there. Some clients are religious, some are interested in nature, and some are interested in building bridges. You never know whom you are going to get as a client. It helps if you can be as broadly informed as possible."

"Wow," said Austin. "You mean I may get to travel around meeting clients?"

"We'll see. Anyway, that's all way down the road. Way down. Managing money is like any other profession. Engineers need to learn about gravity and physics, lawyers about law, doctors about medicine. You need to learn about money and that means learning about people. Only then can you help your clients."

Austin was pleased.

"I'm happy to help, Austin."

After his conversation with Johnny, Austin was pumped up more than he could ever remember. This was the prefect time to go see Professor Williams. Thoughts of traveling around the world to discuss his clients' portfolios gave Austin the sort of charge he got only when playing in his band. He never thought he could feel that way doing something other than playing. Ordinarily, Austin shied away from encounters or conflicts, but he headed straight off to see the famed Professor Williams and undergo his inquiry. Dammit, he thought, I'll convince him.

As expected, the interview was difficult, even rough. Bernie Williams was no pushover. It was his class and his right to set high standards for admission. This attitude and tone was seen in his every publication. It was no wonder many members of the humanities faculty found him offensive. He didn't go along with all their attention to "political correctness." The class wasn't about politics, he insisted, but about human behavior and he'd be damned if he'd let it be contaminated with whatever current cause was in vogue at the moment.

Williams was tough—no doubt about it—but immensely popular with his students. They liked the rigid structure of his lesson plans. But they also attended his "optional" open discussion groups every Friday afternoon that continued until the students couldn't handle any more. In short, Professor Bernie Williams respected his students enough to tell them straight out when they were wrong. Like it or lump it, this was Bernie Williams.

At first, Austin was thrown off balance by Williams' questions. They made no sense. Williams asked Austin questions about what sports he liked, what his parents did for a living, how Austin felt about being orphaned, what novels he read, what music he preferred. What threw Austin most was the seeming irrelevance of Williams' questions to the topic of the class, human behavior.

Austin struggled until he remembered Johnny's advice—find the continuities. It was also the perfect opportunity to drop Johnny's name.

Austin went for it. "Well, Dr. Williams, just as someone might say your questions seem irrelevant to taking a course in human behavior, I'm interested in taking your course as preparation for my job in finance." Austin sat back and looked Williams right in the eye, just as Johnny did to him countless times the week before.

Williams raised his eyebrows. "Really? Interesting. Tell me about that. Why am I asking you these questions?"

Austin thought for a moment, trying to figure the continuities. He saw himself sometime in the future, seated at a table with a client and he let loose with a quote he had memorized for this meeting. "First of all, understand that human behavior in general can be understood only as it is manifested in our daily activities, not in some sort of universal value system. Therefore, it does matter what my father did, and what I eat, and whether or not I like blondes."

Williams engaged immediately. "So Marx argued. But are you really dismissing out of hand the existence of innate behavior patterns, say an innate need for hierarchy?"

Austin started to sweat. But he let fly another shell. "You're right. Because on the other hand, there is some sort of innate need for order amidst the chaos. Like my mentor at First American Investors says—need continuity, create continuity."

Austin sat back and watched Williams say, "Hmmm…you'll be working for First American? It's a good firm."

"Yes, I'll be working for Johnny Long. In case you don't know-"

"I know him." They sat in silence, staring at each other. Austin had no idea what his quote about order from Marx meant. It just sounded good. He hoped Professor Williams wouldn't ask him about it because he didn't have a clue. But as a musician he knew about order. What was music without it? How would Professor Williams react?

So Austin found himself in the midst of yet another continuity—the connection between Johnny Long and Bernie Williams. Austin somehow hit the right note with Professor Williams and got into the class. Some people have a good ear.

Three weeks passed before Austin heard from Johnny again. Johnny called this time to advise Austin to sell his 400 shares of Toll Brothers and replace it with Microsoft.

"No problem," said Austin cheerily. "How much did we make?"

"Let's see," answered Johnny. "You bought 400 Toll Brothers at $20 and we're selling it now for $15. With the proceeds, we will buy 120 shares of Microsoft at $50 a share."

"That means I lost money!" protested Austin.

Johnny's voice was suddenly stern. "Austin, remember what we talked about when you were in Philly? You'll inevitably take losses on stocks. You must accept that, OK? We're buying Microsoft in the hopes that it will become a big winner for you."

Austin was depressed and even a little disillusioned. True,

Johnny mentioned taking loses, but Austin never felt a loss before. This was the first time and he didn't like it. "Are you sure?" Johnny didn't let up. He was training Austin both as a client and as a future employee. "Austin, we're buying Microsoft. And if the earnings are reduced, we're selling it—whether it's up, down, or even."

Austin began to think that Johnny didn't care one way or the other. This annoyed him and he began to think it was a good thing he only gave Johnny $100,000. "But Johnny, how do you know Toll Brothers won't go back up?"

"Austin, I thought you knew better. When our analyst lowers his estimates, you should sell. Right now, we can get $15 for the stock. If he lowers estimates again, you'll have a $10 stock on your hands, and so on. Better you cut your losses than sit around hoping for good news that might never come."

"I don't know…"

"No," said Johnny. "But I do. Bad news is usually followed by more bad news."

There wasn't much Austin could say. He gave Johnny his money to manage and he guessed he just had to trust him, at least for the time being. "OK, Johnny. Do what you have to do. I don't want to worry about it. How are the rest of the stocks doing?"

Your portfolio is currently worth about $94,500, including Toll Brothers."

Austin was aghast. Shock and disbelief hit him smack in the face. He got nauseous. "What! Oh my God, you're kidding me, right? Tell me you're kidding."

"It's normal market fluctuations."

"That's $6,500 I'm down already, and we just sold a stock at a loss!" He started to pace with the cordless phone. This was a disaster! Johnny spoke plainly and without emotion. "It's normal, Austin. Sometimes, people start with $100,000, and it goes up to $110,000 within a few weeks. The markets will fluctuate. You have to look at the long term. Next month, your portfolio may be worth $105,000."

"But-"

"Austin, the toughest thing is to stick to the Strategy. Come on now, I explained this to you clearly when we met."

Austin was about to raise his voice, but managed to hold it in. "Whatever, Johnny. Go ahead and make the changes. Whatever."

"OK," Johnny said, "remember to stick to the Strategy and it'll come out right. Always does. Have a good week," and he hung up.

Austin hung up the phone and went out for pizza. He was very stressed and bewildered. He couldn't get over how much he had lost—just vanished. The Strategy was supposed to make money, not lose it, dammit, he thought. Austin was attacked with doubts and glad he had invested only $100,000. Thank God the other $900,000 was safe in a bank.

Johnny made the trades and took Moira to the Balzac Club for lunch. Chef Jacques was introducing a new pate. He wasn't at all worried—and not because the losses were someone else's losses. He had seen this a thousand times and knew Austin would come out of it in great shape.

Five weeks passed before Austin heard from Johnny again. This time, however, the news was better. "Austin! How're you doing? Are your classes going well?"

"Hi Johnny. Things are going great, especially Professor Williams' class. We sit riveted in class. You could listen to him talk for hours. And we do!"

"Great."

"But more importantly, how's my portfolio doing?"

"Right to the point, huh? Well, let's see, your portfolio is worth $112,000," said Johnny.

"Really? That's great! Good job, Johnny. You made back the money I lost and then some. Maybe we should sell everything and put the twelve percent aside? Money in the bank, and then do it all over again. What do you think?"

"Austin, you and I have a great deal to talk over," replied Johnny in a dry tone. "You've got a lot to learn—a lot. In the meantime, why don't you just worry about graduating and leave the money to me, huh?"

"But all I need is fifteen percent per year and you've got twelve already. Why not take the twelve percent, park it safely and go back after three percent more? When we're up fifteen, maybe we could put everything in cash."

"We do this for three years, Austin?"

"Sure, why not?"

Johnny laughed into the speakerphone. "Are you finished?"

"I guess."

"Thank God. There are some changes that need to be made. You need to sell Tidewater. We lowered estimates recently. We bought it for $42; it's trading at $40."

It was amazing how much better Austin felt this time around. "No problem, go ahead. What do we replace it with?"

"You should buy 130 shares of Hershey Foods at $60 per share. Oh, remember that Microsoft we bought for fifty bucks?"

"Yes! I noticed in the paper that it's trading around $80. Nice job, Johnny. $3,600 profit in a little over a month's not bad."

"Yeah," said Johnny. "Too bad it was like pulling teeth when we did the trade."

"What do you mean?"

Johnny laughed again. "Never mind. Enjoy your classes. I'll call you if there's anything else we need to change."

Chapter 8

AUSTIN'S senior year flew by. He had himself the time of his life and not just because of the girls or the million. That was all good—well, more than good! Austin felt free for the first time in his life and had a sense of security he hadn't had since childhood. For the first time in his memory, he was really happy and felt secure. When he played his sax before, it was partly to help forget, to lose himself in his music and put things behind for a while. Let's face it. It was an escape, Austin knew. But now he went about every day with a sense of discovery, an enthusiasm for everything. He felt alive.

He finished his courses and, like most things in life now, he enjoyed them very much. Those in finance and Professor Williams' course in human behavior were especially valuable. Graduation day came and Austin looked ahead with hope—and admitted to himself with some fear that he might not live up to Johnny's expectations. But, he thought, I'll make it. Dammit, I'll make it!

Austin called Johnny from the airport en route back to Philadelphia. "I'm on the way, Johnny. I hope you're ready for me. By the way, how's my portfolio?"

"Well my friend, your portfolio's value is.... let me see.... is... $130,000."

"Are you serious?" cried Austin. "A $30,000 profit in nine months? That's awesome, Johnny. Awesome. Great work."

"Yes, Austin. It's been nine months. Not every day's been up, and not every stock was a winner, but over the last nine months, your portfolio's done better than the market as a whole. The S&P 500 is up 22%. We're up 30%. I like beating those averages," Johnny said.

"Really? That's great. What's the S&P 500?"

"Austin, you've got so much to learn. The S&P 500 average is the collective value of the largest 500 companies in the United States. Investment advisors use the S&P 500 or the Dow Jones Industrial Average to measure their performance."

"I see. So we can tell if I'm making money simply because the overall market is going up..."

"Or if you're making money because your investment advisor is adding additional performance. It's the latter, Austin, in case you didn't notice."

Austin laughed. "Of course! Thanks, Johnny."

Johnny laughed. "Yeah, whatever."

When he hung up Austin should have been happy. Instead, a terrible realization started eating away at him. He'd made a big mistake—a very big mistake—not giving Johnny the full million to manage. He didn't know Johnny that well and wanted to be cautious, but now it could cost him dearly. If he hadn't been so doubtful, Austin could've accomplished in nine months what he was hoping to achieve in three years! He could've had that 30% profit on the whole million! He started to panic and with good reason. He had a very big problem, he realized. Although his portfolio with Johnny was up some thirty percent, his total million was only up seven percent, including the interest he was receiving on the other $900,000. Worst of all, almost an entire year had passed. The clock was running. Now, Johnny had to get about twenty percent a year to make up for the lost year. The flight back to Philly and his new job should have been a triumphant moment for Austin. Instead, he felt he was flying into the face of a disaster. How could he ever make up for the year he'd just wasted?

Austin had arranged for an apartment in the same neighborhood as Cathy's. He couldn't see Cathy yet, though. He was trying to deal with both his new job and a moment he really dreaded—telling Johnny the truth about the million dollars. After settling in, Austin went downtown to Boyd's to buy a few suits. He hadn't worn one in years. But what the hell, he thought, a lot of things were going to be new from now on.

When Johnny greeted Austin this time, things were different. He was a client and new employee, one of Johnny's family. Johnny introduced Austin to some key people around the office—the sales manager, office manager and his two key people, Moira and Rory.

"Moira," explained Johnny, "is my personal assistant. She handles all client contact and correspondence and keeps the machine oiled and running smoothly. Right, Moira?" Johnny was always gracious to the people who helped make him what he was.

Moira blushed but accepted the credit all the same. "Well, I try," she said modestly. Austin knew she was a powerhouse who made the right things happen. Johnny put his full faith in her and for good reason.

"And this," continued Johnny, gesturing to a woman whom Austin had not met, "is Rory." Rory and Austin shook hands cordially. "Rory is in charge of the daily research on the stocks the firm covers. You and Rory will be working closely together over the next several months. She really knows her way around the analysts' reports, so it should work out well." Rory smiled at Austin.

Both Moira and Rory looked very professional and reserved. Both were single women in their early forties, impeccably dressed, well spoken. They fitted the solid, professional image of Johnny and his office. Very few of the other brokers had their own assistants, and if they did, it was usually one woman scrambling to answer phones and process paperwork. Moira and Rory loved working for Johnny. They believed in him and in his message of discipline and structure in the midst of all the noise of so-called investment "advice" being slung every which way. Johnny's team was solid—right down to his University of Pennsylvania interns who eagerly grabbed any chance to work close to someone like Johnny. And like any good leader, Johnny shared the victories with his team. Not just with praise, but also at bonus time. It was a good team and a good atmosphere.

"Austin," said Johnny, "come over here. Welcome to the salt mines. This is where you'll earn your bread by the sweat of your brow," gesturing to a small office with barely room for a desk and chair. "Spread yourself out anyway you want. It's all yours."

Austin was thrilled. His first job out of college, and he had his own office. "This is great, Johnny. Now put me to work. I'm rarin' to go."

"Go ahead, take the chair for a spin. It's all yours," Johnny laughed. Austin sat down behind his desk like he was sitting down behind the wheel of a new Ferrari. He was revved up and ready to go.

Suddenly all business, Johnny sat facing Austin and got right to the point. "The work you'll be doing will be broken down into three parts. First, you record every change our analysts make in their earnings estimates."

"The analysts do the real research, right?"

"Yes. Like I said, we organize and use the research our analysts do. I'm not an analyst; I'm a money manager. The analysts are the real driving force behind what I do here. We never see them. We only sometimes hear them. But without them, there's no First American, there's no investing, and there's no strategy. For me, well, I sometimes feel I'm part of a dance team—like I'm dancing with the analysts."

Austin laughed. "Good analogy."

"The second thing you'll be doing is culling all the research to build a list of stocks that have had at least two earnings estimates increases in the past six months."

"That's the list of stocks you buy, right?"

Johnny smiled. "That's the list, Austin. It's as good as gold, my friend. Our analysts make those estimates of earnings increases and we dig them out, find them and present them to our clients. That's what we do here. Got it?"

"Right. Make continuities."

"That's it, Austin. That's what I'm talking about. After you make the list, you'll then be continually adding new stocks and removing stocks whose earnings have been..." Johnny paused to let Austin answer.

"Reduced," Austin completed his sentence. "At that time— and that time only—do we sell the stock."

Johnny was pleased. "Precisely. Yes! And third, you'll track an entire portfolio of up to 15 stocks to learn how an actual portfolio looks and feels."

"Sounds exciting."

"Well Austin, at first it might be a bit boring, locked up in there with all those numbers. But it's kind of like being the Karate Kid—a lot of waxing on and waxing off. In time, it'll become almost like an instinct. That's important. I speak from instinct where the Strategy is concerned."

"Yes, Mr. Miagi," joked Austin. "I certainly have my work cut out for me, huh?"

"It should take you about three months to complete the entire project."

"That's not too bad."

Johnny became serious. No more joking. "Austin, it's absolutely crucial that you do this right. If you make a mistake, you'll have to redo a lot of the work. So ask Rory or me any questions you might have. Got it? Accuracy is everything here, down to the penny. To the penny, Austin."

"No guessing."

"No guessing. Is that clear?"

"Yup. Where are the research materials?"

"They are all in the large filing cabinet near Rory. Start with January 1990." Johnny placed a thick bound research book on Austin's desk. It contained all of First American's awesome research for January 1990. "The firm publishes a new book every month. Every change for every stock we cover is officially recorded here," he said, tapping the cover of the book.

Austin took the book with reverence. It was thick and the print was small. "So this is the goose that lays the golden egg, huh?"

"Sort of. Remember, the analysts produce all the numbers, so in a way, they're the golden geese. Anyway, you'll follow every change in every company. Exhausting detail and accuracy is what my clients are banking on. Remember that. It's your responsibility. Don't let them down."

Austin nodded. "OK. I understand."

"So if you're going through the book, and you notice an earnings increase for, say, Apple Computer, mark down Apple on a list as well as the market price at the time of the change, as recorded in the book, and the date the earnings estimate was raised."

"There are going to be a lot of changes, aren't there?" asked Austin.

"Sure. What's important with Apple, for example—or with any stock—is to track how often the analyst raised estimates over the last decade. Because, remember what I taught you..." he paused again to let Austin answer.

"The more frequently the estimates are raised, the bigger the winner."

"Right," praised Johnny. "The big winners are those stocks that have several estimate increases over time. Remember, we're catching these stocks early—after two increases within a six-month period—and holding them until..."

"Until the earnings are reduced."

Johnny slapped his hand against the desk. "There you go!"

"So," said Austin, "the stock should go up a lot over time."

"How about skyrocket? Sometimes 2,000%! Once you find out what the perception will be for a particular stock, you're home free."

"It all depends on the analysts, doesn't it? They're about as close to a crystal ball as we'll ever get," Austin said.

"Good way to put it. Each analyst covers several stocks, usually in the same industry. Based on consumer trends and the particular things Apple, say, is doing, the analyst will estimate Apple's profits and growth, and issue a report as frequently as he or she deems necessary to justify the estimates and changes."

"So the analyst for Apple will also cover other companies in the computer business?" Austin asked.

"The competition, yes. Sure. Let's say that Compaq comes out with a new product which people start buying. What do you think might happen?"

"He might raise estimates for Compaq."

"And...."

"And lower them for Apple?"

"Right. They're connected. One might affect the other. We don't guess. We follow the changes the analyst makes once they are recorded in this book. You mentioned a crystal ball. Well, look at it another way. In the military, there are soldiers who go ahead of the rest."

"Like scouts, spotters."

"Right. Their duty is to look out for any upcoming hazards and report back, or just the opposite, if things look good. An analyst looks ahead—always ahead—and if things don't look good with a particular company, the analyst lets the troops know. That's us. We're the troops."

"Or if things look particularly good," added Austin, "they'll report that, too."

"Of course. And by using these scouting reports to answer those three questions—what to buy, when to sell, what to buy with the proceeds—we put investors where they don't suffer big losses or miss large gains."

Austin smiled. "It's beautiful, Johnny. But I guess it all depends on how accurate our analysts are."

Johnny nodded. "Well, they certainly make mistakes. That's part of the game. There's no perfect system to picking stocks, Austin. You know that. But just buying GE and holding it doesn't guarantee your return will outperform even the S&P 500 either."

"Do you have your favorite analysts?"

Johnny laughed. "Sure. It's like any other profession. You have good and bad doctors, good and bad baseball players. In the world of brokerage, you have good and bad analysts."

"So you give more weight to a good analyst's estimates?"

Johnny shook his head. "No, that wouldn't be possible. Think about it. You'd end up buying an overwhelming number of stocks in the same industry or sector just because you like the analyst who covers it. No good. Either way—good or bad—you have to rely on all of them as a team."

"So in a nutshell, the analyst establishes the earnings estimate—I think you called it a 'perception'?"

"Right...."

"And the changes in this perception change a stock's price?"

"That's right," said Johnny. "The perception is the horse and the stock price is the wagon. The perception is up front pulling the wagon—the stock price—up the hill or down the hill."

"Right, because a stock's price is pulled by those estimates, not pushed."

"That's it. It's not rocket science, Austin. It's pretty simple. For the time being, though, you'll only track increases in perception, or earnings. Later, you'll track decreases."

"Oh yes, knowing when to sell is more important than knowing what to buy."

"You bet. If repeated increases in earnings estimates cause a stock to go up, I want to reconfirm the fact that multiple decreases cause a stock to go down."

"Yeah, I remember you said that."

"And the research you're about to do for me will prove and reprove the Strategy over and over. We've back-tested every part of the Strategy. That's why you're going back to 1990. There are no empty promises in my Strategy, Austin. Everything I tell my clients about the Strategy is supported by thousands of pages of research."

"Do clients always believe you, like when you tell them that a company will go down?"

"Well, I tell my clients that any stock might go down if their new estimates of earnings decreases. I can't tell the future. I can only go by what's likely to happen, based on the analysts' reports. The fundamental assumption of the Strategy is what could happen—not what's guaranteed. That's the best we can do."

"And some clients fight you?"

"Sure! Clients often don't want to believe that a stock that's made them money in the past or they feel emotionally tied to will go down in the future. They simply can't, or won't, believe it."

"It's a sort of denial."

"Yes! Good word for it."

Austin laughed. "I learned it from your buddy Bernie Williams."

Johnny laughed too. "Good guy, that Williams. Anyway, the simple fact is that Wall Street is littered with companies that can no longer compete or have gone out of business entirely."

"You're losing me, Johnny."

"OK, let's say you're an analyst for First American and you follow a toy company. One of your responsibilities is to visit the company every so often. You ask how things are going and, of course, management tells you, 'hey, everything's just fine.' The future looks promising, they tell you, so you can go on back and write a good report. People buy the stock."

"And the price goes up."

"Exactly. But, as you know, management comments are not always a good indicator. So you decide to hire some college kid to go out to the company and secretly record the number of delivery trucks coming and going from the shipping dock each day."

"Is that legal?" interrupted Austin.

"Sure. Analysts are allowed to verify their opinions. And they do it in a number of ways. At first, the kid sees that an average of 30 trucks leave the shipping dock each day. The analyst visits the company again, and they say things are still just great. But the college intern reports back that now only 18 or so trucks leave the dock, not the usual 30."

"So even the analysts, our spotters, have spotters of their own?"

"Well, all I care about is that the analyst, our spotter, gets the information he needs to make an informed comment on the company—a comment we can count on and put money on. And you know what? They usually find out what they need to know, which, by the way, is what we need to know. And it's all here in these monthly books," Johnny said. "Now, hit the books."

Austin began his work, both thrilled and more than a little afraid he'd make a mistake. Johnny's warning about being exact kept ringing in his ears.

About an hour later, Moira walked in to check on him. "Well, what do you think about all this?" she asked.

Austin dropped his pencil and stretched his arms. "A lot of waxing to do."

Moira laughed. "He uses that Karate Kid analogy on all the new people."

"Why doesn't everyone in this office use the Strategy? I mean, it works. The results prove it."

Moira grimaced. "Who knows human nature, Austin? Maybe pride, resentment or maybe they're just locked into the old patterns—you know, buy on a hot tip or gut feeling, follow the herd. Johnny's very special, as you'll find out."

"That I know," Austin said. "So most advisors..." He held up his hands and shrugged.

"Who knows?" replied Moira. "To tell you the truth," she whispered, "most of these guys have absolutely no idea how to manage money." But the walls have ears in a brokerage office, and she didn't want to be overheard. "It's funny, too, because sometimes they'll come in and ask Johnny for ideas."

Austin thought of Bobby Lane. "The hot stock of the day," he mocked.

"And Johnny tells them to do the Strategy. But of course, they never do. They just all slowly begin to ignore Johnny. He's no use to them because he manages money instead of guessing at stocks—a whole different approach."

"Johnny must get upset being ignored."

"To tell you the truth, I'm not sure myself," said Moira. "Sometimes he blows it right off. Sometimes he gets upset. I remember once he got really upset when one of the young brokers asked him for help and instead of just giving him a pat answer, Johnny offered to take time to teach the guy how to do the research himself."

"That's only fair. And besides, it helps the broker if he learns the Strategy firsthand, like I'm doing."

"Of course. But the guy said something nasty or snide to Johnny, and Johnny got all upset. It happens in this business, Austin. If you've got something special, people won't try to be a part of it. Instead they'll be lazy and try to copy it, without bothering to understand how it works—or corrupt it out of plain spite."

"Or resentment," added Austin, harkening back to another of Professor Williams' theories. "Because people are fundamentally concerned only with their self-preservation, resentment will emerge as a primary means of justifying one's actions while at the very same time denying or masking the selfishness of them."

"That's a mouthful Austin," Moira said. "But so true. You know, Austin, I think what actually made Johnny mad was that the guy had a lot of potential and was just wasting it. Wasted talent is something that gets to Johnny. Take the humanitarian projects Johnny gets involved with—life is more than making money. When you're dealing with making money as a job, it's pretty important to have outside interests, something that gives you a feeling of personal fulfillment. Making money is great, but it isn't everything. I've seen what it can do to some people, and it's pretty sad."

"So, Johnny has humanitarian projects?" Austin was intrigued.

"Oh," said Moira, "he does a lot of good things. But I'm sure he'll tell you when he gets around to it. Anyway, I'll let you get back to work. It's only your first day. Don't want you to get too distracted, do we? You might make a mistake."

"God forbid," said Austin.

"You don't want to make any mistakes, Austin. That could cost you days correcting them. I've seen it happen."

Moira turned to leave, but Austin stopped her. "Moira, do you ever travel with Johnny?"

Moira shook her head. "No, but he does travel a lot. You know, he has clients all over the world, including the OPEC countries. You can see some pictures of Johnny traveling. They're hanging on his wall."

"With clients?"

"Oh, yes. He's got clients all over the world. It's really amazing."

"Have you known Johnny a long time?"

Moira whistled. "For over ten years. Wow, time flies. Not only does he pay me well—a rarity around here—he also lets me get involved in everything."

"Except traveling," Austin joked.

"Who knows?" she said. "Maybe that'll be your job someday. But one step at a time, right?"

Austin smiled. "Right. Do his clients ever push you around or try to intimidate you? I mean, are they all as nice as Johnny?"

"Well, yes and no. I can usually divide his clients into two categories. It's basically a cultural issue."

"I can imagine," added Austin. "Johnny made me take courses in religion and international cultures."

"They'll certainly help. One type treats women as equals. The other type treats women as servants. But even then, Johnny has American clients who treat me like some sort of slave. If they give me too hard a time, I just tell Johnny, and he takes over."

"Really? That's nice of him."

"He actually told a client to take a hike one time. Just up and told him to transfer his account somewhere else because he treated me disrespectfully more than once. And it was a pretty sizable account, too. Well, enough of that. Back to work." Moira left Austin sitting there staring at ninety-six fat books.

By the end of the day, Austin had made his way through only two books—two down and ninety-four to go. Johnny had told him his first project would be tedious and boring, and it was. Still, he had a sense of accomplishment because he knew he was doing something essential and worthwhile. As time passed, Austin became more adept and self-confident, and he was soon able to finish five books a day.

Once he finished with phase one, he moved on to phase two—recording each company that had an earnings increase. If a particular company had at least two increases within six months, he noted the stock price and the earnings estimates. If there was a reduction, Austin would stop following that company. It would be off the list.

For the first two months, Austin started following these changes more closely. He saw that stocks which had their estimates increased a number of times went up in value. In fact, some stocks went up quite a bit after only a few increases. He thought, this is like a golden thread linking the estimates to the prices, pulling them up or down as the estimates went up or down. And it happened over and over. Austin knew his faith in Johnny was justified, and that made him feel much worse about not giving Johnny all the money from the outset. How much would that mistake cost him, he constantly wondered. The whole five million?

About three months into Austin's stint, Austin and Johnny sat down together to review Austin's progress. "Johnny," started Austin, "for the last few months I've seen literally thousands of earnings estimates. I think I'm going blind."

Johnny laughed. "Well, just don't be blind to the obvious, my friend."

"Well that's just it, Johnny. I've seen the numbers over several years—thousands of companies—and I see the connection between earnings estimates and prices. Your strategy is bang on."

"Gee, thanks Austin. Of course its 'bang on,' as you called it. What did you expect to find?" Johnny laughed. "You're funny, Austin. I enjoy having you around. Anyway, go on."

"Well, it's old hat to you, but it's like a revelation for me. I can't believe it. It's one thing for you to tell me, but it's another to see it over and over in those pages. Now that I actually see the numbers and research behind what we've been talking about for over a year, I'm even more overwhelmed. It's beautiful. Well, now that I see the light, so to speak, when do I move up to work directly with you?"

Johnny held up his hand. "Not yet," he laughed. "You're progressing just fine, but you've still got a lot of work and learning in front of you. You can barely walk, and you want to run? Don't worry, Austin. You'll have your day. We've got big plans for you. Patience, my boy."

Austin crocked his head. "We?"

"Never mind," said Johnny. "Have you finished all the years I asked you to review?"

"Yes."

"Good. Now you still have to track each company that qualifies. Then you need to track a sample portfolio or two. We can't rush your development when people's money is at stake, Austin. I can't let that happen. And besides, it's lazy and not living up to your potential, just riding my coattails like that."

Austin felt deflated. "Sorry."

"Now go back to work. Go and see Rory about the tracking. She'll set you up with what you need. It should take you about two weeks to do the tracking. Come and see me when you're done."

Rory showed Austin how to track each stock as each month progresses, and then calculate the investment return as well as that of the S&P 500. Austin pulled up a chair, and they began to do a test run together.

"OK," said Rory, "let's compare notes. How many estimate increases were there for Ford Motor Company?"

Austin checked his notes. For the last ten years, there were ...let's see, twelve increases."

"Good. How about Compaq Computer?"

"Oh, twenty-five."

"Now Austin, you need to be sure you're doing this right," Rory said emphatically. "There's no margin for errors. None. For example, you know you have to track each company separately. Just because there are a lot of increases over a long period of time, doesn't mean there were no decreases. There might be one hidden in there. That's what you have to be careful of, and it would totally invalidate your research if you didn't take that into account."

Luckily, Austin had considered that. Actually, by doing his research systematically as Johnny had instructed, Austin avoided this problem. That was why Johnny didn't warn Austin about this beforehand. It was a test of Austin's discipline.

Chapter 9

AUSTIN decided he had to face his big mistake of not telling Johnny about the rest of the money. After about a year, Austin's portfolio was worth $135,000. The bulk of his money—the $900,000 in the bank—was still earning a paltry 5%. Austin hoped Johnny would take it as good news and not get insulted by Austin's lack of faith. He made a lunch appointment with Johnny. There was no way to delay any longer. My God, he wondered, how will Johnny take it? Stupid, stupid, stupid!

Over lunch, Austin began to reminisce in an attempt to soften Johnny up. "Johnny, remember the last time we went to lunch, over a year ago?"

"Ah yes, the Balzac Club. What a Dover Sole, huh? And the same day, you gave me your life's savings to invest. I don't forget those kinds of things. It took a lot of trust on your part. And now look, you're working for me."

"I'm very happy with the way the job is going, Johnny. I want to tell you that. Not to mention the 35% my portfolio is up!"

"That's only a drop in the bucket if you stick with the Strategy. More importantly, are you learning anything?"

"Am I learning anything? I can almost feel stocks moving in anticipation of an earnings increase. Doesn't that tell you I'm ready for bigger things?"

"You are ambitious and impatient," Johnny said, laughingly. "But you still have to finish the project, Austin. Once you've finished the earnings increases, you need to do the same for the earnings decreases. Remember, I want you to be able to quantify the difference between good and bad news. Got it?"

"Uh-huh. So far, it's coming along fine. I'm already halfway through the decreases. I should be finished in about two weeks."

"That was fast. Good job. When you're totally finished, you and I will sit down and have a long talk. As for now, I want your full attention on getting this project finished. Don't half-ass me now just to get through it."

Austin feigned dismay. "Why Johnny, I never…"

"Yeah, yeah" said Johnny. "We'll see. Let me inspire you by saying that if you do the job well, we'll take a trip together so that we can talk uninterrupted for a long time."

Austin was surprised. "Take a trip just to talk?"

"It's my way, Austin. When you get this job done, you'll have earned it. And I'm a great believer in finding the right setting for important moments. I think maybe the Bahamas this time around."

"Johnny, I like your style. All business, but damned if it isn't the most pleasurable work I've ever done. The Bahamas, huh? Sounds great to me."

"Well, let's just say that a long time ago a complete stranger gave me the secret to wealth and making people happy, especially if they're less fortunate."

"That reminds me," Austin said, "Moira once said something about all the charitable work you do."

"We'll talk about all that later. It's all secondary to learning the Strategy. Without the Strategy, there's no helping anyone. So be patient, if you can," he laughed. "It's one step at a time for you, OK?"

Things had gone so well at lunch Austin just couldn't risk it all by dropping the bombshell news of the other $900,000. He knew it was a mistake to delay any further, but he just couldn't risk it now. He didn't want to offend Johnny and blow his chances at whatever Johnny had in mind for him. Later is always convenient—and always costly— Austin would learn the hard way.

He finished the project and was left reeling from so many months behind pages full of numbers. But Johnny reviewed his work and the output and was very pleased. "It's off on a break for you, my boy. The Bahamas."

Before he knew it, he was checking into a hotel the likes of which he had never seen. Johnny sent him to the Bahamas a day early so that Austin could treat himself to a full day of nothing—just sun and fun. When Johnny planned to do business, business was done. Why not let the kid have a little fun first, he reasoned.

Johnny was right about one thing. Important moments in life—really important moments—come along only so often, and most of the time we miss them. And he'd learned that a big moment should have the right setting. For example, how many people remember a career-making discussion they had in their car while stuck in traffic? Odds are, you'd probably remember the traffic first. But have that conversation somewhere special—somewhere conducive to creative thinking, for example while sitting like Austin on the terrace of a suite overlooking the crystal-blue ocean surrounding the Bahamas—and things are different.

To Johnny, the Strategy was like a silver chalice passed down to him from another. It was something ceremonial, not to be taken lightly. Any serious discussion, such as he had in mind, needed a setting worthy of it.

The effect was not totally lost on Austin. True, he'd spent four years in beautiful Palo Alto, California. But he certainly wasn't treated like a king from sun up to sun down, as he was here in Johnny's favorite island fantasyland. From the moment he stepped off the plane into the limo that awaited him, he knew things were going to be different—like he felt after he met Johnny for the first time. Ironically, their first meeting was over coffee in some greasy-spoon diner. But now, the background music had changed. Long gone was the din of crashing dishes and frying cheese steaks. This meeting with Johnny would be set to the soothing music of steadily breaking waves accentuated by rustling palm trees.

Austin was aware that something important was about to happen, and so prepared himself mentally. As the hectic hustle-and-bustle of Philadelphia faded into the background, Austin moved deeper and deeper into what might be called his "zone," where a person stops analyzing and calculating and just "lives," as Johnny says. Austin was right where Johnny wanted him.

Johnny wasn't due to arrive until tomorrow, leaving Austin free to live like a king for the day. On arriving at the hotel, he was greeted by a number of cheerful islanders who brought him a cold towel to cool his face and a glass of punch to soothe his spirit. A beautiful woman escorted him to a VIP desk so he could check in more quickly and privately. She waited by his side while he completed the paperwork.

"Your room is lovely," she said. "You're a bachelor I see," she nodded to his empty ring finger. "You'll make them all jealous."

Austin loved the attention being lavished on him. After all, he was only 23 and a bachelor. What young guy wouldn't want to live like this? Sure, he knew he'd have to work for it. But for Austin, as for Johnny Long, working was the best part. People like Johnny, however, worked for the sheer joy of it. And no one was more creative than Johnny Long when it came to spoiling his employees. Just look at this trip! Johnny rewarded his people for their loyalty and dedication, for their commitment to him and his vision.

The breaking surf was a mere twenty yards away and the rocking of the waves was hypnotic. The view of the endless turquoise horizon took Austin further and further away from himself as he used to be—evasive, defensive, afraid of commitment and sometimes bitter.

Austin lit one of the Cuban Romeo and Juliet cigars Johnny had waiting for him in his room, mixed himself a drink at his bar, and watched a group of three tanned women meander topless along the beach. This, he thought, is the stuff of dreams. Austin found within him a new thirst for success, just as Johnny had expected. Austin would work for that success pouring through the thousands of pages of analysts' research. He'd mine those pages doggedly, religiously—not ever knowing who the analysts were or what their children looked like, or what they ate for dinner. He had learned to respect their every calculation with something close to reverence.

No coattails for him. He would earn every penny by hard work and he'd remember this island paradise in his mind long after he left. His reactions were just what Johnny knew they'd be. He knew how to bait the hook and reel the fish in. Whatever he was going to propose, Austin was already softened up for the kill.

Softened up?

Hell, he was jelly.

Chapter 10

THE phone rang shortly before noon the next day. Austin picked up the phone after two rings. "Hello, Austin speaking."

"Austin, hi. It's Johnny, your friend and benefactor."

Austin ran his hand through his wet hair. He was just back from a swim in the ocean. "Hail to thee, great chief. Johnny, this place is wonderful."

"Just a little slice of my dreams, Austin. It gets better from here. Hey, did you get the massage I ordered for you this morning?"

Austin grinned and cast a glance into his bedroom. His masseuse, a beautiful French woman with a taste for the islands, was still changing back into her clothes. She was a masseuse, but sometimes things between a beautiful woman and a young man, well…things just happened. Austin caught a glimpse of her bronzed body as it glowed against the bleached white walls. "Words couldn't thank you enough, Johnny."

"Hey, the Romans had nothing on me, my friend. But I'm not interested in words. I appreciate your commitment to me, and now it's time to move."

It sounded to Austin like Johnny wanted to work rather than play, so Austin changed his tone while addressing his boss. "So what's on the agenda now that you're on the island?" The Parisian masseuse picked up her portable table, kissed Austin on the check, laughingly pulled his towel off, and left without a word. Austin would find her card waiting for him on his pillow.

"Meet me in the bar of your hotel in two hours. Is there anything you need in the mean time?" asked Johnny.

Austin laughed. "Not a thing."

"OK. We've got work to do, my friend. See you soon." Austin hung up the phone and walked out onto the beach to catch some sun before the meeting.

Johnny was already at the bar when Austin arrived. "Looks like you got a little suntan, Austin." Austin just smiled. "Beats the hell out of the fluorescent pallor of office life, doesn't it?" quipped Johnny.

Austin pulled up a seat next to Johnny. "Let's just say that the island has been... good to me thus far. What're you drinking?"

"Don't bother," said Johnny. "We're going to find a nice little spot where we can sit and talk for a while. I know the perfect place. The view... well, it changes your perspective on things."

"More changes in perspective. Johnny, I don't know if I can handle too much more."

"By the time I'm done with you my boy, life will become just one big change for the better. Every damned day!" He slapped Austin on the back. "Come on, let's go."

Johnny had the concierge order a cab. "We're taking a taxi?" asked Austin?

"Yes. A very good client of mine has a house on the top of one of these hills." Johnny gestured toward lush, green slopes in the distance. "It overlooks the ocean. I told him we were coming down, and he insisted on our stopping by. We can talk there for a while without interruption or...distraction of various sorts, huh?" he said, as Austin's eyes followed a girl heading for the pool in a bikini. Her looks could kill.

"Good idea."

The cab crawled along the winding roads. The driving, like life on the island, was slow. No rushing, no worries. It was a far cry from Philadelphia where they would try to run you over if you were even one step off the sidewalk into traffic. Occasionally, the taxi van would speed around slower traffic racing up to a whopping thirty miles an hour or so, then slow back down to cruising speed. They continued wending their way up the hill.

"Geez," complained Austin, "do you think this guy can drive any slower?"

Johnny smiled. "What's the hurry? The house will still be there when we arrive. Anyway, why let the seconds pass you by, Austin? We often calculate our life in years the way we calculate our portfolios in bottom lines, but you still can't change the fact that the years are made of seconds just like the profits are made of earnings. Try breathing once in a while."

Austin sat back and tried to relax. "Who's the client?" asked Austin.

"His name is Henry Hart. He used to own the Philadelphia Eagles football team. You've heard of him, I suppose. He's something of a walking Philly tradition."

Austin was excited to meet a celebrity. "I love football, but that must've been before my time," said Austin.

"Well, some things are indifferent to time—like the Strategy. Some things never change."

"Look for continuity," added Austin.

"Look for continuity," agreed Johnny.

"Will we be meeting Mr. Hart?"

"Yes, we will," answered Johnny.

"Tell me what I need to know about this guy."

"Henry and I go way back. He made his money in food packaging back in the 50's. Like a lot of my clients, he became wealthy after selling the business off to some corporate giant. In this case, he got something like $20 million. Now this is back in his day."

"That's a lot of money back then."

"Sure. Still is! We were introduced around 1980, I think, by a mutual friend."

"You know, I've noticed that a lot of your big clients were introduced to you."

"That's important, Austin. Referrals are the lifeblood of the business."

"It must be nice to have someone refer big clients to you. Keeps your business growing."

Johnny nodded. "Sure, it's important to bring in new business. But don't overlook the fact that referrals are an expression of trust and respect. Someone is putting their good name behind me when they send a wealthy friend or colleague to invest with me. I never forget a good referral, Austin. It's a gift of trust—the greatest gift a client can give you. Do you understand?"

"I do, I guess."

"It's early in your career, I know. But you'll see what I'm talking about in time."

"Just like everything else, Johnny."

Johnny smiled. He loved to be appreciated. That's what he worked for—to earn respect above all else. Everything else, including money, followed from there.

"Anyway, at the time, he had his money invested with various local banks. Needless to say, his returns were low. They usually are. Shortly after we met, he gave me a small piece of his portfolio to manage."

"Is that usually how it starts?" asked Austin, feeling better about his own mistake of not giving Johnny more money to manage.

"Sure. But more always follows. That's also how it works. You get what you earn. Within a few years, Henry gave me all his money to manage. Best thing he ever did, and he knows it." Johnny paused to let that sink in.

Austin fed off Johnny's confidence. "You must've made him a lot of money."

"He's had some great years. Wait 'till you see this house. I think it costs him something like three million dollars back in 1985. That was a good year for him. He built the house on just the profits we made."

"My God," exclaimed Austin. "No wonder he likes you."

Johnny quickly turned the boasting into a cautionary lesson. "Sure. But never forget that it's his money, Austin. I only manage it. And believe me, wealthy clients are usually seasoned businessmen, control freaks. Sometimes, they'll call you up out of the blue, regardless of how much money you're making, and challenge the entire thing—even the very strategy that's making them money. Figure that out."

"That must be pretty upsetting."

"At first I used to get mad. Now I simply understand it as part of a successful personality."

"Well, I guess you're like that with your strategy, too," commented Austin.

"Who me?" Johnny laughed. "Austin, I'm so sure the Strategy works, I always hold the upper hand. I'm at the point now in my life where I don't work for money. I work for a sense of achievement. The money follows. The worst thing I can do to a client is close their account and send them back to working with some broker like the one they used to have. That's another beauty of the Strategy."

"I wish I could feel that way."

"I'm sure someday you will, Austin. But like everything else....."

"I know, I know. I have to earn it."

"There you go. Anyway, Henry and other clients are really hiring First American Investors. The firm, in turn, gives me a cut. First American won't let you forget that, either!"

This started Austin thinking. "What if some really rich person asked you to work for them and them alone? Would you leave First American?"

"Actually, that offer has been made a number of times by some extremely wealthy and famous people. But I like having different clients, having variety and diversity in my business life. I don't know that I'd like to work for only one person. I think I'd lose too much leverage. Anyway, I'd be too dependent on a single person. As with the stocks in the strategy, I need diversity in my clients."

"Boy," Austin said, "the Strategy certainly has its parallels in life."

"Like you said earlier, 'seek continuities.' Living a successful life is way too hard to be haphazard, Austin, no matter how you define success."

They sat quietly for a while in order to admire the surroundings during their final ascent up the hill. The foliage was thick and harbored a wide variety of bird life. When they reached the top, the taxi was almost at a forty-five degree angle. The view was as breathtaking as Johnny promised.

"The view's incredible," gasped Austin. "The ocean looks like glass from here. I swear I can see a hundred miles off."

"Easy now, Austin. We're only visitors."

The front door opened and Hart stood looking at them, hands in his pockets. "Johnny! How the hell are you?" greeted Hart.

"Hey there, stranger," said Johnny. They met in the doorway.

"Mr. Hart, I'd like you to meet Austin Montgomery, my protégé. He comes to us from Stanford. Very solid."

"Nice to meet you, Austin."

"Nice to meet you, sir," said Austin.

"Johnny has told me a lot about you."

"He has?"

"Certainly. You sound quite impressive. It's a pleasure to meet you. Come on in."

As they walked through the house, Austin's jaw almost hit the floor. The house was filled with expensive art and sculpture. It must have been at least fifty-feet wide, providing enough room to admire the artwork. Austin and Johnny followed Hart out onto the balcony with a view of the ocean worthy of a great master's landscape. A butler asked if anyone would like a drink. Austin accepted a soda. They sat down around a table and chatted.

Henry Hart was no nonsense and plunged right into Austin's affairs. "So Austin, Johnny tells me you are interested in learning how to manage money. Is that true?"

Austin felt like he was back in front of Bernie Williams. This time, however, he was wiser for the wear. Hart was no pushover, but neither was Williams. Moreover, this was Johnny's client, and Austin would be damned if he would allow himself to look bad with Johnny's name behind him. "Yes, it's true. I'm frankly fascinated by the whole process..."

Hart interrupted him. "See that, Johnny. They teach you to say things like 'frankly' at Stanford. I like that." Johnny and Hart had a little laugh, but Austin was undaunted.

"Since Johnny took me under his wing, I've learned a lot about the Strategy. But I'm still learning. "

Hart was unimpressed. "I see. And so what do you think is the most important thing to do when you invest? What is more important—knowing when to buy or when to sell?"

Austin fired back without hesitation, "Without a doubt, knowing when to sell is more important than knowing when to buy."

Hart nodded. "Good. You've learned that lesson well. Quite a difference from most young people nowadays, huh Johnny?" Hart didn't wait for a response. "Johnny is a good teacher. The best. You should feel very fortunate, young man."

"I do, sir," answered Austin humbly.

"Yes, well, all this," he said, waving toward the beautiful interior, "is a result of Johnny's work. This place wouldn't exist without Johnny's guidance. Do you think you could do it if you had to pick up without Johnny tomorrow?"

This question caught Austin off guard. "Umm... sure. Yes, I do. It'd be a great challenge, but with a little time, I could do it."

Hart laughed. "Well, we shall see one day, won't we?"

"I hope so, yes. And let me say, sir, your house is exquisite. It's like a palace. Do you stay here all year?"

"No," said Hart. "I only stay here when we have special guests. So you see... you must be special."

Austin drew some strength from his position alongside Johnny. "I've noticed you've said 'we' several times now. Do you and Johnny both own this place?"

Hart laughed and Johnny rolled his eyes. "No, Austin. This is entirely mine. But Johnny and I do share other interests."

Austin knew he'd put his foot in his mouth. "I hope I'm not prying."

"No, not at all," answered Hart. "I'm a straight-forward guy. I believe Johnny has a gift—a special gift. Now, you think I mean the Strategy, don't you? But you'll learn it's more than that. Johnny's gift is not about money all the time. It's also about people." Hart gestured to Johnny Long. "This man here has used his talents and his energy to help people. And that is the mark of a special man—very special."

"We both know that Johnny's got big shoes to fill."

"Austin, making money in life is easy. And, heaven knows, so is losing it. Making money is nothing in my estimation. Then again, I have it, so what do I know? But growing as a person isn't simply a matter of a bank account. It's a lot more than that. It's what God put us on this Earth for in the first place. Don't forget that."

The butler came out with an assortment of Cuban cigars. Everyone took one. Austin welcomed the lull while everyone quietly lit their smoke. The pause gave Austin time to reflect. By this time he liked being grilled by successful people—it only made him smarter and stronger. Sitting there, talking with the former owner of the Eagles football team, nestled in an exquisite house atop a Bahamian cliff, Austin's deep complex about being a musician and liberal arts major dissolved into the warm tropical breeze. He felt comfortable facing men like this. Not arrogant, but at ease.

He was also struck by Johnny's silence. He'd said little. Was he afraid to offend a client? No, not Johnny. That was the first time Austin ever saw Johnny as someone's employee. He had always seemed so independent. What was going on here? Austin wondered. Maybe this grilling by Hart was part of Johnny's training. Well, he'd just be himself—no pretensions. Hart would either like him or not, as he was.

After a few puffs, Hart broke the quiet. "Where was I? You know, Johnny has used his talents in more ways than just helping me get this house. Helping people. All this..." He gestured around him. "All this is only glass and mortar, so to speak."

Austin jumped at the chance to score some points for his mentor. "Yes, Johnny's Strategy works, Mr. Hart. I'm in awe of it."

Hart spat out a bit of cigar end. "Son, haven't you heard a word I just said?" He turned to Johnny who was choking back his laughter. "Johnny, did I say your wisdom was helping people or not?" Johnny nodded, red in the face from holding back his laughter. "I thought I did. See that, son. You're making my advisor choke. That'd be bad."

Austin recognized Hart's humor and flowed with it. That's the trick to getting on with wealthy businessmen—in their mind, they're always funny, witty, or ironic, like the greatest writers only wished they could be. He'd try to turn the conversation towards Hart. "That's interesting. What do you mean?"

"What I mean is that Johnny knows that money can be used to help people in a positive way. For example, in addition to making good, sound investments, Johnny also helps me maintain this house year round."

Austin was a bit confused. "I thought you owned this house yourself?"

"I do. But Johnny and I use this house to comfort people with special problems."

Hart looked at Johnny, who picked it up from there. "Austin, Mr. Hart and I offer certain people help and comfort. It's really what we work for these days. For example, we open this house to people who need some time to reflect and find solace. It's all for them. Everything."

"My wife died of cancer," said Hart. "Toward the end, she wanted to leave a sort of legacy to others suffering like she was."

"Since then," continued Johnny, "we've opened this house to people suffering the last stages of cancer. You'd be surprised how they welcome the change in perspective this house offers. It helps in so many ways. Henry, you know Austin's mother died of cancer."

"That so? My condolences."

"Thank you," said Austin. "I appreciate it." But he was intrigued on a personal level and wanted to hear more. "Please go on. This is fascinating."

Johnny continued. "It's quite simple. With the money I manage for Mr. Hart, we're able to cover our operating expenses here."

"In other words," added Hart, "Johnny's using his gift to help others."

"And Mr. Hart is gracious enough to help others, too," said Johnny.

Austin was moved. With all the money issues, and the story about his father, and graduating, and the new job, Austin really hadn't really worked through his mother's death. There was no closure and now it was hitting him like a ton of bricks. "This is amazing," was the only comment he could muster.

"No need to say it, son," said Hart. "I know how you feel.
I've been there myself, remember."

Johnny continued. "For about ten years, we've had
arrangements with twenty or so cancer treatment centers around the
world."

"How do you decide whom to select?" asked Austin.

"Tough question," said Hart. "I'll let Johnny answer that
one."

"I actually do research on each patient, Austin. To be honest,
I find out whether or not the person in question has lived a good and
honorable life."

"We all have our skeletons," said Hart, "but you get our drift.
No criminals and the like. It's not our way. We invite people who
have lived good and charitable lives. Otherwise, we rule them out.
It's tough, but obviously, we have to draw the line somewhere. It
might sound cold," said Hart, "but it's necessary."

"Let me spin it this way, Austin," said Johnny. "Mr. Hart and
I believe that people should help others if they have the means to do
so. It's a moral and ethical obligation."

"I ...think I understand," said Austin.

Hart grew more serious. "Austin, the reason we are telling
you all this is because we're interested in you. That's why I was
grilling you so hard. Otherwise, we'd be talking about the view. Do
you understand that?"

"Yes."

"Good, because we're serious here. This is our life's work
we're talking about—and it's my wife's last wish."

Austin looked to Johnny for more clues. Johnny smiled.
That eased Austin. "Austin, Mr. Hart and I have been looking ahead
a few years. You know, nothing's for sure in life. Illness, airplane
crashes—who knows? We want you to learn how to manage money
so you can continue with this house and our work, in the spirit of
our beliefs."

Austin was stunned. Nothing had prepared him for this. But
he knew special moments like this came only rarely and had to be
recognized for the breakthroughs they were. This was the moment
he'd been waiting for—a level of responsibility worthy of his very

best. It was about making money, yes, but much more. He was overwhelmed and deeply moved.

Hart and Johnny walked Austin through the house, pointing out the more notable works of art. Austin took it all in like a dry sponge. The island, the art, the talk of a higher cause—this all propelled Austin far from the petty world he'd known before. He felt humbled by all this, not proud. What a vote of confidence these two men had placed in him! He had to live up to their expectations. Nothing—absolutely nothing—in Austin's short life had shoved him into maturity and seriousness like what had just happened. Grow up, buddy, he said to himself. Get serious. You're in it now!

"The art is something else, isn't it?" asked Hart. "It's inspiring, especially for the people who come out here."

"There's a great variety," said Austin.

"Precisely. The diversity of work here is intentional. There are at least several pieces that will appeal to someone from just about any cultural background."

The three of them sat down in a large, bright salon called simply, The View. There, they took cognac, cheeses, and pate. The air was heavy with contemplation. This was a special moment, a window of opportunity not to be passed up.

They held up their snifters in a toast. "Johnny, would you," said Hart.

"Certainly. Here's to people. And here's to Austin's developing gift." They clinked glasses. It was a very fine cognac.

"My what?" asked Austin. He'd never felt so... special, and he was wondering what he did to deserve all this.

"You have a gift, Austin," said Johnny.

"Like Johnny," said Hart.

"You grasp the Strategy as if it were commonplace," Johnny said, "like it is simply the way of the world. I saw glimpses of that after our very first conversation. I saw the potential."

"Austin," said Hart. Austin looked right at him. "Tell me something."

Austin knew another test question was coming.

"How successful is the Strategy?"

"I've just finished researching five hundred thousand estimate changes, Mr. Hart—five hundred thousand—stretching over the last decade. It's unbelievable. It's like a golden cord connecting earnings estimates to stock prices. The estimates pull them up or bring them down. It's like a law of some kind—that's what Johnny calls it. How successful is it? Very, Mr. Hart. Very."

"Right. And how many consultants in your office follow the Strategy?"

Austin shrugged. "I don't know."

"Johnny?" said Hart.

Johnny frowned. "Not many, Austin. Very few, in fact."

"But I thought the Strategy was available to everyone in the firm on the computer."

"It is, Austin. For now, at least. That's what we mean. Fewer and fewer of the young consultants are doing the Strategy, and the older guys are too far gone to make a difference."

Hart put his drink down and rapped the table for emphasis. "I don't understand why on God's good earth people don't get in line and follow Johnny. I'd love to sit in a room with one of those dusty old brokers who think I should buy GE and AT&T and never worry again. Let'em have my kind of money? No way. Let'em earn the kind of money Johnny has earned me—then let's talk."

Austin seized the moment to get on board with these men. "I believe in what you and Johnny are doing. I think it's very special. There was silence for a moment. "So tell me more about what you want me to do."

"Excellent. All business. I like that," said Hart.

"First," said Johnny, "let me tell you about some of my clients. Many are people or institutions that share the same values as Mr. Hart and me—professors, doctors, some lawyers, and even some politicians. They're from all walks of life, but have a common belief in doing some good with their money. Also I handle some hospitals, charities and even some businesses, if I like them."

"Many of these people, and some businesses, donate money to worthy causes," said Hart.

"My goal is to help these people and businesses by managing their money. This gives them more money, some of which is used to help others. Is that clear?"

"Sure," said Austin enthusiastically. "You know, my mother did a lot of volunteer work. I mean the real dirty kind that others didn't want to do. She did it for years."

"We know that Austin. And we're counting on you being something like her," Johnny said.

Hart stood up abruptly. "Good. That's what I like—a man on a mission. Never let it go, son. Fight the good fight 'till the day you die." He put his glass down. "I'll leave you two alone to discuss whatever it is you financial types talk about. I'll see you at dinner. Say around seven?"

"That'll be fine," said Johnny. Once Hart left, Johnny turned to Austin. "Now you see why I wanted you to come here. If using the Strategy to help people has been the light in my life, then this place is like the lighthouse. I thought you should see it. Managing money, Austin, is like any other profession. I only hope that you take what I have to give you and do the right thing with it."

"I will, Johnny. You know I will."

"We'll see. I'm a man with a purpose, and to be honest, at this point in my life, I really only want to be with like-minded people."

"So your clients share your desire to help people?" asked Austin.

"As many as possible. If they don't, we eventually part ways."

"It's their loss," said Austin.

"Yes it is," agreed Johnny. "Financially and spiritually."

"To you, they're sort of connected, aren't they?"

"No, Austin. There are many, many wealthy people who simply don't care what happens to others. They're just not my type. Fortunately, I can be selective with the people I choose as friends and clients. That's another benefit of the Strategy."

"I'll add it to the list."

"Now, let's get down to it. I want to start with a summary of your research to date. What have you found? Tell me."

"I went back over ten years and recorded every single earnings increase. I noted each company that had at least two increases within a six-month period."

"What did you find?"

"Well, for one, the analysts change their earnings very often."

"Yes. And what about that?"

"What about that? Well, the most obvious thing was the relationship between the stock price and the estimate increases."

"Go on."

"When the analyst increased his estimates, the stock price would usually move higher."

"And conversely?"

"For sure. If the analyst lowered his estimates, the price usually moved lower. But I noticed something else, too."

"Really?" said Johnny. "Tell me."

"Sometimes, not often, the price seemed to move before the analyst made his changes up or down. It's almost like someone knew the news was coming before it was made known."

Johnny nodded. "First of all, you're absolutely right about the effect of estimate changes on the price of a stock. As for the market activity before news comes public, well that's not anything we take part in. That's rumor or illegal inside information. Another thing, many analysts have institutional clients of their own. They don't want to be the first or the last to announce bad news. Likewise, they want to be the first to announce good news. When the analyst publishes their changes, that's what we use. No harm, no foul."

"I wish we could know what stocks to buy beforehand."

"No you don't, Austin. Don't get involved with that kind of stuff. Get rid of any client, big or small, who wants inside information, Austin. They're not the kind of people we're looking for."

"OK, I'll remember that."

"I hope so, Austin, because it's like a drug. Don't get caught up in it. You always lose in the end. And anyway, like I've been telling you, all stocks are correctly priced at the time you buy them. The secret is knowing when to sell."

"If you do that," said Austin, "you'll hold on to the stocks that go up and up and up. I've followed a few of those and it's really amazing. But if someone was watching only the price, they'd have most likely sold it with only a 10% profit instead of holding it for a 100% profit."

"Or a 1,000% profit," added Johnny.

"Yeah! I tracked several of those over the past ten years, too."

"Amazing, isn't it?"

"It is. But it's also reassuring. Especially when you can remove yourself from the daily fluctuations and feel confident that every stock you own has had, or is still having, good earnings. It's much calmer," Austin said.

"It's also much smarter," Johnny replied. "Successful investing for growth requires patience and research. Most people have neither. Most people don't have reliable research. True, they can go on-line, but First American has the best research team. You get what you pay for, and I mean that. The best is the best, and that's that."

"You know, I noticed another interesting thing," Austin said. "It sometimes takes time for some stocks to move up a lot. They move, but it sometimes takes time."

"Well, like I said, patience is everything. Without a proper strategy, your average investor might not feel comfortable waiting three years for a stock to go up 300%. Instead they rush into this or that hot stock hoping to make 50% in a month. They buy it for no sound reason, and end up holding a stock that does nothing but go down. If they make a buck, they should feel lucky."

"Do you think people know the earnings of the companies they invest in?"

"Ha!" Johnny exclaimed, "ask your average—or even a so-called sophisticated—investor what the earnings are expected to be for his IBM stock, and I bet he hasn't got a clue. Ask most brokers. I'll bet they've got no idea what the earnings are for the stocks they're buying and selling every day."

"They're just guessing!" said Austin.

"If you can make them see that, you can save them. If you can't make them see that, then cut'em loose."

Austin liked having rules of thumb like this. It gave order to his life. But there was still something Austin didn't fully understand. "OK, tell me why past information about a company is no good to use."

"It's useless. In an airplane, the pilot needs to see the weather 30 to 50 miles in front of him—not what's behind him. Logic in this example is simple. Pilots want to know what is ahead. The better the weather forecasting, the smoother the flight.

"What do I tell a client who insists on buying, say Microsoft, if it isn't in the Strategy?"

"Tell them this—let's say you have two companies. Microsoft is expected to increase its earnings 100% for the year. Of course, being public information, that news is already priced into the stock. It will take several estimate increases to move it significantly higher, even though analysts pretty much have Microsoft earnings down pat. You also have a lesser-known stock, expected to increase earnings 10% for the year."

"The client would fight me about not buying Microsoft."

"Right. And they'd be totally wrong. So, let's say you get the client to buy stock in both companies—Microsoft and the lesser-known company. After three months, our analyst says that because of an acquisition and trouble in Asia, Microsoft will only grow earnings by 90% this year—still phenomenal growth, but that is already priced into the stock. There's no such thing as a true value in the stock market."

"So, once again, it really doesn't matter how much a company increases their earnings year to year as much as it matters how often the estimates change?" Austin asked.

"That's right," Johnny said. "In the case of Microsoft, they have to grow earnings by an incredible amount year after year in order to dramatically increase their share price. No thanks. I'll just wait until their earnings are increased twice in a six-month period. Because, like I said, the price at which you buy the stock is irrelevant. What matters are…"

"The estimate changes," said Austin.

"Right. Let's say our analyst for the lesser-known stock you bought raises estimates from 10% to 15%. Three months later, Microsoft estimates are again reduced, this time down to 80% due to a one-time restructuring cost. The other company is raised from 15% to 20% and so on."

"So the only thing to watch is whether or not earnings are disappointing?"

"Yes, but only using our analysts. We have to draw the line somewhere, you know. The size of the growth—in this example, 80% and 20%—is secondary to increases and decreases. That's the hardest thing to explain to clients. Usually, faster-growth companies are harder for the analyst to predict, so you see more changes. Larger companies like Microsoft are established and easier to predict, so you don't get as many surprises. Which do you think will have the most surprises? Fast-growing companies, of course. It's all about expectations.

"Also, there is no risk in using historical data. Think about it for a second—risk versus return. Where there is risk, you will find a return. Of course, the return could be negative or positive. Is there any risk in using historical data? No. It's not likely that the prices in the Wall Street Journal for last week were printed incorrectly. History is history. Because there is no risk in this historical data, there cannot be a return earned from it. You are only rewarded or punished by future events being different three months from now."

"Expectations, yes," agreed Austin. "But that makes for more volatility, doesn't it?"

"Of course, because they're harder to predict. That's why the 'new economy' or faster-growth companies are more volatile. But so long as you know the earnings are there, what's the problem? Then you've got all those novice day-traders, trading on the Internet and watching those TV shows. They watch the shows and jump in and out based on someone's hype and 30-second sound bites. That creates a lot more volatility, too. That's another big problem you'll have—explaining to a client that market volatility means nothing, that the price means nothing."

"That's why we have a discipline to fall back on."

"That's right, Austin. That's exactly right. And it's also why we diversify. But use your common sense."

"So I shouldn't worry about all the bad news I hear on TV about tech stocks crashing, high stock prices, evaluations and stuff? Sometimes it really stresses me out."

"Well it doesn't worry me. That should tell you something. It's all media marketing. As I told you before, it's intended to increase their audience. What better way to do it than by scaring the crap out of people and getting them hooked on irrelevant information? Irrelevant information, Austin."

"Sure, especially since a stock price itself is really a red herring."

"Since you mentioned it, let me say something more about this new wave of TV investors and on-line traders. They can be greedy, jealous people, Austin—not the clients we want."

"How do you mean? I have a number of friends who trade on-line. They're not so bad."

"They might not even realize it, but these are greedy times. I'll give you an example. Imagine you're one of your friends, OK?"

"No problem," said Austin.

"Imagine you buy a stock for $20 a share, and you sell it for $30."

"Why did I sell it?"

"You have no real idea. You made some money, and you're taking profits. That's why. You're not using the Strategy, so there's really no rhyme or reason to buy and sell. Now, what do you want that stock to do after you sell it?"

Austin thought for a moment. "Well, I wouldn't want it to go up after I sold it."

"Of course not," said Johnny sarcastically. "After all, you need affirmation that your judgment is right, the illusion that you know what you're doing."

Austin laughed. "Sure. That'd be comforting. Then I could tell all the girls what a great investor I am."

"There you go," said Johnny. "But think about it for a second, because there is a moral good and a bad when it comes to investing. And I'm not talking about breaking the law. I'm talking about actually wishing ill on others because you don't know what you're doing."

"Interesting." said Austin. "So I sell the stock. Go on."

"You probably want that stock to go down after you sold it, which means you want something bad to happen to that company that will make its stock depreciate. Now you're thinking negatively."

Austin shrugged it off. "I guess so. Is that a problem?"

"Is that a problem? You're young, Austin. Maybe you don't have a firm idea of ramifications and accountability. But negative thinking is contagious—very contagious—and it infects everyone around you who drops their defenses."

"Is it really that big a deal to want the stock I just sold to go down?"

"Well, now suppose you sold your whole portfolio. I've seen it happen more often than I care to remember. What would you want to see then?"

"I guess I'd want them all to go down. You know, like people say, I'd want the market to go down."

"So now you're hoping for a depression, or world war, or an assassination of a world leader—things that make the entire market go down. And for what? So that you feel better about yourself."

"Unless you knew about the earnings," said Austin."

"Right, and then you wouldn't be worrying or wishing any ill. You wouldn't be selfish. You'd be letting the Strategy do the work for you."

"No wonder my friends were always happy—or pissed off— depending on how the market did that day."

"If you listen to these people, you'll be appalled at some of the things you'll hear. About three years ago, I had this client named Joe Sherman. He just loved to trade stocks. He used to call me at least ten times a day to make trades. This was before on-line trading. He was a close friend of a good client, so I humored him as long as I could."

"So you fired him?"

"One day, he called me up to complain that a stock he'd sold a week or so earlier against my advice kept going up and up. Now most of my clients owned the stock in the Strategy."

"Which one?"

"Kohl's."

"You owned Kohl's in the Strategy three years ago!" exclaimed Austin, figuring quickly that many of Johnny's clients must have made about 800%.

"You should know that, Austin. And I'm still holding it. But this guy insists we sell it, so I did. And he calls me to complain and say something like, 'that damned stock, I hope the thing just blows up.' As always, he felt it necessary to accentuate his call with an impressive array of vulgarity and general vitriol. The man was negative Austin—that's my point. I made a mistake taking him on because I let an existing friendship get in the way of good business sense."

"So he actually wanted one of the most successful retailing stocks to just plain crash. Boom! Just like that?"

"Sure. Screw everybody else. That's how these day traders are. Like you told me, Austin, people will almost instinctively act out of self-interest, and resentment colors their entire world view."

"But you think it's possible to do good with one's wealth? I'm confused."

"Think of helping others, Austin, as an attempt to grow beyond your own human limitations and instincts. I don't know if it's really possible to do it, but we have to try. That's how Mr. Hart feels, too."

"You know, I still can't get over how simple the Strategy is."

"Austin, most truths which have profoundly changed things are simple. That's why people either overlook them, or don't appreciate them. They think if it's good it has to be more complicated. There's got to be more to it than this—and they miss it. And remember, there's no bank vault anywhere locked more tightly than a closed mind."

Johnny went on, "There's a tremendous difference between simple and simplistic. Simple is clear, direct, uncomplicated—like the Strategy. But simplistic means ignoring complexities, taking shortcuts. As for your comment about making something as difficult and convoluted as the stock market seem easy to understand—well, thanks. That's quite a compliment."

Austin smiled. "Johnny, another one of your talents is being able to explain things in a way people understand. I did, at our very first meeting."

"Well, you had an open mind. Not everyone does. I can tell you this, those who do see the light often see something else, too—big success in the market. Then we move on and start helping others with our shared good fortune. Now, that's when it becomes fun. And how many 50 year-old men can say they have fun at work every day? Think about that, Austin."

Austin hoped he'd say that very same thing when he was Johnny's age. "It's pretty clear you're satisfied with what you're doing because you feel it works."

"Not 'feel' Austin. It does work," interrupted Johnny.

"OK, because it works. But aren't there other strategies out there that work? I hope it doesn't offend you Johnny, but someone's going to ask me—so I should ask you—are you right and everyone else wrong? I mean, what about all the books on investing? Are they all wrong?"

"Austin, it's hard to find a good book on investing. They're few and far between. Occasionally, though, one comes along that opens some eyes. The problem is that people have been successful in the stock market for many different reasons. Now, let's get one thing clear. I know my strategy isn't the only way to invest money. I'm a pure 'growth investor,' but there are a lot of other investors who have used different strategies, and successfully. I've got literally shelves full of books containing all their innermost secrets."

"What are the most popular strategies out there?" asked Austin.

"Let's see," said Johnny. "Well, some say buy stocks that have low price to earnings—P/E ratios. They call this 'value investing.' They look for stocks that have relatively cheap prices compared to the S&P 500. Often the prices are cheap because the companies have had a period of poor earning and are hoping to improve someday."

"Why would I want to invest in a company that's done badly for years?"

"Good question. That's what I'd like to know."

"It seems to me," Austin added, "they're just guessing good news will come because so much of the past news is bad."

"Well, a little more than that. They're also depending on the company's positive comments about the future. All that's pretty 'iffy.' I'd rather wait until our analysts have actually increased their estimates two times in a six-month period. Then, count me in."

"What are the other theories?"

"Well, some say buy the 'big guy'—huge, large-cap companies that dominate their business. Others say buy the companies that have the best management, but how can you tell that except by higher earnings? You name it—I've had it used against me. But my strategy keeps cranking higher. And you know," said Johnny, "I've yet to read a book about when to sell a stock. Now that would be valuable to the investing public. Not some esoteric discourse on market timing or other such 'voodoo' investing. Yes, a book on what to buy and when to sell..." Johnny slipped into thought.

"Maybe I'll write it someday, Johnny."

Johnny looked up suddenly. "Yes, Austin. Maybe that's not such a bad idea. We'll keep that in mind."

On the spot, Austin decided that someday he'd write a book on Johnny's strategy—something more than just a boring manual on investing. He'd write the story of Johnny Long and the simple strategy he'd uncovered while looking for the answer to those three questions, and what good could be done by reaching beyond the world of gain, moving into the world of putting that gain to good use. That'd be a glimpse into living itself.

"Do you understand that?" Austin, deep in thought, heard Johnny ask.

"Huh?" Austin snapped out of his thoughts. "Sorry, could you repeat that?"

"I said, do you understand that in the long run it's useless to try to 'time' the market—when to move in and out, based on timing. That's another popular obsession, thanks to the recent boom in day trading."

"Isn't that what technical analysis is for? Even First American publishes its technical analysis."

"Yes, but just think about it. Technical analysis is a historical, mathematical model of the market. It does not take into account the future earnings of a stock. Don't get me wrong. I'd love to come up with a strategy for market timing that actually worked— getting out when the stock is at a high and getting in when the stock is at a low. I'd love to learn that trick! But I've yet to meet anyone who can time the market consistently. Sometimes, yes. Sure, if the market's in a correction, of course all stocks are lower and that would be a good time to buy the stocks that meet the Strategy. That's a no-brainer. But consistently, reliably time the market? No way! For one thing, the downside risk of letting go a big winner is far too great."

Johnny went on. "I mentioned a correction. Corrections happen. The whole market goes down—the good, the bad, the indifferent. A lot of people sell out during a correction. People panic. They want out before they go even lower—to salvage whatever they can, usually hoping to time the market and get back in at the 'right time'—whenever that is. But my research shows that being out of the market loses far more money than is lost staying in the market when it corrects or goes down. Why? Well, all corrections end and they usually end suddenly and often move up fast—up a lot in a short period of time. You miss that and you've lost more money than the 'paper losses' you had by staying in. So, don't try to time it—you can lose big. Stay in the market, have a good strategy, use the best research you can get—and be patient. Well, now you know what I think about those who try to time the market. Good luck—and timing is just plain luck."

"Simple," said Austin. "But not simplistic."

Johnny smiled. "Right. And smart people will pay you for that information, Austin. You'll make them rich and, guess what, you'll share in their success."

By the time Johnny finished teaching Austin these finer points of the Strategy, Austin suddenly realized he was fatigued. They'd been going for hours, but he still had to break the news to Johnny about the rest of his money. And he had to do it now. He couldn't go on deceiving a man who'd put so much trust in him. He had rehearsed the speech he'd prepared—he had been a client first and he'd just done what other clients, including Mr. Hart, had done. He tested the abilities of Johnny Long before committing all his money—that was the speech. My God, he was nervous!

"Johnny, there's still one thing I want to talk over with you before dinner."

"I think I can manage one more issue," replied Johnny. "What's on your mind?"

"When I came to you about a year ago, I told you I had $100,000 to invest in keeping with my father's trust and so on. That much is true. But I also have more than that."

"Right. Your account is up around $135,000 today," Johnny said with a smile.

"I know. That's great. But I mean I actually have more money in the bank—a lot more. My mother died, and I came to Philadelphia for the funeral. I was then called in to attend the reading of a will I didn't even know existed. You remember that, I'm sure. It was a weird time for me. Anyway, the trust I told you about stipulated that I was to receive an initial $1 million, not $100,000 like I told you. I was to invest that initial million and, if I averaged fifteen percent per year over three years, I'd receive an additional five million dollars."

Johnny was floored. "Wow! That's a far cry from the numbers we discussed. So you're a millionaire, are you?"

"Trying to become a multi-millionaire. I realized too late that if I'd given you the full amount, I'd be looking great about now. Unfortunately, though, I was afraid and I'm slipping behind now."

Johnny looked concerned. He wasn't upset or bitter. He was afraid—genuinely afraid—there wasn't enough time left. "Austin, this isn't good. Not good at all."

"Johnny, I'm sorry," pleaded Austin. "I didn't know what to do. You said yourself that most clients start you off with only some of their money."

"Austin, your prudence or inexperience—whichever we wish to call it—isn't my worry. Your beating the challenge of the trust is. Are you telling me, then, that the other $900,000 has been sitting around in a bank account collecting simple interest?"

Austin felt ashamed. "Yes. By my calculations, I've earned about 7½ % on the total amount so far. So now I need to earn about 20% per year for the next two years in order to average-"

"To average out the 15% a year. Yes, I know. That's what worries me."

"Do we have a chance?" asked Austin.

Johnny thought for a moment. This was not good news. OK, he knew Austin had to learn, but this lesson might be a very expensive lesson—a five million dollar lesson. "Well, this is certainly a new challenge. OK, that's how we'll look at it. Put a positive spin on it, Austin. We'll do our best."

"Are you mad at me for not telling you sooner, Johnny?"

Johnny smiled and said in a soothing voice, "No, I am not mad at you. I'm a little confused though."

Austin wanted—needed—to explain. "In the beginning, I spoke to different people about investing the money. The whole thing was confusing and overwhelming. I spoke to real estate people, mutual fund people and other brokers. The more they said, the more confused I got. It was getting ridiculous. Try to put yourself in my shoes. Most of the people I spoke with were either too inexperienced or else they made me nervous for one reason or another. I just got a bad vibe, you know. And I didn't want to blow the million I did have. I woke up in a cold sweat more than once, thinking I'd lost the million trying to get the five million. I can't tell you how lost I felt. That's it—lost. When I met you, that all changed. I felt comfortable and confident, but I still thought it'd be a good idea to be careful. You know. Just in case."

Johnny nodded. "I understand, Austin. But let this be a lesson for you. I only hope it doesn't turn out to cost you five million dollars."

"I know. So what do we do from here?"

"As soon as we get back to Philadelphia, transfer the money to your First American account. If we don't get around 30% this year, we're going to have to crank it up and get more aggressive in the third year. Austin, how many times have I told you this is a long-term strategy? It sometimes takes up to three years to get the most out of it. It takes time—and that's something we don't have a lot of. It's certainly not too late to accomplish your goal, but we may have to be more aggressive. Do you understand what I'm saying?"

Austin was totally out of his league here. "Whatever you say, Johnny. Just let's make the numbers, OK?"

"Well, we'll see Austin. That's the best I can tell you."

"But if we only need to average 20%, why do we need to shoot for 30%?" asked Austin.

"Because we need a cushion," replied Johnny. "One of these days, the market could go down for an extended period—a correction or even a bear market. Right now, your portfolio is worth $135,000 or so. If we leverage you up with margin, you could own almost twice that amount."

"Margin...what's that?"

"For every dollar you invest with First American, we'll lend you an equal amount and charge you interest. For example, you invested $100,000, but you actually could have purchased almost $200,000 in stocks by borrowing, or margining, the other half. If you'd done that, your account would be worth some $270,000 now."

Austin was confused. "Let me get this straight. If I give you $100,000, you could buy $200,000 worth of stock? If the portfolio appreciates 35% or so, it'd be worth $270,000. That's a return of 70%!"

"Right. But you have to deduct the yearly interest of about nine percent, but, yes you're right— $270,000."

"Well, why didn't you do that from the outset?" griped Austin.

Johnny rolled his eyes. "Because it's a double-edged sword, Austin. If your portfolio goes down 10%, let's say, you'd be down twice as much, plus interest. That's the risk you take when you leverage up like that. It's riskier than what you're doing right now. But we've got to look at that if we're going to get you higher returns."

"But, I shouldn't worry, though, huh...because we're using the Strategy, right?" asked Austin.

"My job is managing risk, Austin. Leveraging up increases that risk. But we could also use options."

"Options? Everyone says stay away from them."

"There's a time and a place for everything, Austin."

"How do they work?"

"Options are basically another form of leverage. Options are contracts that give you the right to buy or sell a block of 100 shares of a stock at a pre-established price. These are call options. Each call-option contract gives you the right to buy 100 shares of stock at a specific price for an agreed upon time. Let's say you own a contract on IBM. Right now, IBM is selling for $100 a share. With a call contract, you have the right to buy 100 shares of the stock at

$100, good for the next six months. For that right, you pay the owner of that stock a premium or fee—in this case, probably about $800. Now, if IBM appreciates to, say $120 a share sometime during the next six months, you still have the right to buy the stock from the seller for $100 a share. You paid him a premium for that right. Follow me so far?"

"Yes."

"So you paid $800 to make $2000. Not a bad return. Of course, if IBM doesn't break 100 over the next six months, your contract expires worthless, as most do, and you lose your premium to the seller. We could use this approach if we need to. We still have time to consider it."

"OK, I'm still a little confused. Just do what you think is best."

"Well, the important point is that both of these strategies make money if stocks go up in value. As such, they fit within the Strategy. In fact, in some cases they fit in very well. We'll go over things in more detail when the time is right."

What should have been a great trip turned into a constant worry for Austin on how to beat the clock. He tried to push it into the back of his mind and concentrate on his visit with Mr. Hart. Clearly, Austin was being drawn into something very big and very important. It had been an eventful, even wonderful, trip. But at the same time he pictured the ticking clock and five million dollars slipping away.

Hart's dinner stories were funny and fascinating. What an incredible and wonderful world men like Hart and Johnny lived in. They prospered, enjoyed life and did good things for people. And they'd invited him into their world. Austin knew he'd have to do a lot better than he'd done so far to deserve a place beside men like these.

Chapter 11

AUSTIN flew back alone, and thankfully it gave him a few hours to think about everything. He had no doubt that his life just took a turn for the better despite his holding out on Johnny. It happens that way sometimes, thought Austin. You make a mistake and stumble, and a handful of good people are there to help you along with the next step. He realized that's what Johnny meant when he said a person had to try to overcome what's most human— bitterness, resentment, self-interest. True, it might never happen. But living is in the trying.

All in all, things went well for Austin over the next few months. He was still doing the research, but Johnny was bringing him more and more into the actual investment decisions. Austin prepared the lists and double-checked everything before Johnny recommended a stock. He'd moved his other $900,000 over and Johnny had invested that. He was fully invested and in a race against time. Time was moving on and things were getting tense for Austin. He was making money—just not enough.

Things were also getting tough in the world arena. There were mounting tensions between OPEC and the emerging South American oil producers. They were clandestinely producing more oil than agreed on, driving down the price of oil through over-supply. The Arabs were incensed, or so the rhetoric went. To make matters worse, the United States seemed to be supporting the South American producers, although nothing official had been announced. This new tension was causing the markets to move down steadily for a couple of weeks. This was putting tremendous short-term pressure on Austin's returns and his "paper profits" were going back down again. In the long run he felt things would be fine. But he didn't have a long run.

In fact, he only had four more months until the deadline and he was barely averaging 14% growth—1% below the critical amount. Just one "down period" for the market in general, however short-term, could drag him down, and he'd lose the whole five million. He was a nervous wreck.

To try to relax he took a long weekend in Miami. He needed to blow off some steam. Not only was this market getting to him, but also Johnny was stepping up his demands on Austin's time. Johnny was getting ready to share some accounts with Austin as preparation for sending him out to meet with important clients. There'd also been a jump in the number of advisors using the Strategy at First American and Johnny needed someone to go to various offices and present the Strategy. Austin had to be ramped up faster than originally planned and the pressure was on.

Austin managed to have a good time in Miami. On the way back he had a sense of misgiving and unease about the market. Time was very short and he was just barely under the amount he needed. With his luck, he thought, something's bound to happen. The market would probably fall out of bed just before his deadline. It was the familiar chorus of his life.

The Philadelphia airport was its usual busy self. On his way to the baggage claim, Austin noticed a crowd of people hovering around a television at a terminal bar. You can always sense when there's something big happening—people crowding around for the latest word. Austin stepped off the people mover and joined the crowd. The news reporter was summarizing the effects of a new oil production quota just announced. This was serious stuff. OPEC was cutting back on their oil shipments to the West, just as they had done back in the 70's.

With the supply cut, prices would skyrocket until they found the level of maximum efficiency. The looming disaster got worse when the reporter announced that only halfway through the trading day the price of oil jumped from $12 a barrel to $40.

Johnny was right about people. Nobody around Austin seemed to care about why OPEC was doing what they were doing. People were angry. Gas for their gas-guzzling sports utility vehicles would be ridiculously expensive. Airfares for their trips down to Palm Beach would skyrocket, and the market—their stocks. Austin thought, oh my God, the stocks.

The Dow was down 525 points. Austin was instantly nauseated. If he lost his five million dollars because some oil producers decided to flex their muscle, he would…he didn't know what. He was so mad and so scared. Oh, my God, he thought. He whipped out his cell phone and called Johnny.

Johnny answered his own phone, which meant that Moira and Rory must've been tied up with other callers. "Johnny Long speaking," he snapped. He sounded stressed.

"Johnny, its Austin. What the hell's going on?"

Johnny was not in the mood to go through his handholding with another caller. "Reduced oil production. Huge market drop. It happens. Where are you?"

"I'm in the airport."

"Well, get the hell in here. It's Monday. Time to work. Let's go." He hung up.

Austin rushed back to the office as fast as he could. He was distraught about his own money. He knew he was losing big today. But he was still one of Johnny's team and would do what he was told. If nothing else, it would take his mind off his losses.

Back in the office, Austin immediately saw the look of panic on everyone's face. It was borderline hysteria. Phones were ringing off the hook. The younger brokers were standing up in their cubicles gesticulating wildly while their clients berated them on the phone for not anticipating the fuel crisis. People were in a panic and selling as fast as they could. Everyone was speaking at the top of his or her voice.

Let's get out now… Hey, at least we can cut our losses… Look, I have no idea when it'll end. What do I look like, Nostradamus… I…I just don't know what to do.

The managers were nowhere to be found. Austin's office manager was away on vacation. And the sales manager, the man who was supposed to guide the brokers—especially the young ones—through crises like this one, well, he was chained to his desk, sleeves rolled up to the elbow, sweat stains soaking through, trading stocks as fast as he could. Whatever his clients wanted to do. Buy or sell. Today it was all sell—sell everything. He let the client make the decisions. This way he wouldn't get into trouble. Rule number one—cover your ass. Austin dropped his bags in his office and went straight in to see Johnny. "I'm here."

Johnny was on the phone; several other calls were holding. He covered the mouthpiece of the phone. "Oh good. The market's been waiting just for you," he muttered a little sarcastically. He pointed to a seat. Austin sat down and watched his mentor at work in the midst of a full-blown crisis.

Unlike most of the others, Johnny Long was unconcerned with the long-term implications of the new oil production quota. Yes, the short-term impact would be severe. But the good stocks—like the stocks in the Strategy—should come out with their earnings intact and rebound and keep going. Of course the increase in energy costs might affect some of those earnings, so they'd keep a close eye on those earning forecasts. If any earnings estimates were reduced, he'd sell. If not, hang in there and trust the Strategy—no market timing. Johnny was more stressed over the number of panic-stricken clients calling than he was over anything else.

"Trust the Strategy. You've got good companies. Earnings are going up. Fundamentals are still great. The economy's still sound. Be patient...this thing will pass, don't bail out now, whatever you do." That was his theme over and over to the desperate callers.

Johnny hung up the phone. "Welcome back, my friend. You missed a hell of a morning."

"This is crazy," said Austin, now caught up in the emotional turmoil. "Everybody's doing his or her own thing. There's no system in place. It's chaos."

Johnny looked concerned. "That worries me more than anything else. Today, it's a new oil production quota. Tomorrow, it will be something else, and so on. It's the lack of any clear strategy that'll kill a client on a day like today."

"Well, what does the firm say?"

Johnny closed his eyes and shook his head. "Nothing. They're still 'analyzing' the situation. Just when you need the advice of professionals the most, there's none being offered. We're on our own."

Austin could hardly believe what he was hearing. "How can that be? Even the analysts?"

"Well, the analysts are watching for earnings changes, not the macro-economic picture. We've got other people for that, but they're M.I.A. The analysts are still working with us. When they make decreases, we'll sell. Until then, we stick with their existing estimates."

"Got it. OK. That helps."

"Listen to me, Austin."

Austin leaned forward. "Yes?"

"Most clients are going to get killed today because their advisors have no idea why they buy and sell stocks. OK?" He paused.

"OK."

"But others, Austin, will make a killing precisely because their advisors do know why and when to buy and sell. Like my clients. Today is my day, Austin. A day like today is when I can really be of help to my people."

"Thank God someone's got a clue. What should I do?"

Johnny slapped his hand on his desk. "Buy! I've seen artificial corrections like this before. I'm buying aggressively here."

"What do you mean by artificial correction?"

"By artificial I mean a correction which has nothing to do with a drop in earnings. A bear market is legitimate. It's for real and happens when there's a drop due to steadily decreasing earnings. A bear market is when earnings are going down steadily. That's a real bear market. That's not what's happening here.

"Earnings are still high and in some cases growing. Fundamentals are still solid. This is an artificial correction, my friend. Artificial corrections happen because of a scare—an oil scare, rumors, a regional conflict somewhere. It all gets down to fear—and sometimes that fear is caused by so-called experts on television shows talking about disaster. That draws the crowds and can be self-fulfilling. They shout 'fire' and everyone rushes to the exit—and to the television screens. No, this is a classic artificial correction—fear-based—not earnings-based. Like I said, the earnings and fundamentals are all solid. So we buy, my friend. We buy."

"You're advising your clients to buy?"

"Yes. To buy the stocks in the Strategy, of course. I'm advising my clients to buy, and they'll soon see why they hired me."

"So give me the game plan."

"Do you remember when we talked about options?"

"Yeah. You said we had time to decide what we were going to do regarding leverage."

"Well, the decision is made. It's time to make a move, Austin. We're putting $250,000 into options. If things work out, you should make about half-a-mil in three months. We're also buying $350,000 worth of additional stocks on margin. Your portfolio is currently worth about $1,300,000. Normally, I would never recommend you buying options or stocks on margin. Both of these are very risky and should be used only in special situations. Most investors should invest for the long term and pay 100% for their stock purchases. In our case, this is the right time."

Austin gasped, shocked. His account had been up around $1,480,000 when he left for Miami. It had dropped to $1,300,000 in just days! A $180,000 loss in a few days—my God, how could this be? He knew it'd go back up after the correction, but that would be too late for him.

"So this correction erased about everything I recently made?" he asked, fighting his panic.

"Yup, for now. When there's a general market decline it takes the good down with the bad. That's why patience is key to the Strategy. These are good stocks. They've got the earnings increases. They'll go back up…and then some."

Austin was distraught. "I can understand why people wish they could time the markets."

"Please," said Johnny. "I've been hearing it all morning. I'm pretty sick of it by now. If I have to hear one more client demand to know why I didn't know about this oil problem before it happened, I'm going to scream."

"So these buys could really catapult me forward in about three months?"

"They should, but you never know, Austin. Trust the Strategy. Things will work themselves out in the long run, one way or another. When the market goes back up, I'm looking to get back up to $1.5 million and change in order to collect the rest of the trust. This should do it. The short-term return should do the job. Are you with me?" He handed Austin a sheet of paper.

Austin didn't know what to say. When he started out, he was simply buying some stocks. Now he was leveraging, and using margin and buying options, and paying back debt. He was in over his head. But it was either trust Johnny and his Strategy or not—in or out. Austin gathered his mettle. "That's why I hired you, Johnny. You get what you pay for, right?"

Johnny sensed Austin was looking for some much-needed reassurance. "If this doesn't work, Austin, I frankly don't know what does. Let's get it going. And look at it this way—even if you had given me all your money at the beginning, the investments would still have gone down. So nothing gained, nothing lost. We've got a clean slate and we'll see what happens. Let me get back to work. I've got other clients to manage along the same lines."

"OK, do it," Austin said. "I agree with your portfolio recommendations. Hopefully, when D-Day gets here, I'll reach my goal."

Austin returned to his office knowing full well that this was it. This was the make-or-break decision. Not only could he earn an additional five million, he could also very well lose a substantial part of his original million and the five million as well. The stress was immense. Would he one day be able to make decisions on a scale like this?

Austin threw himself into his increasing workload for the next three months. He was scared—much too scared—to check the value of his portfolio. He didn't want to know. He could just click on the computer and see how much his portfolio was. That click was like the click of death to Austin.

Once when checking on a client's portfolio for Johnny, he clicked the wrong button and his own portfolio came up on the screen. In a panic, Austin covered his eyes so he couldn't see the screen—and clicked anywhere, just to get out. He didn't want to know. Too much was at stake. But the ignorance was far from blissful. There was no way he would die a thousand deaths by checking. He knew if he started checking, he'd wind up checking daily—or even hourly. He'd live or die by every bounce or drop. He just couldn't live that way. He would just wait until the time had run out and go to Johnny for the bottom-line—did I make or lose five million dollars?

Chapter 12

JUST as Johnny predicted, the new oil production quota was short-lived—just a little scare by OPEC. After all, how long could they go without selling their oil to the West? Accordingly, the market recovered and kept moving up another ten percent as the United States economy gained strength. Most investors were happy just to see their portfolios stop going down. Many had sold at a big loss. Others who held their stocks were starting to break even again. But there was the minority of investors—people like Johnny's clients—making a lot of money.

D-Day came and Austin turned up his courage and went into Johnny's office. Moira was there, shuffling some papers—she wouldn't have missed this moment for anything. Rory stuck her head in the door, watching.

"This is it," Austin said. Today's the deadline. How'd I do?" He was mentally prepared for the worst. My God, if he could just have his million back!

"Well, let's see," Johnny said as he pulled Austin's account up on the screen and looked at it.

"Hum...uh oh...how did that happen? Oh well, we really tried, I guess."

Austin's heart sank. He knew he'd missed. He'd felt it for weeks now.

"Johnny, don't torture me. How much have I got left?"

"Well, let's see. Well, well... guess what, folks? I'm talking to a multi-millionaire! You did it! You made it, my friend." Moira suddenly beamed. Of course, she and Johnny had already known and cooked up this little performance for Austin.

Austin jumped up, "Oh my God. I can't believe it! Oh my God." He leaped up and hugged a startled but smiling Moira and rushed around the desk to give Johnny a big hug.

"Thanks Johnny. What more can I say? And you, Moira and you too, Rory. Oh my God. Thank you! You guys are like a family to me. Thank you."

"Austin," Johnny said, "Calm down. You earned it. You trusted me. You trusted the Strategy."

The $250,000 options portfolio Johnny bought him was now worth about $410,000. The stock portfolio was worth a little over $1.2 million. All told, Austin made his fifteen percent over the past three years. He had his five million dollars!

All he had to do now was call Parkinson and get on with the audit and verification. The rest was history. At the age of 24, Austin Montgomery was worth over $6 million and was apprenticed to one of the most successful money managers in the world. All this, thanks to a father he barely knew. And thanks to Johnny Long.

Moira faxed a copy of Austin's statement over to Parkinson's office. A couple of days later, Parkinson called to confirm what Austin was waiting to hear officially—he'd done it. That evening, it was his great pleasure to take Johnny, Moira and Rory to the Balzac Café for an exquisite dinner. It was his turn to reciprocate. What he'd said in his outburst of joy was true—they were like a family to him.

At dinner, Austin toasted them. He told them the obvious. Without Johnny Long he'd have been lost. Not only had he passed his father's test, but he'd also gained a family of sorts. Both made it the best evening of his life.

At the end of a wonderful dinner, Johnny said, "Well, Austin, you've done well, very well on your investments. You passed your dad's test. He'd be very proud of you. Now I want to see how my investment is doing."

Austin didn't get it.

"What investment is that?" he asked.

"My investment in you. In case you've forgotten, I've got a big investment in you. You've got your payoff. Now I want to see how mine is doing."

The next two years were very hectic for Austin. Busy as he was, he began to notice a change taking place in his own personal life. He was no longer afraid of getting close to anyone. He'd met a wonderful girl named Geraldine, and had fallen in love with her. They'd gone together for almost two years, which was a record for Austin. She was a sweet, intelligent girl and everyone in Johnny's office loved her. She was majoring in education and loved children. And Austin had lost the remoteness, bitterness and resentment he'd had most of his life.

He'd learned to trust people. Good people. He still enjoyed his solitary moments from time to time, but he now actually enjoyed being with people. He realized that maybe being involved with people wasn't as simple as being alone, but it was a lot more rewarding. And his "family"—those close to him—saw Austin growing as a person at the same time he grew professionally. They were relieved that the money—more than six million—hadn't changed him one bit. It certainly did with some people, and they were anxiously waiting to see what happened. They didn't have to worry. Austin was the same old Austin, just growing.

In addition to the new clients Austin had brought in on his own, he was beginning to take care of some clients Johnny had moved over to him. This freed up Johnny's time and also allowed Austin to continue honing his money-management skills. The clients didn't mind. So long as Austin did the Strategy, they were happy. He made a few trips to the house in the Bahamas to check on things, and was always moved by the good work Johnny and Mr. Hart were doing—work he'd have to take over someday.

Johnny took the next step and sent Austin overseas to speak to First American brokers on the Strategy. At first, it was a trial run. The feedback was excellent. Soon, it became common for Austin to hop on a plane and head for London, Paris or Zurich. Nothing talks like success, and word of the outstanding success of the Strategy spread throughout the firm, worldwide.

By using Austin to do his in-house presentations, Johnny was getting his protégé ready to take over the cause. More clients would be next. Austin hired two assistants of his own to cover things when he went away. Thanks to Johnny, Austin was making good money now, and he saw the advantages to hiring competent help. No man is an island, not even Johnny Long. He learned that from Johnny. Austin took his research one step further than Johnny. He actually had his people monitoring not only First American's research changes, but the research changes of the other major firms as well.

He still used only First American's analysts when making investment decisions. He discovered that the other firms' research just confirmed how good First American's analysts were. He had extraordinary success using this technique to win new clients from other firms. His ability to innovate and fine-tune the Strategy Johnny Long had developed was his main strength. It was exactly what Johnny hoped the new blood and an open mind would bring.

One day, Johnny called Austin in to send him to the Allentown, Pennsylvania, office. The manager there, Frank Deason, was a long-standing friend of Johnny's. Recently, Deason decided to offer the Strategy aggressively in his office. It was not a particularly large office, so this was perfectly feasible. It was Deason's prerogative as manager, but it was still a very big move. Obviously, his brokers would have to get on board and be as well versed as possible with the Strategy. If it caught on and his people did a good job with it, everybody in Deason's office, including the clients, would make more money by using a systematic, proven method.

Austin was happy to go. He was still single, but he wondered, for how long? He also enjoyed traveling. Anyway, it was part of Johnny's philosophy to help people. He'd always generously shared his Strategy with anyone interested. So Austin carried on this tradition, feeling an obligation to any of the firm's advisors who called on him to help.

Austin arrived in Allentown around 10:30 the next day. As expected, a lunch meeting was called so that he could speak to the entire office. First American advisors were used to a barrage of these lunchtime meetings. Week after week, representatives from mutual fund families—even First American's own funds—rolled in to peddle their wares. In exchange for the staff's time, they usually paid to have the office lunch catered by some neighborhood deli or pizzeria. This was supposed to win the brokers' allegiance in hopes that he or she would put their clients' money into the *fund d' jour.* This business never ceased to amaze him.

By noon, the main conference room was full. There were all kinds of brokers in the room—new guys, seasoned vets, even the sales manager. Frank Deason certainly wanted the Strategy to take off. Austin assumed they were already bored, so he liked to start off with a bang.

After being introduced by Deason, Austin walked to the front of the room and stood silently for about thirty seconds—then a minute, then some more. The silence was uncomfortable. He could feel every broker stirring in his chair. He knew what they were thinking—they send this kid? This is what Frank pulled us away for? This is the new "miracle strategy" that's going to increase our business tenfold? And that's just what Austin wanted them to think. He remained silent while looking each person square in the eye.

He cleared his throat to let everyone know he was doing this intentionally. He learned the art of the dramatic pause from the master himself, Johnny Long. It was time to begin. "Silence. Saying nothing—that's what you do every time you advise a client to buy or sell a stock without knowing our analysts' earnings estimates, especially how they've changed. And if you don't know what the estimate changes are, how can you know what to buy or when to sell?"

There was quiet in the room. Austin had their attention. "My name is Austin Montgomery. If you don't know who I am, that doesn't matter. If you don't know Johnny Long's Strategy, well, that certainly does matter, because you're doing yourself and your clients a great disservice. That's what I'm here to say." Austin paused for a moment to let the weight of what he just said sink in. "Now, let me start by giving you an example of a pretty common trade. Buying shares of Merck. Merck's a good stock, right?"

"Right," said several of the brokers. "It's blue chip all the way." These meetings were all two-way interchanges. That's the way Johnny wanted it. It drew the brokers in and led to some pretty intense exchanges. Good.

"Well, I'm certainly not going to argue with that. But when do you sell it? Would your client take a 15% profit?"

"Sure," said someone. "That's more than the average S&P return over the last twenty years."

"Well, why not 20%?"

"Sure, why not," said the broker sarcastically. Everyone laughed.

"Well, then why not 30%? Why not 40, or 50, or 1,000%?" Everyone laughed. "The answer is, it doesn't matter when you buy a stock. The fact is that if you don't know when to sell, you're costing your clients a huge amount in potential profits. OK, no one likes to take losses. But that's nothing compared to the opportunity costs of selling a big winner too early. For example, think how many of your clients sold a stock with a 20, 40, even 100% profit. Looking back, we all know they sold too soon—much too soon. So when do you sell a winning or losing stock? If you don't have a strategy for that, you're hurting yourself and your clients everyday you walk into this office."

Suddenly, the brokers sat at attention. They'd never heard anything like this before. Austin continued, "As most of you know, First American has many different products to offer. But throughout the years, our most marketable product is our research." There was a general murmur of agreement. For years, First American was known to have the premier research team on the Street.

"Whoever has the best research should have the best investment returns—if we use it right. Information is the key. There are four kinds of research—great research, good research, poor research and no research at all. I'd guess that most people, maybe 95%, make their investment decisions using the last type of research—none at all. The way you can tell is by asking them the projected earnings for any of their stocks."

A hand went up. Austin gestured toward a young man. "So you connect our research directly with earnings?"

Austin laughed to himself. He remembered the days back when he didn't even know what a mutual fund was. "For me, the firm's research is all about earnings estimates. I've found that the price of a stock today is determined by the existing estimates of the company's future earnings. When those estimates go up, so does the price of the stock—and conversely. Know those estimates. Keep your eyes on them and you'll see exactly what I mean. And those estimates of a company's future earnings are available to you and me. When you get right down to it, our analysts primary function is to forecast what they think the profits of a company will be in the future."

"Austin," said Deason, "can you give us an example?"

"Sure. Ask a client what stock they like. If they say Microsoft, for example, ask them if they know what the profits are expected to be next year. If they don't know, they're just guessing. If you don't know, you're guessing. Knowing the future earnings of a stock is crucial because it's the perception of tomorrow that determines the stock price today. If the analysts on the Street think Microsoft will earn $500 million next year, then that's more or less why Microsoft is trading where it is. It's already priced in."

Austin noticed some confused looks. He quickly drew on one of his favorite analogies. "Put it this way. Imagine the perception or earnings forecast is the horse and the stock price is the cart. It's the perception—those estimated earnings—that pulls the price up or down. Looking at the price instead of the earnings is putting the cart before the horse. Why? Because if the future doesn't look as promising as it did two months ago, the price will decline to reflect the new estimates. But if the future looks more promising than the analysts expected two months ago, the stock price will go up to reflect the increase in estimates.

"Our team has researched more than 500,000 analysts' reports"—a gasp went up—"and this happened in almost every case. Think of that. In almost every case, prices were pulled up or dragged down by those earnings estimates. You know those estimates and you've got a good idea where the stock is going. We're not talking speculation here."

"So you keep track of all this?" asked a middle-aged man.

"Yes. Over a twelve-month period, you should record what our analysts are saying about the future profits of a company. You'll see that as they increase their earnings projections, the stock price will follow upwards—like a golden thread pulling it up—or dragging it down, if the estimates are lowered. So I never buy a stock on its name or its price. In fact, I don't care what the price is when I buy it. I buy a stock only on its estimates. Just take a look at your biggest losers. If you go back and look at what our analyst was projecting about the company's earnings during the time of the stock's decline, you'll almost certainly find that he lowered his estimates—probably many times. Every one of those lowered estimates was a shout to you to 'sell' before it went even lower—but did you hear it?"

Austin paused a moment. Everyone was thinking of their big losers and they were getting it. He continued. "If you want to be successful at First American, you have to do two things well. First, you need to get more money from your clients. Second, you need to get more referrals from your clients. Using First American's research, as our Strategy does, accomplishes them both. As you make money for your clients, you can ask them for more and for referrals. The Strategy sells itself because it works very, very well. It'll generate good returns and new business."

A young woman raised her hand. "So, you're trading stocks based only on our analysts' estimates?"

Austin shook his head. "No. I'm not trading stocks; I'm making informed investment decisions. There's a big difference. Let me explain. Many people who call themselves 'investors' are really 'traders.' The difference is that traders look at the price of a stock as the key to buying or selling. Buy low, sell high. Catch the timing. That's a trader—in and out based on prices. Investors look beyond the price to what actually makes prices move. Not the prices—but what makes them move up or down. The two are very, very different approaches. Traders usually want to make small profits very quickly. Investors want to make large profits, over time if need be. But this doesn't mean that investors simply buy and hold stocks. Nothing could be further from the truth.

"Ask a trader what he paid for a stock, and he might say $30 a share. Then ask him when he'll sell that stock. He'll usually say something like $40. So then, ask them why not sell it at $200 a share?" Everyone laughed again remembering Austin's earlier comment about Merck. "They'll look at you like you're crazy. But the simple fact is that they don't know when to sell." Heads were nodding in agreement. He had their attention. "All they know is the price of a stock. That stock could move from $30 to $40, back down to $30, then back up to $45, then down again to $40, up to $55, and then down to $40 again. This roller-coaster ride can drive you totally insane. By the way, any nuts here?" The group roared with laughter. They'd all been there.

"On the other hand, the investor looks at something else—namely, the perception of earnings to come, not the stock price. If over a period of two to three years, our analysts have increased their earnings estimates many times, that stock may very well have appreciated some 1,000%. That's right, 1,000%."

Now there was a real gasp from the audience.

Austin continued, "I tell people that my specialty is advising clients when to sell. They can even pick the stocks, as long as they're on our list. But I'll tell them when to sell. That's where money is made or lost. Some of you might do hours of research on buying stocks, but not know when to sell them. What happens is that often you sell your losers too late and your winners too soon. The Strategy—based on our company's research—gives you the clear, loud buy and sell signals. They're right there in the earnings estimates. Can you imagine investing $25,000 in a stock and still owning that stock three years later for $250,000?" More murmuring. "Can you imagine that? Do you have any idea what this can do to your returns? I hope you see what I'm driving at. Using First American's research in a disciplined, structured way—that's what the Strategy is all about."

Austin looked at his watch and noticed he had been speaking for about half an hour. He was totally engaged in his subject matter and didn't notice how much time flew. But nobody was asking questions. They all stared at Austin. He was used to this by now.

Finally, someone asked, "Mr. Montgomery, how many stocks do you follow in your Strategy?"

"I follow all the stocks that First American follows, about 3,500 companies. I then narrow this list down to a select few by using different screens."

"Can you tell us what those screens are?"

"I select companies that have had at least two earnings-estimate increases within six months. Our firm must also have a good general opinion of the company. Using these two screens narrows the list down to a manageable 50 or 60 stocks."

"Wow," someone said. "Out of 3,500 stocks, you wind up with 50 or 60? That's incredible."

"The important thing," said Austin, "is that I've prevented my client from buying the other 3,450 on a hunch. Think about that." People shook their heads in silent agreement.

"How many stocks should a client own in the Strategy?" asked someone else.

"The ideal number is around 15 stocks. You should have one big winner with 15 companies. Plus, with 15 companies in many different sectors, you'll be diversified. In fact, you will use a very formidable net to catch your big winner. You know—the one that didn't get away. It's very important to be diversified. This way you can customize the strategy to each individual client. That's an important element of the Strategy. It's very flexible. Measuring a client's risk level is always risky. Just listen to how they scream and shout at you sometimes." They laughed again. "But with around 15 stocks, you should be able to reduce the risk of owning a bad stock. It sometimes happens, but the risk is far less."

"Do you ever use margin?" asked an older gentleman.

"Yes," nodded Austin. "But only on special occasions. Most of my clients just want a good return on their money. Sometimes, I have clients who want to speculate with a small portion of their portfolio. In those cases, I'll use margin and/or buy call options on the stocks in the Strategy. If the clients follow the discipline of the Strategy using call options, they should be very happy with the returns."

The presentation with the advisors continued on for over an hour. Success breeds interest. Light a fire, and people will come. Success also breeds success. First American's advisors were the firm's foot soldiers. What they wanted was something to believe in, something that worked. That's what they and their clients wanted.

All of Austin's office visits went like this. Most people would guess that First American advisors were successful and set in their ways. So why would they need to make radical changes and risk upsetting the apple cart? That's what people outside often thought. In reality, though, advisors could fall victim to the market's deceptions as easily as the greenest investor.

Where First American excelled beyond all others was in their research—in the strength of their analysts. First American advisors were among the most motivated and intelligent brokers in the world. But the two had to be brought together to really reach full potential. To Austin and Johnny, it was a dream come true, especially since First American was rapidly expanding its research into burgeoning global markets. The potential was endless!

Word spread quickly through the management ranks of the firm. Any big firm was like that. And once word got out that Austin Montgomery was helping offices generate millions in additional revenues, as well as bringing clients unparalleled returns, everyone wanted a piece of the pie.

Johnny had been keeping close track of Austin's visits throughout the firm. He had been around for thirty-odd years and knew most of the managers well. They'd report back to him with news of the Strategy's success. It seemed everywhere Austin went over the next three years, people began to thrive, as long as they followed the Strategy.

Soon enough, managers were calling Austin directly. Johnny encouraged that. The amount of traveling Austin did was unusual for a broker. For a money manager, however, it was par for the course. Geraldine understood and supported him. To Austin, he was simply sharing with others a Strategy that had changed his own life.

Chapter 13

ONE day, Austin came in to find an email from Johnny. "See me when you get a chance."

Austin settled in for the day and went in to see his mentor. "What's up, Johnny?"

"Hi, Austin. Grab a seat." Austin sat down for what he hoped would be good news. "I want you to go to the Middle East and visit with some clients in Saudi Arabia."

"Really! Great! Who? Tell me more."

"I want you to call Malek Taqi in the Bahrain office. They border Saudi Arabia. Malek is a good friend of mine and has been doing the Strategy for some time. He acts as my contact in the Middle East. Be prepared to make a presentation to the brokers in his office. He'll give you the details, I'm sure."

"Should I have Moira make the arrangements?"

"Yes. You'll need a visa and some other things. Can you go next month?"

"Absolutely," said Austin enthusiastically. He'd been waiting for this moment for years. "Give me the accounts for review, and I'll prepare a nice presentation."

Being in Bahrain was like being in another world. From the oppressive heat, to the style of dress, to the women who chose to cover their face in public, cultural differences abounded. Located on the Arabian Gulf, the Bahrain airport is small and well-traveled, a hub for international business. More noticeable, though, was the humidity. It was almost as if the breeze picked up moisture over the Arabian Gulf and efficiently deposited it under your clothes. It made waiting in the passport line in a suit and tie almost unbearable. Austin laughed at himself. No wonder everyone was wearing cool, white robes, called Thobes, instead of the constrictive Western suit and tie.

A representative of First American named Omar Ali met Austin at the baggage claim. Unlike the others, he was wearing a blue suit, but looked unaffected by the intense heat and humidity. How did he do that, a perspiring Austin thought. Omar was warm and gracious, all smiles. He escorted Austin into a gray Mercedes awaiting them just outside the baggage claim. Austin and Omar sat in back while their driver quietly whisked them to The Royal Meridian hotel.

Americans have a way of equating every foreign landscape with some place in the States. It makes them feel at home, perhaps, less of a stranger in a strange land. It's just another form of the cultural colonialism that keeps America on top of the food chain. To Austin, the surroundings of Bahrain resembled the countryside of Southern California—flat and treeless. He was immediately struck by the newness of everything. The roads, the buildings, even the streetlights were newly erected or still in the process of going up. Construction was everywhere. Boomtown, he thought.

And Austin was surprised. Like many Americans, he'd developed his own stereotype about the Arab world—all those terrorists and everything. He expected to see sheep and camels wandering the streets, nomads and hot winds. In fact, there was none of this. He quickly realized his stereotype was way off base. Quite the contrary, Bahrain was an exploding Mecca of business as was the Middle East as a whole. Johnny had always spoken of the Middle East as if it was a dream. The American in the Middle East for the first time has absolutely no idea of the riches he can see if he's welcomed into the circle.

Americans are not accustomed to royalty. We know about the decorative, ceremonial royalty in Britain, for example. The average Saudi, though, could never imagine living exposed without a monarch to buffer and protect them from an uncertain, confusing and dangerous world full of violence, drugs and crime. Royalty was protection. Royalty was assurance and stability in a highly unstable world. That's how the Saudi sees it. The eyes of the American see only the spoon-fed images given them—the kind that Austin had before he went there.

The degree of opulence was unrivaled. Johnny knew this when he sent Austin to meet his clients. He knew Austin would return from this place a changed man, a dazzled man, but more than anything else, a humbled man.

To complement the sheer girth of Royal wealth were cities like Manama, Bahrain—burgeoning centers of business rapidly getting their piece of the capitalist pie. Real estate, for example, was exploding in Bahrain, as it was throughout the region, explained Omar. The Royal Meridian hotel was just one example of the sort of money being made those days. Local businessmen built the palatial hotel for some $50 million only a few years before Austin's arrival. It was sold within months for over $100 million. Now this was the kind of place to develop a client base.

Omar escorted Austin to the front desk and then bid him good-bye. Austin's room was a beautiful extension to the hotel. Marble floors graced his feet. His walls, like those in the lobby, were adorned with the finest art. Mosaic tiles offered splashes of color against the crisp, white walls. Donald Trump or Steve Winn couldn't have found finer Persian rugs to soften their hotel floors. It was the embodiment of luxury—a mere hint of things to come. A fruit basket was waiting for Austin when he arrived at his room, compliments of Malek Taqi, the Bahrain office manager. There was a message attached from someone named Aref Kamal, a First American vice president working out of the Bahrain office. Aref became quite successful using the Strategy, one of the first in his office, so he was the natural choice to accompany Austin on his trip. Aref would meet Austin for a drink at 9:00 that night.

Aref was what they call in Bahrain an expatriate. That is, he was not native born. Aref was born in Lebanon. Blonde and blue-eyed, he carried his Oxford education with authority. There was something distinguished about Aref Kamal, a finer quality that escaped words. Wealthy people felt comfortable with Aref, like he was one of their own. Perhaps it stemmed from his English training. Whatever it was, Aref's network of the wealthiest Arabs was extensive.

Aref worked hard to maintain his reputation, and his affiliation with Johnny Long was part of that. Aref was sharp and direct. The Strategy worked, and he knew it. He derived a sort of ethical imperative from the Strategy that preceded him in the room. In other words, the man had presence. Wealthy people responded to Aref Kamal. But what catapulted Aref to the top of First American's ranks was the Strategy. Aref had a way with people, true enough, but with the Strategy in hand he also had a way with money. The combination made Aref a natural choice for success.

Aref was becoming more and more successful every year. When Austin met him, Aref was the fifth largest producer in the firm thanks to the Strategy, and growing every year. That's the sign of a successful advisor at First American—someone who grows their business every year, just like the stocks in which Johnny Long invests. Aref was, as they say, on a roll. He was making more and more money, as were his clients, and he liked it. He was aggressive and loved being rewarded for his investment advice. But he never forgot to show his gratitude to Johnny. His surprising humility was one of his finest Lebanese traits.

Aref and Johnny worked together. Aref would bring in the clients and Johnny would provide the investment insights and do presentations on the Strategy. Everyone was happy, especially Aref's clients. And the client list was impressive. Austin was about to get just a taste of Aref's prowess. Johnny and Aref already managed money for what could only be termed the upper echelon of wealth and power. Most brokers would be happy gaining a $100,000 account, but using the Strategy, Aref and Johnny managed money for financial institutions! When financial institutions come to you for investment advice, then you know you're on to something special—something extraordinary.

According to local law, Aref could work and live in Bahrain, but as an expatriate, he was forbidden to own property. He had to rent his house from a native-born citizen. Such a restriction was vigorously enforced, as were all laws in the Middle East. Any western visitor had better take heed. The net effect of laws such as these is twofold. First, they are intended to protect the dominant Islamic culture that forms the spiritual, legal and ethical bedrock of the region. Considering the rapidity with which Western—read American—culture is influencing and dominating other cultures throughout the world, the need for people to preserve their own culture seems obvious. Second, those strict codes of laws restricting international investment assured natives the right to own everything that could be owned.

Saudi Arabia, for example, is a Kingdom and proud if it. They have embraced what might be called "controlled capitalism," a far cry from a free and open market. But then what capitalist economy is really free and open? People tend to define free according to their particular needs and prejudices. The Saudis lead their Middle Eastern kin in being acutely aware of this irony. With over $200 million of oil money flowing into the Kingdom each day, it is easy for people to interpret "freedom" to their own advantage.

Chapter 14

AUSTIN was waiting in the lobby promptly at nine that evening. He didn't know how Bahrainians regarded lateness, and he feared offending Aref. A cheerful-looking man in a blue suit walked in and came right up to Austin.

"Hello, Mr. Montgomery. I am Aref Kamal."

"Hello. It's a pleasure to meet you," said Austin. He shook hands nervously.

"I trust everything is fine with your accommodations."

Austin smiled. "To say the least. This place is phenomenal."

Aref laughed. "It is one of the finest hotels in the world, yes. But wait until you see some of the homes we'll be visiting. They humble this."

Austin raised his eyebrows. "Really?"

Aref smiled. "Come. Let's sit at the bar and chat a bit. I would like to review your schedule for tomorrow." They walked over to the bar and sat down. They were immediately waited on.

Austin had done his research. "I thought alcohol was illegal in these parts?"

"Ah, you've done your homework. In Bahrain, liquor is allowed. In Saudi Arabia, where we will be doing some business, it is not. There, it is strictly forbidden according to Islamic law. Even the President of the United States himself could not get you out of trouble if you are caught with alcohol in Saudi Arabia. Drugs, too. I assume you will have no drugs on you."

Austin shook his head. "Just aspirin," joked Austin.

Aref's dry English humor showed. "No problem. Actually, Bahrain is a popular place on the weekends—Thursday and Friday for us. Many Saudi men come over the bridge to party. Look around, what do you notice?"

Austin took a good look around. "Aside from the nicest furnishings I've ever seen... wow, the women."

Aref smiled and nodded. "That's one of Bahrain's finest natural resources. The beautiful women flock to places like this, especially on the weekend."

"Looking for rich men, huh," said Austin.

Aref nodded. "They are just like us, Austin Montgomery. They know how to fish where the fish are."

They ordered another drink and chatted about Aref's family and the ways of the Middle East. Then Aref outlined Austin's schedule for tomorrow.

"I will pick you up at eight in the morning. We'll go straight to the office, so eat breakfast first. You'll do a walkthrough, and then address the entire office from about 9:30 to 11:00."

"That's perfect," said Austin.

"You know, you have quite a fan in the office."

Austin smiled. "You mean Reza?" Reza had been doing the Strategy for some time. Reza got Aref into doing the Strategy, and it was the best decision either of them ever made.

"Yes. Reza talks about you all the time. He's quite excited to finally meet you. As am I, I might add."

Austin blushed. "That's kind of you, really. I am looking forward to meeting Reza at last. Nice guy."

"He is. Real salt of the Earth," said Aref. "But don't let him monopolize your time." They both laughed. "No, I'm serious," continued Aref. "Everyone is enthusiastic about meeting you tomorrow. They will all want your individual attention. That's why I thought a walkthrough would be good. I know you don't have much time to spend with us, and I have a rather demanding schedule laid out. You and I will be spending most of the time together. We will fit in the others when we can. But I would appreciate making our visits your priority. The others will have to understand. I have business lined up for us."

"Yes. Good idea."

"And I also want you to spend some time with Malek Taqi, our manager. He's the person in the office you need to impress the most."

"No problem," said Austin. "The Strategy sells itself."

"Actually, Malek heard you speak in Paris a couple of years ago."

"Did he?"

"Sure. He's the real reason why you're here. Reza can create interest, but Malek calls the shots."

"Is that all for tomorrow?"

Aref laughed. "Yes. We will have lunch with some of the top guys in the office, compliments of Mr. Taqi. After 3:00, you'll have some free time to take a nap or whatever. At 7:00, you'll be making a presentation to a group of investors we've lined up. We advertised and worked the phones very heavily for you. We're expecting a nice turnout."

"Excellent. How many are you expecting?"

Aref smiled happily. "We have about 300 confirmed."

"Really? That's great." This would be one of Austin's largest audiences.

"Sure. And afterwards, there will be a cocktail party in your honor. The audience will be invited to attend as well. So you see, we are expecting great things from you, Austin Montgomery."

Austin played it off. "Well, the real thanks should go to Johnny Long. And to the Strategy. I'm just presenting what Johnny developed. The Strategy is the real star—not me."

"The cocktail party is where I expect most of the real business to be conducted. Something you will notice quickly about wealthy Arabs—they do not like to ask questions at large public presentations. They will reserve their questions for a more intimate meeting with you."

Austin liked that way of doing business. "I'll see what I can do."

"Oh, and listen. I'm sure Malek will discuss this with you. He already talked with Johnny about it. Any accounts that are opened will be opened through our office, OK?"

This was First American's policy, and Austin had no choice. He was out of his District, not to mention out of his country. But he didn't care. He was there to help his colleagues and their clients be better investors. "That's no problem with me."

"Good. I guess the last thing I'll say is, thank you. We really need your help. As you can imagine, there is so much business to be done here. But most of these people have been very badly advised. You'd be amazed at how some have been taken advantage of by slick talkers from the United States and Europe. You have your work cut out for you."

Austin was flattered. "I wouldn't have it any other way. Now if you don't mind, I want to get a good night's sleep. I'm kind of tired."

"Of course," said Aref. They said their good-byes and went their separate ways for the night.

Austin awoke the next morning feeling tired. He could have slept another five hours easily. He was still on Eastern Standard Time. It felt like 12:30 at night to him. Austin drank as much coffee as he could stomach and met Aref at 8:00 sharp. A chauffeured Mercedes transported them to the Bahrain office where Austin did his walkthrough. True to Aref's word, everyone was thrilled to see Austin. They were already waiting for him when he arrived.

"Some of the guys from the Dubai office are here, too," said Aref. "Word spreads fast around here."

"Everywhere," said Austin. "That's how it works. Now you know why referrals come in faster than you can handle them when you use the Strategy."

"Tell me about it," said Aref.

Malek Taqi met them in the reception area. For the next six hours, Austin lived up to his renown. The questions were all the same, but the exuberance of this particular group was second to none. Aref was not exaggerating when he said his office needed Austin's help. Investing in the United States equity markets was still relatively new in the region, and a lot of money had been lost. "Experts" had swept through from the United States and Europe, promised a lot but delivered little—sometimes only huge losses. If getting referrals came easily using the Strategy, losing accounts came even faster without it. This group of advisors from the Bahrain and Dubai offices had a genuine thirst to do better, to be better. And Austin helped satisfy that thirst.

Austin sat beside the podium as Malek introduced him to over 300 concerned investors. Austin was impressed with the turnout. Malek's people did a great job setting things up. Malek's introduction caught people's attention quickly. Austin was not here to talk about what stock to buy. No, he was here to discuss when to sell a stock. There was a hush.

Austin took the podium and began as he had done a hundred times. Only now, he looked out over a sea of white Thobes. Not a single member of the audience was female. This was simply not their realm. At first, this shook Austin a bit. It wasn't his way, but he knew he shouldn't judge them by totally different and foreign standards. With all of our drugs and crime, who were we to lecture them, Austin thought. He also remembered Johnny's thoughts on cultural difference and focused on the continuities, on what they all had in common, regardless of culture—namely, good investing. No doubt there was a great deal that morally offended these Islamic men about American culture. Not to mention the fact that each of them prayed five times a day. Good and bad was in the eye of the beholder. Putting that aside, Austin went about his business with confidence and authority.

As Aref predicted, there were no questions following Austin's presentations. Once in the hospitality suite, however, people squeezed around Austin to hear him field questions. For each question answered, Austin was rewarded with a business card and a request for a follow-up call. Austin ran out of his own cards within ten minutes. Some of the more established men even invited Austin to stay at their home for a night. They wanted him. But as Johnny Long might say, what they really wanted was what Austin had—the Strategy.

Toward the end of the reception, Malek complimented Austin one last time before leaving. "I just want to tell you, Austin, what a great job you did today. Before you came to us, people thought we were just some sort of trading house which couldn't match up to the Swiss bankers. But you made us come across as an investment firm armed with the wisdom of the ages."

Austin returned to his room and fell fast asleep. He felt rejuvenated when Aref picked him up. On their way over the border into Saudi Arabia they passed a large, forbidding sign – Drugs Are Death.

"By the way," said Aref. "I don't know if I told you, but if you are caught bringing drugs into the country, you will automatically be sentenced to death. Period. You wouldn't be the first young businessman executed for possession of pot or coke. I know how you brokers are."

"Not me," said Austin.

"We shall see," joked Aref.

They were stopped by the border guards and questioned as to their business in Saudi Arabia. They began checking Austin's bag. How stupid of him, he thought. He hadn't had the foresight to check his bag before putting it in the trunk of the Benz. What if, like Johnny said, certain people wanted to stop him? Would they ever go so far as to set him up? If he could think of it, they could think of it.

But the search lasted only a few minutes, although in the hot sun, it seemed like hours to Austin and they were back on their way. Aref quickly briefed Austin on their first visit.

Mohammed Talal was in his mid-forties, slightly overweight from his love of the good life, and worth over $50 million. Aref and Malek wanted Talal in the Strategy in the worst way. Not only was Talal valuable to them, but also the referrals he could bring would amount to a nice piece of business indeed.

Austin and Aref were escorted in to see Talal. His house reminded Austin of The Royal Meridian. Austin could hardly believe that a man could actually own such a house. "House" wasn't even word enough for this place. That's what Westerners don't understand if they've never been visiting with the wealthy in the Middle East. For people like Talal—and Talal was worth only $50 million—wealth was not an adjective, and it was not a life's goal. It was a means to an end. Arabs view wealth as a creative force—a way of life that generates thoughts and acts that fit the religious beliefs they hold so dear.

Arab wealth was a creative force rivaled by little else short of Allah Himself. It created its own values and yet acknowledged the need for something more, at one and the same time. No wonder Johnny loved his Saudi clients.

A servant brought the three men some refreshments and then quietly left the room. Talal began the conversation. "Aref here tells me you are a famous man in the investment community. Do you think the market will continue going up?"

Austin decided not to play humble with Talal. "Yes, over the years I've developed a strong following, and I do work with the best equity analysts on Wall Street. With regards to the United States market, it should continue to go up. The economy is very strong. When I talk of investing, though, I am talking about a two or three year time horizon. Predicting the next six months is not my specialty."

Talal took it all in. He was sizing Austin up. He'd been through all this before with Aref. "What kind of stocks do you like?" he asked.

"I like companies that go up," joked Austin in an attempt to break the ice. They all laughed. "Seriously, though, I don't have one or two favorites or any hot stocks like you might hear about from other brokers. I manage money, which means I use a clearly defined discipline for buying and, more importantly, selling growth stocks."

"Do you have any specific recommendations?"

"I recommend that your portfolio include about fifteen different stocks in many different sectors. We buy only stocks that have had at least two earnings estimate increases in the last six months. From there, we hold those stocks—and we hold them until the earnings estimates are reduced. Then we sell it and move on. The goal is to never hold a loser and, sooner or later, hold one or two stocks that increase 500% or 1,000%. Have you ever had a stock that went up that much?"

"No!" said Talal. "But I would like it. Right now my brokers call as soon as one of my stocks goes up two dollars! They advise I sell it and take my profits."

"If you want a big profit," said Austin, "you must be patient. To do this, you must know when to sell a stock or more importantly, when not to sell a stock."

Austin and Talal sparred with each other for about an hour. When Austin felt he'd said enough, he went for closure.

"That's what I believe to be the most successful method of growth investing. If you decide to become a client, you will have to stick with it. I only manage money using the Strategy."

"I would like that," said Talal.

Aref and Austin were delighted. "I thought you would. You may open an account for five million."

Talal responded quickly. "Five million is more than I have available right now. Can you send me a proposal for three million for the time being?"

Austin didn't bat an eye. "No problem. By the way..." He looked at Aref, then at Talal. "Do you ever get to the United States?"

"Of course," said Talal. "I am in New York at least twice a year."

"Good. You must let me see you the next time you are there. We'll have lunch at our World Headquarters. Have you ever been down to the floor of the New York Stock Exchange?"

"No! You can arrange that?"

"For you," said Austin, "yes."

With that, Aref and Austin were off to their next appointment.

They sped off to meet with Sheikh Abdulla.

Sheikh Abdulla would be different from Talal. Talal was a long-time friend of Aref's and was already well versed in the ways of the Strategy. Moreover, compared with Abdulla, Talal was a little fish. Abdulla was a whale.

Sheikh Abdulla owned a large cement company based in the Eastern Province. The recent building boom in the region flowed like a river through Abdulla's pocket. He was the "concrete king" of Saudi Arabia. Sheikh Abdulla was one of those men who didn't just stick with the family business until it was bought out by some larger conglomerate. No, the Sheikh amassed his wealth by positioning himself and his people where the money was going to be. It just so happened that construction was the place to be. Cement was the intermediary. But becoming the intermediary was no mean feat. Abdulla was a wealthy man precisely because he could become an intermediary. When cars became more affordable in the Middle East, Abdulla was in the car business. Wherever there was a demand, Abdulla was there. Because of his talent, he was worth upwards of $150 million.

Austin would have to lure Abdulla away from his Swiss bankers. This, in itself, was no particular problem. By Aref's estimation, Abdulla probably made about seven percent a year. Abdulla and men like him liked the service they received from their Swiss bankers, but he felt no loyalty to his bankers where stocks were concerned. The problem for Austin was that the United States had no loyalties to its Arab investors. The United States Government could legally freeze foreign assets overnight, so the Americans lost the business to the Swiss.

Johnny had complained of this several times, so Austin had planned and strategized in preparation for this moment. He had the answer. He had found a way to manage Arab assets using the Strategy while holding the assets at foreign banks in Switzerland, the Caymans, the Bahamas, and so on—safe from some arbitrary or politically motivated seizure. That put the Arab investors at ease.

"Thank you for taking the time to see me. I think the time will be rewarding," said Austin.

Abdulla was straight faced. "For whom? For you or for me?"

Austin looked Abdulla squarely in the eyes. "For the both of us."

Abdulla returned Austin's gaze. He conceded the point. "I have it from Aref that you are special. I trust Aref. That is the only reason you are here."

"You trust Aref?"

"That is correct," said the Sheikh.

Austin nodded. "Hmm...I see. That's good. But as I understand it, you've yet to open an account with him."

There was an uncomfortable silence. Abdulla breathed deeply. "Yes... what's your point, Mr. Montgomery?"

Austin moved on the opportunity. "My point is simply this. Aref is a great guy. But what do you care about great guys? What you care about where your financial advisors are concerned is making money. Returns, plain and simple. Am I right?"

"You are correct. Continue."

Aref tried to interject, but Austin silenced him immediately with his hand. "By himself, Aref cannot bring you the returns you are looking for. And neither can your Swiss bankers, I dare say. But I'm here now. And I'm here to tell you that you have at your disposal, compliments of First American, a Strategy that will earn your business. And it will earn your trust. And it will earn your respect."

There was another uncomfortable pause, uncomfortable, that is, only for Aref. For Austin and Abdulla, however, it was a moment of uniting; a realization that an alliance was about to be struck, so long as they both remained true to their word.

"You know, Mr. Montgomery, I am an Engineer by trade. I received my degree from MIT. I have had a very good taste of Americans. I know what is good about your country and I know what is bad. I like discipline. I like order. Tell me about yours."

That was it. Austin knew he earned a new account. And as Johnny always said, once you get your foot in the door, the Strategy would pry it open the rest of the way.

"Just make sure that my returns are better than eight percent when we meet again."

"When would you like to meet again?"

"I expect to see you one year from now at the Dorchester Hotel in London. I expect to see better returns than I am getting today at my Swiss bank. If so, I will certainly reward you with more and more money. Is that a good enough challenge for you?"

Austin nodded. "Yes, and we'll start with five million dollars."

"Yes," said the Sheikh. "We will."

Austin and Aref thanked Abdulla for the check and left for their next appointment.

Chapter 15

THUS far, things were going very well. Assuming Talal would come through with the money, Austin brought in eight million dollars in two visits—not to mention the tens of millions that would no doubt follow with the Strategy's success, as well as any accounts that were opened as a result of Austin's presentation.

The evening's work was drawing to a close. By the time they finished with the next four meetings, they had commitments for over twenty-five million dollars in new assets for the strategy. They were running on adrenaline. Twenty-five million dollars buys a lot of enthusiasm. Aref was ecstatic; Austin remained focused on tomorrow's whale, the biggest of all—Sheikh Abdul Khaleq.

Abdul Khaleq was already a client of Johnny's. But he was no ordinary client. The man had his finger on the pulse of the world. He was one of the best-informed men in the world. For two hours each day, Abdul Khaleq did nothing but read faxes from his people positioned around the world. He demanded information be delivered to him in a consistent stream. His entourage and security attaché was immense. When he stayed at a hotel, he occupied an entire floor. The man was brilliant, informed, deeply religious and a man who always kept his word.

There is a saying in London about rich Arabs: If you can't own the oil, trade the oil. In Saudi Arabia, Abdul Khaleq was the master of oil commodity trading. Abdul Khaleq was estimated to be worth over one billion dollars; his father, twice that. How Johnny met these people, Austin didn't know. What did it matter? Not losing them was the important thing.

After talking with Johnny, Sheikh Abdul Khaleq planned a luncheon in Austin's honor. Johnny arranged it so that about a dozen of the Sheik's friends and colleagues would be attending, all of whom were interested in learning about the Strategy. To call this even a "luncheon" was a gross understatement. It was going to be a banquet the likes of which Austin had never seen. When most people think of a banquet, they think of a wedding or some such event where every serving is pre-calculated, the schedule pre-ordained, and so on. But in Saudi Arabia, a feast of this sort was intended to be excessive. For example, food enough to feed half a village was prepared. Chickens, steaks, seafood, fowl, pastas, soups, salads, cheeses, breads, cakes, you name it. What was not eaten by Abdul Khaleq and his guests would go to other villagers such as the chef's friends, the less fortunate. It was the tribal embodiment of trickle-down economics.

Early the next afternoon, a bright new Rolls-Royce arrived to pick up Austin and Aref. This was Austin's first ride in the prestigious car. He felt like royalty, but he knew better. He knew he was working. There was a job to do. The Sheik's mansion was heavily guarded. The gated driveway was long and intimated the lengths to which one had to go to gain an audience with the Sheikh. Not to mention the fact that the driveway was made of mosaic tile to rival the Alhambra. Austin's car assumed its place behind those of the other guests.

The Sheikh was waiting out front for Austin. It was time for a personal tour of his house. Austin behaved as if he was in a museum, and rightfully so. Once domiciling his grandfather's harem, the entire house could be opened to the public as a monument to Abdul Khaleq's wealth. That was the point.

Following custom, Abdul Khaleq personally introduced Austin to each individual member of his family. This was a serious moment, and Austin respected the trust Abdul Khaleq was putting in him. Indeed, Abdul Khaleq introduced Austin to his wife, Mariam. It was a rare act according to Islamic custom.

"You will not see her again for the remainder of the day," said Abdul Khaleq. "But I wanted you to meet her today. She is my life."

Austin didn't know whether to shake her hand or what. He kept his distance and just said "Hi." She was beautiful, lavishly jeweled and eloquent.

After their hellos, Austin was shown into a spacious dining room. The large mahogany dining table seated thirty, each place marked by a jeweled gold chair. The other guests filed in behind him. Austin was seated next to his host who was himself seated at the head of his table. From there he introduced Austin as "his financial advisor". He bade them listen to what Austin had to say, for it was a pearl of wisdom worthy of all due respect.

First they would enjoy some appetizers, however. A delicious array of lambs, hummus, eggplant, fowl, and more varieties of chicken than Austin had ever seen on one table. When they finished with the appetizers, the dishes were whisked away. The guests rose from their chairs and left the room.

"What's going on?" Austin asked Aref.

"Nothing to worry about. It's prayer time. Five times a day."

"That's right," said Austin. "But I didn't think they'd leave in the middle of a banquet."

Aref smiled. "These are religious men, Austin. Anyway, is what you have to say more important than their faith in God?"

Austin paused a moment. "You're right." Then he smiled. "Wait until you hear what I have to say this afternoon. I think you'll be pleasantly surprised."

The men returned within fifteen minutes and took their next courses. The eating went on for about two hours. After strong Turkish coffee, it was Austin's turn to address the men. This was the moment he'd been planning for almost a year. Arranging to manage money housed in foreign banks was easy. What Austin was going to announce took hundreds of hours of research by his interns. More importantly, it required Austin to care about doing business differently and do it better.

Austin stood up, thanked them, and proceeded with his usual presentation of the Strategy. Except this time, he concluded differently. "One of the most important characteristics that separate us from other living creatures is our ability to worship God—each in our own way. The important point is that each of us chooses how and why we worship. I respect this." They all nodded. "I respect your differences, because they demonstrate your commitment to an ideal. The Strategy you've all heard so much about...I am committed to it. Not because I'm shallow and worship money, a false God, but because making money for you helps enable you to help others."

There was a murmur of agreement. "Yes. It's wise of you to see that so quickly," a guest said.

"With this in mind, I have spent over a year researching and preparing a version of the Strategy especially for you. The primary objective of what I propose is to invest in industries that benefit humankind. To do this, we will avoid industries that are not suited to your religious beliefs, while still providing you with above average returns through the Strategy my own teacher, Mr. Johnny Long, developed. It is, I feel, an opportunity to combine financial and spiritual reward."

The men were shocked. This was the first time any of these men had been addressed by a Western advisor in their terms. Austin's plan went far beyond some banker looking for their money or a broker with hot stocks. Austin's Strategy reflected a level of understanding beyond what they'd seen or heard from the bankers. And it wasn't a sales pitch. He had spent nearly a year researching how to adapt the Strategy to these unique men and their ideals.

One of the guests felt compelled to speak. "Sir, are you suggesting that you can invest our money in accordance with our religious doctrines?" The other men murmured similar interest.

Austin nodded. "Yes sir, I am. You know, when I was a student at Stanford University, I always believed in broadening my horizons. At the time, of course, I really didn't know why. I just knew there would come a time when things would fall into place. Well now they have."

The man scratched his head and laughed. "You mean you have been planning for us for so long a time? Surely we are blessed." The others laughed along with their friend, for they all knew what he said was more truth than not.

"I have come a long way, gentlemen. And I want you all to know that I consider this Strategy to mark the high point of my career. I am proud to bring you a means for advancing both your financial and spiritual needs. This is, I think, the true potential of money."

"Abdul Khaleq," said one of the guests, "where have you been hiding this young man?"

"Yes, indeed," answered Abdul Khaleq as he glanced at the others. "Austin, why do you care so much about our cultural beliefs? They must seem quite strange to an American, no?"

Austin cleared his throat. "Let me make something very clear. I am nothing short of proud to have—with the guidance of my mentor and friend, Mr. Long—moved beyond the petty greed that characterizes my field. And I mean that. It's something I'm proud of."

"So you feel that as a money manager, you can help your clients live better?" asked a man seated across from Austin.

Austin nodded. "So long as their pursuits are honorable. Most people know not what they do for a living, so to speak. But I seek to work with people who know they want to live better lives by spreading their benevolence."

"This is what you work for?" asked Abdul Khaleq. "It is honorable, I agree. Excellent word…honorable. A rare quality in this day and age." Abdul Khaleq looked at his friends knowingly. They all nodded as if they had seen too much conflict, too much cheating and too much hurting—on all sides. As devout Muslims, this was no surprise.

A gentleman seated next to Abdul Khaleq broke into the conversation. His voice carried a tone of authority as old as the deserts themselves. It was clear he had seen much. In fact, he had. Unbeknownst to Austin and Aref, here sat the Deputy Director of OPEC, a man on a first-name basis with heads of state the world over. Alan Greenspan returned his calls without a second thought. This man was powerful and commanded both wisdom and consistency. He was no stranger to politics and conflict. But he was always a man of deep commitment to his country's religious and cultural beliefs.

"Mr. Montgomery," he said. Austin turned to him, as the others grew silent. "Make no mistake about it, sir, this is a matter of respect." The others nodded. "Do you understand what I mean?" Before Austin could respond, the Deputy Director continued. "For as long as I can remember, for as long as we have been a people, we have had to play by others' rules—namely the West. It is a matter of respect. I dare say we have all had our share of being ordered to and fro. But I am talking about Western countries continually treating us as if we were subordinate. Subordinate—less than them. Do you understand?"

The man's tone was calm and measured. It set Austin at ease. "Yes, sir, I do."

"You are evidently a smart man. If it were not for our oil, we would have disappeared long ago. But we are a powerful people, and it is about time someone like you acknowledged that in our terms, with respect for our values, instead of forcing us to accept Western codes and ways. Do not take us for granted. We are a powerful people, believe me." He stopped abruptly. Everyone waited. "This is something, sir. You impress me. Yes."

There was a palpable sigh of relief. Austin's proposal would mean nothing if he failed to gain the Deputy Director's approval. He carried great weight with his friends, and for good reason.

Austin sensed it was his turn to acknowledge the Deputy Director's approval. "I am flattered. Obviously, you speak from great experience and have been wronged in the past. Precisely how and by whom, I cannot say. But your graciousness bespeaks your wisdom. Perhaps like you, sir, I have fulfilled my potential because I understand that individual people have individual needs that must be both respected and satisfied. It is an honor for me to develop an investment strategy that respects and satisfies your religious beliefs. And that, I hope, distinguishes me from other advisors you have met."

"Please understand," said one of the guests. "We are accustomed to dealing with bankers who are far more rigid in their ways. Your Strategy seems so flexible to me."

Austin smiled. "That's exactly right! The Strategy can accommodate your particular needs. It can help achieve your financial and spiritual needs for just that reason. The Strategy actually embodies the fine balance between money and spirit, to which all of us here this afternoon aspire."

The men applauded and turned to their host to express their collective gratitude.

"This is certainly something," said Abdul Khaleq. "You can imagine how many advisors come to us courting our business. Ordinarily, we must turn away from our customs if we are to be included in a financial world directed by Western mores and standards. I think I speak for everyone present here this afternoon when I say that never has an advisor come before us to present a means of giving us access to the United States market and still maintain the sense of spiritual reverence which is so obviously important to us."

That said, words of thanks circulated around the table. In a world torn apart by institutionalized mass destruction, Austin's proposal reflected a human compromise. The world was not going to change, but these men all realized they now had access to something that made their worlds better. And sometimes, that is the path to personal fulfillment—changing what we can and making our individual worlds a better place.

The Lord knows, Austin thought, my world has changed since I met Johnny. "It is my pleasure," said Austin.

"Yes. But not so much as it is ours," said Abdul Khaleq. He beckoned Austin to give them some details. Austin described how he tailored the Strategy to exclude tobacco, firearms, liquor and so on. The harder part was trying to develop a list of companies that adhered to strict debt-to-equity ratios. That had taken countless hours of research. Austin respected their beliefs. Needless to say, though, more important than the individual stocks was building the desire to help others, the singular will to become far more than a greedy young man. Austin was right in one thing—everything else followed from there.

Chapter 16

WHEN Austin returned to the office, Johnny was the first to congratulate him. The fact that Johnny Long hadn't devised such a plan was a testament to Austin's own creativity. More importantly, though, the religious strategy was a declaration of commitment to his mentor's ideals. When Johnny Long first spoke with that insecure, confused and frightened young man sitting at the counter having a cup of coffee, he had no idea what would follow. At the time, Johnny and Hart were looking for someone to carry on their torch. They couldn't actively search out the one for whom they were looking. You don't place ads to find such a person. Their torch could not be given; it had to be taken—by a gifted person. Johnny Long and Austin Montgomery found each other that day in the diner—not by looking, but by just living.

Johnny always figured Austin was a free agent and should be left to make his own mistakes. But Austin used that freedom to choose to learn and grow, as a person and in his work. Others who at first seemed to be right had left the firm for a quick signing bonus at another firm. Or they cared nothing for the well being of others. Or they simply couldn't see the benefits of the Strategy and ended up among the scores of brokers like Bobby Lane.

Austin, however, never veered from the path of Johnny's ideal. And it was certainly clear after his meeting with the Arabs, that Austin and his mentor shared the same ideals. It's the kind of thing you can't explain. Call it serendipity, Kismet, fate or Karma. The ancients Greeks thousands of years ago posed the question— Fate or Free Will? As Johnny said, there may not be an ultimate answer to this question.

For the Arabs, it shows up in balancing "wealth" and religion—a search for the perfect harmony between worldly and spiritual riches. For Johnny and Austin, it is the very soul of the Strategy—something far more than merely buying and selling stocks.

In one way, when Austin took the creative initiative and redesigned the strategy especially for his Islamic clients, he was taking a bite out of life and letting his mentor, Johnny Long, savor the juice. This was what Johnny was waiting for. Austin was now ready to move beyond his teacher. For Johnny, this was not a sign of his own faltering, but the pinnacle of his career. His protégé had become a new master himself. Johnny had fulfilled his role—to help a fellowman move past him in the ranks of humanity. Because, as with the Strategy, the moment such growth ceases is the moment to sell stock in humanity.

Humanity is organized as a 'society' so we can reward those who work to fortify and develop this order of things. It is a matter of survival. If a man like Johnny Long is punished by his society for the positive contributions he makes, it's a step backwards for humanity. If he is rewarded, it is a step forward. And conversely, two things can happen to those who are bitter and resentful. Either they are punished, and that's a step forward, or else they are rewarded and humanity falters, if only imperceptibly.

And there was news from New York—staggering news. Johnny was told First American would aggressively offer the Strategy. Purely out of self-interest—to ensure its own survival— the corporate giant was at last doing the right thing.

To save face, the firm formed a Committee to study the Strategy. The Committee announced it was worthy. It was all window-dressing of course to avoid having to admit that one man with a vision came up with the strategy and stood behind it—until no one could deny its power.

Sometimes, good things have a way of working out.

Austin and Johnny sat down and talked all this over—the trip to Saudi Arabia, the acceptance of the Strategy.

"Austin," he said, "when I met you, you were by your own admission, insecure, resentful, afraid of getting close to anyone and ready to go out and blow your one million dollars. I've seen you come along. And you know what I'm most pleased with—not just your professional or financial growth, but also your growth as a person.

"There's a lot more to life than money, Austin. You can be rich and very unsuccessful in life. We both know some very wealthy people whose lives are horribly messed up. Thank God you realize there's more to success than money. And, let me add, thank God you understand that money can be put to good use to help people. Mr. Hart and I are counting on that.

"Your father would be proud of you. He dangled that five million out in front of you and knew it would make or break you. But I'm sure that in his heart he knew you'd go for it—and in the process become the kind of man he'd be proud of. I know I'm proud of you—and I know he is too."

"Thanks, Johnny. I owe a lot to you. And by the way, you're the best man when Geraldine and I get married."

"Hey, that's great. When's the date?"

"Soon, Johnny, soon." Austin and Geraldine were very much in love and planned to have several children.

"Well, never think you're in charge of your life. Life has a dynamic of its own. You can only respond to what comes next. Is it fate or free will that everything turned out this way? How did I happen to meet you in that diner? Who knows? It's sort of like dancing with the analysts— they lead in time with the music of the market, building with the tempo, synchronous, in flow with the music of the ages."

"You know something I've learned," Austin said, "If you grab whatever life brings you—and make the most of it— *that's really living.*"

The End